CW01498488

Christmas at Mistletoe Lodge

Sweet Colorado Romance – Book 1

AMY RAFFERTY

Copyright © 2024 by Amy Rafferty

All rights reserved.

No part of this publication may be reproduced, stored, distributed, or transmitted in any form or by any means, including photocopying, recording, or other electronic or mechanical methods, without the prior written permission of the publisher or author. For permission requests, contact the author.

The story, all names, characters, and incidents portrayed in this production are fictitious. No identification with actual persons (living or deceased), places, buildings, and products is intended or should be inferred.

Images inside were designed using resources from canva.com and bookbrush.com

First Edition 2024

Subscribe Here!

Don't miss the
Giveaways, competitions,
and 'off the press' news!

Don't want to miss out on my giveaways, competitions,
and 'hot off the press' news?
Subscribe to my email list.
It is FREE!
Click Here!

CONNECT WITH AMY RAFFERTY

Not only can you check out the latest news and deals, you can also get an email alert each time I release my next book.

Follow me on BookBub
I always love to hear from you and get your feedback.
Email me at ~ books@amyraffertyauthor.com
Follow on Amazon ~ Amy Rafferty
Sign up for my newsletter and free gift, Here
Join my 'Amy's Friends' group on Facebook

CONTENTS

1. CHAPTER 1   1

2. CHAPTER 2   14

3. CHAPTER 3   26

4. CHAPTER 4   45

5. CHAPTER 5   61

6. CHAPTER 6   77

7. CHAPTER 7   90

8. CHAPTER 8   111

9. CHAPTER 9   128

10. CHAPTER 10   146

11. CHAPTER 11   161

12. CHAPTER 12   176

13. CHAPTER 13   192

14. CHAPTER 14   213

15. CHAPTER 15   232

16. CHAPTER 16   255

17. CHAPTER 17   278

18. CHAPTER 18   303

19. CHAPTER 19   329

20. CHAPTER 20   352

21. CHAPTER 21   374

22. EPILOGUE   398

CONTINUE READING...   411

SWEET COLORADO ROMANCE SERIES   435

MORE BOOKS BY AMY RAFFERTY   436

AMY RAFFERTY VIP READERS   440

CONNECT WITH AMY RAFFERTY   441

A NOTE FROM AMY RAFFERTY   442

REVIEW   444

CHAPTER 1

Avery Hawthorne sat at her desk, surrounded by paperwork and a laptop. She was deep in concentration as she worked on finalizing a merger deal that needed to be completed by the morning. Suddenly, a video call from her parents popped up on her screen, pulling her out of her work.

Glancing at the clock, she was surprised to see that it was nearly seven thirty in the evening. Realizing she hadn't eaten since breakfast, Avery's stomach growled as she answered the video call.

"Hi, Mom," Avery greeted her mother on the screen.

"Hi, sweetheart," her mother, Judy Hawthorne, replied. "How is everything In Los Angeles?"

"Oh, as usual, I'm busy preparing presentations and researching my next project." Avery's stomach took that moment to protest its hunger once again.

"Honey, please tell me you've eaten dinner," Judy expressed her concern.

"I'll grab something after our call," Avery promised.

By the tone of her mother's voice and the way she was fidgeting with her necklace, Avery knew something was wrong. Her breath caught in her throat when she realized what time it was in Colorado and that her father didn't appear to be home.

"Is everything alright, Mom?" Avery asked worriedly.

"There's been an incident," Judy blurted out, and she continued the story before Avery could say anything. "Frank Harland's Zamboni crashed through the Hardware store's window late this afternoon."

Avery's jaw dropped, and she gaped at her mother. "Did you say a Zamboni crashed through the store's window?" She squinted in disbelief. "Was anyone hurt?"

"Yes, I did. I'll send you the pictures," Judy told her. "No one was hurt." She shook her head in dismay. "Luckily, the store was closed, so there were no customers. Only your father and Matty, the new cashier, were there."

Avery was still in shock over the news. It seemed so surreal and was something that happened in cartoons or comedies, not at her father's hardware store.

"I'm glad no one was hurt," Avery said, relieved that her father, his staff, and the Zamboni drivers were okay.

"I am, but your father has to see to the repairs of the store," Judy said woefully, "which means we're not going to be able to make it to Los Angeles for Christmas this year."

Avery's heart sank. She loved spending Christmas with her family, who had spent it with her in Los Angeles for the past twelve years. Avery couldn't remember a Christmas she hadn't spent with her family, and it seemed like this year would be the first she would be spending alone.

"Oh, no, Mom!" Avery exclaimed, feeling terribly deflated. "That's terrible news. But I understand."

Judy asked hesitantly, "Avery, is there any way you could come home for Christmas?" She looked at Avery hopefully before adding, "Your father would be so happy to have you home."

Avery hesitated for a few minutes. She hadn't been back home in twelve years. Avery did miss the cold winters and all the fun holiday season activities of her small hometown. But one terrible day overshadowed all of her pleasant memories of Frisco.

A day that Avery had pushed to the back of her mind and locked away. She saw the plea in her mother's eyes and knew that she couldn't say no. Avery knew she'd have to go back there one day and face her demons, and maybe facing them in the midst of Christmas cheer would make it less painful.

"Okay, Mom." Avery saw the joy burst in her mother's eyes, and a big smile spread across her face. "I can't make any promises because I don't know if my boss will let me change my leave this late."

"I understand, honey," Judy said. "And thank you for at least wanting to try to get here." She reached over and picked up her tea, taking a sip. "Your father will be so relieved. His biggest panic wasn't the store. It was about how it was going to affect our plans of seeing you."

They spoke for a few more minutes before her mother had to leave to go and take food to her father, who was still cleaning up at the store. Avery promised to speak to her boss in the morning about changing her holiday leave.

When the call ended, Avery sat back against the plush cushions of her sofa and stared up at the ceiling. Her mind raced with thoughts of going back to Frisco, and flashes of her eighteenth birthday tormented her. It was supposed to be the happiest day of her life, but it turned out to be one filled with heartache, betrayal, and pain.

Avery had been engaged to be married on her eighteenth birthday, but her fiancé had stood her up at the altar with a note that said, *you deserve the big future you've always dreamed of.* She had grabbed her bags, left Frisco for Los Angeles, and never looked back. But now it seemed like a freak accident at her father's store was dragging her back home.

Maybe it's a sign that it's time to put the past behind me, Avery thought and sighed. *It would be nice to have a cold winter again.* She looked at the clock on the wall. It was getting late, and Avery needed to finish her presentation so she could land this account for her firm. Avery really wanted the promotion at work and had to make sure she went the extra mile since she was up against the CEO's nephew.

As Avery got ready for bed three hours later, she couldn't shake the feeling that going back to Frisco would be a turning point in her life, and she wasn't quite sure if it would be for better or for worse.

· ♥ · ♥ · ♥ · ♥ · ♥ ·

The next morning, Avery's presentation went well, and after some discussion with the customer, they signed with her firm, Grimes Mergers & Acquisitions. After the client left, Avery went straight to her boss, Harry Monk's, office.

Avery knocked on his office door and stepped in when he called for her to.

"Harry, could I have a word, please?" Avery stood at the door.

"Avery, you must've picked up on my thoughts," Harry told her, leaning back in his plush office chair. "I was about to call you to my office." He gestured toward the chair in front of him. "Please come in and take a seat."

"Oh!" Avery raised her brows as she walked over and took a seat in front of his desk. "Is everything okay?"

"Yes," Harry assured. "It couldn't be better, especially after you landed the Holland Corporation account." He smiled. "Well done on that."

"Thank you," Avery said, feeling elated. The firm had been trying to get the account for years. "Harry, I was wondering if I could change my annual leave."

Avery explained the situation to him and said that she'd like to go home to help her father and spend the holidays in Colorado this year.

Harry sat looking at her in disbelief, and Avery's heart sank as she thought he wasn't going to let her change her vacation dates.

"A Zamboni drove through the window of your father's store," Harry said in amazement. "Good grief. That's not something you hear about every day."

"I know." Avery sighed in relief, realizing he was looking at her like that because, like her, he couldn't believe things like that actually happened.

"I'm sorry to hear about your father's store," Harry condoled, "but it must be fate!" He smiled. "Because I have a great opportunity for you that I was going to wait to offer you in the new year." His eyes narrowed as he thought. "But in all honesty, the sooner we can get this deal done, the better it will be for the company." He raised an eyebrow. "And it will give you the boost you need to get the promotion to take over my position in the new year."

Avery's brows creased. "What opportunity?"

"Pembrook Hotel, Resorts, and Spa's Group is looking to acquire a lodge for their new mountain resort chain," Harry explained. "They want their first Mountain Resort in or around Breckenridge, Colorado." He steepled his fingers in front of him. "They have two properties they're interested in around that area."

"Oh?" Avery's stomach clenched with excitement.

Pembrook was one of Grimes Mergers and Acquisitions' biggest clients. She had to stop herself from holding her breath while she waited in anticipation for Harry's next words.

"The instant Sully Banks from Pembrook mentioned Breckenridge and Frisco, I knew you were the person to close the deal," Harry said. "As I said, they're interested in two properties, but their first choice is this one."

Harry pulled a folder from the pile he had on the side of his desk and handed it to her. The folder was labeled *ML, Frisco, Co.,* and a tingling sensation made the hairs on her arm stand up. Avery knew before she even opened the folder what the property was.

"This one is their favorite." Henry tapped on the document. "It's close enough to Breckenridge yet far enough to have an isolated mountain feel to it." He steepled his fingers again. "It also has a lake, trails, and enough land."

Avery stared at the name on the top of the page—Mistletoe Lodge. It had been twelve years since she'd been back to Frisco. But the name of that lodge still had the power to make her feel like she'd had the wind knocked out of her. It was where she was supposed to get married, but instead, it was where she'd had her heart shattered into a million pieces and been jilted.

Avery knew that after David Carlisle passed away about three years ago, his two children had taken over the running of the lodge. His daughter, Emily, had been Avery's childhood best friend, and Avery would love to see her again. It was Emily's older brother that was the problem—Ryder Carlisle, who also happened to be Avery's ex-fiancé.

"Avery?" Harry asked, looking at her curiously. "Are you okay?" His frown deepened. "You've gone pale."

"Oh, no, I'm fine," Avery assured him. "I know the owners of Mistletoe Lodge." She cleared her throat and decided not to tell Harry about her history with Ryder. "Emily Saunders, a part owner of the lodge, is my childhood best friend."

"Oh!" Harry's brows shot up. "Is that going to be a problem for you?"

"No, not at all," Avery lied, hoping her voice didn't sound as shaky as her insides felt at that moment. "I'm just shocked to see how badly the lodge is doing." She paged through the documents and glanced at some of the figures. "It was quite a prosperous business while I was growing up."

"These have been some difficult times, Avery," Harry said. "A lot of companies haven't fared well and have had to close or sell."

"That's true," Avery agreed with him.

"Maybe if the owners know you're handling the deal, they'll be a little more forthcoming." Harry leaned back in his chair. "The few times I've tried to talk to them, they haven't been too cooperative."

"Mistletoe Lodge has been in the Carlisle family for generations," Avery explained. "I guess it's hard for Emily and her brother to find themselves in the position they're in."

"Yes, that is understandable." Harry nodded. He was quiet for a few seconds before saying, "This is a huge opportunity for you, Avery. Land this deal, and the promotion plus the company's five largest client accounts will be yours."

Avery knew Harry was right. This was a huge opportunity for her career. And she couldn't let her past with Ryder and Emily get in the way of that. Avery would also ensure that the Carlisle family got the best deal she could get for them.

"I'll do my best," Avery said determinedly.

She knew that if she was going to go back to Frisco for the holidays, she'd have to face her past head-on, but she hadn't realized she'd be doing so by making them an offer on the lodge. Avery knew it wasn't going to go down well with the Carlisle family, especially Ryder.

CHAPTER 2

Ryder Carlisle sat in the small back office of Mistletoe Lodge, rubbing his aching neck. He had been staring at the computer screen for hours, reviewing the lodge's finances. Ryder's sister, Emily, and her husband, Hank, moved back to Mistletoe Lodge four years ago to care for their terminally ill father.

When Emily took over the running of the lodge, she was shocked to find how badly it had been doing for over a year before she moved back.

Ryder and his eight-year-old daughter had moved back to Mistletoe Lodge a month after his father passed away three years ago. Since then, he and Emily had struggled to pull Mistletoe Lodge out of the red and make it turn a decent profit like it once did.

To save the lodge, Ryder invested a large portion of his free capital into an orchard of fruit and mistletoe. He also fixed up the lodge and holiday cottages, but it wasn't enough. Corporate hotel chains were trying to acquire Mistletoe Lodge, but Ryder and Emily were determined to save it and keep it in the family.

"I hope your deep, thoughtful stare means the Annual Winter Mistletoe Festival revival is all sold out." Emily walked into the office carrying two steamy mugs of hot cocoa topped with a tower of cream stuffed with mini marshmallows and a candy cane stick.

"If you tell me one of those festive season beverages you've been designing is mine, I'll give you an update," Ryder bargained with her.

"Deal." Emily handed him one of the mugs before taking a seat in front of him. "I put a bit of chili spice and cinnamon in the hot chocolate to give it a warm, spicy flavor."

Ryder took a sip of the cocoa and was pleasantly surprised at how good it was.

"Em, this is delicious," Ryder told her. "I hope you'll include it on the hot beverages list for the festive season."

"I've put it on the menu already," Emily told him before taking another sip and putting the mug on the desk. "Hank thinks it's the best cup of cocoa he's ever had."

"Of course, Hank would say that. He's your husband," Ryder teased her. "But seriously, it is delicious, and so is the peppermint cream coffee you made this afternoon."

"Thank you," Emily said proudly. "Didn't you promise to give me a winter festival update?"

"I did." Ryder nodded. "Let's see. We need two more trail guides for the winter trail hike."

"I think I know two people to fill those positions." Emily took a pen out of the pen holder on the desk and found a piece of scrap paper to start a to-do list. "I'll speak to them tomorrow morning."

"Thank you." Ryder breathed a sigh of relief to have two more items off his list. "We have two people getting back to me about booths at the festival, leaving only one booth to fill."

"I think I may know the perfect person for the spare booth," Emily told him.

"Really?" Ryder felt the tension start to drain from his aching head. "Who did you have in mind?"

"Jim Hawthorn," Emily shocked Ryder by saying.

"Are they not going to Los Angeles like they do each year?" Ryder asked curiously and then berated himself for sounding too enthusiastic about what it might mean if the Hawthorns stayed in Frisco this year.

"Haven't you heard?" Emily looked at her brother in amazement.

"Heard what?" Ryder frowned. "Has something happened that I was supposed to know about?"

"The entire town knows about the Zamboni incident on the Main road this afternoon." Emily picked up her cocoa.

"Zamboni incident?" Ryder's frown deepened. "Did something happen to Frank Harland's Zamboni again?" Ryder couldn't believe how careless Frank Harland could be, leaving his Zamboni parked at the side of a pond the town used as an ice rink during the winter. "Didn't it go through the ice last year?"

"That was the year before. Last year someone stole the Zamboni," Emily corrected him.

"What happened to it this time?" Ryder asked.

"Frank's grandson and friends struck once again and took it for a joy ride that got out of control." Emily filled Ryder in on the story. "They jumped off the machine when they couldn't control it, and the Zamboni went through Hawthorn's Hardware window."

"Oh no!" Ryder stared at Emily in disbelief. "Was anyone hurt?"

"Luckily, no." Emily took a sip of her cocoa. "But poor Frank has a huge mess to clean up, and the Hawthorn's had to cancel their annual trip to visit Avery in Los Angeles."

"Does that mean Avery is coming home this year?" Ryder tried to keep his voice neutral and act like nothing more than a concerned friend.

"I don't know," Emily told him. "I haven't spoken to the Hawthorns yet. But I'll probably find out tomorrow when I ask Frank if he would like the last booth in our Mistletoe Lodge Winter Festival Revival."

"Do you have a backup if Frank won't take the booth?" Ryder asked.

"Yes, us!" Emily surprised him by saying.

"Us?" Ryder raised his brows. "What would we sell at the booth?"

"Apples, mistletoe, Christmas trees, and we can pass out flyers for the opening of Mistletoe Lodge Orchard." Emily put her cocoa down and reached over the desk to grab a folder she'd left there earlier that day. "Hank designed these to pass out at the festival and leave around the lodge, like on the front desk, the magazine table in the main living room, the guest's rooms, etcetera." She pulled a pamphlet from the folder and handed it to him.

Ryder took the pamphlet and looked at the leaflet advertising the grand opening of Mistletoe Orchard. This was Ryder's, his daughter's, Emily's, Hanks, and his grandmother's future and a new beginning for Mistletoe Lodge. Ryder was confident it would change everything for them and keep the lodge running during the quiet, uncertain times they were currently going through.

But Ryder and Emily had to hold onto Mistletoe Lodge with everything they had. Finding ways to keep it going and out of the clutches of the large corporate hotel and resort chain trying to acquire Mistletoe Lodge.

Two months after moving back to Frisco, the large hotel and resort chain approached Ryder and Emily. Mistletoe Lodge was on prime land and perfect for their mountain resort project. The lodge's proximity to some top ski resorts and adventure trails, the fact that it bordered a lake, and the amount of land it was on were precisely what the company was looking for.

The first executives that had visited them had been pleasant and eager to come to an arrangement that would benefit them all. But when the man left empty-handed after they turned down his offer, the company changed its tactics. It brought a mergers and acquisitions company in to do the negotiations. Which were more like strong-arm tactics that only benefited the hotel and resort group.

Thanks to last year's incredible season, the lodge had a steady stream of business throughout the year. Ryder and Emily had managed to keep their heads just enough above water so as not to drown.

But the lodge cost a lot to run and maintain. Mistletoe Lodge was far from being out of hot water and needed another successful festive season this year.

Ryder's family had a lot riding on it, especially after they had each sunk nearly every cent they had into the orchard business and revamping Mistletoe Lodge.

The website Hank had designed for them was working and giving them the exposure they desperately needed. Still, they needed an edge to hoist them into a more comfortable position for the new year. Last year, they got a helping hand from nature. This year, Ryder felt they needed nothing short of a Christmas miracle.

Emily believed they may just have gotten one! Because while she and Ryder were going through the Christmas decorations for the lodge in one of the storage rooms, Ryder found their old Christmas wreath. Their mother would hang it on the front door to mark the start of the yearly Mistletoe Lodge festive season.

The wreath had reminded him and Emily of the magical Christmases Mistletoe Lodge had been famous for. That's when they got the idea to restart the Mistletoe Lodge Annual Festive Season Festival. The first Carlisle to own Mistletoe Lodge founded the festival. It used to be the highlight of the season for the town. It drew people from all over America and the world each year.

Ryder's father stopped having the annual festival ten years ago when their mother died. Ryder, Emily, Hank, and the lodge staff had worked hard over the past month to ensure they made the festival as magical and successful as his mother had.

Ryder glanced at the letters in the in-tray on the cabinet near the office door. He wanted nothing more than to get into the holiday spirit and enjoy the excitement of it all. But it was hard when Ryder and Emily had an in-tray of letters from their bank and a merger and acquisitions company representing the hotel and resort chain trying to take over the lodge.

Ryder felt like he was living with a sword hanging by a thin thread above his head.

"Ryder!" Emily's raised voice and snapping fingers drew him from his thoughts. "Where did you go?" She looked at him curiously. "Do you not like the pamphlets?"

"I love the pamphlet," Ryder assured Emily. "I'm not sure about handing them out, though. I would rather wait until after the new year when we've got a better grasp of our financial situation and will know if we can keep the lodge."

"I understand your concerns, big brother." Emily reached across the desk and covered his hand with hers. "But if we start advertising the orchard now, we'll start to build a list of potential customers who may also become potential lodge guests," she explained.

Ryder looked over the pamphlet as he pondered the idea for a while.

"Okay, put the pamphlets out," Ryder told her.

Emily jumped up, ran around the desk, and gave Ryder a hug and kiss. "I'll put them out first thing in the morning." She glanced at the clock that hung above the door. "It's late, and I think I'd better get to bed because we have a big day tomorrow."

Emily picked up the empty mugs and walked to the office door, where she stopped.

"You need to get some sleep, too," Emily ordered. She was about to leave but popped her head back in the door. "Oh, and Ryder, I'll let you know if Avery is coming home or not as soon as I know." She gave him a knowing smile before saying goodnight.

CHAPTER 3

Avery wheeled her suitcase behind her as she hurried through the busy Los Angeles airport, hoping that she wasn't too late to check in for her flight. After a restless night of battling with her conscience, Avery had missed her alarm and was running late. Even with her boss calling her with last-minute details about the deal, Avery managed to check in just in time.

As she went through security, Avery's phone rang.

"Hi, Mom," Avery answered, balancing her phone between her ear and shoulder as she stuffed her wallet into her purse and looked for her boarding gate.

"Avery, sweetheart, did you get to the airport on time?" Judy's voice was filled with concern.

"Yes, Mom, I'm on my way to the boarding gate," Avery assured her. "I'll see you and Dad in about two and a half hours."

"That's why I'm calling," Judy told her. "Your father and I may be a little late because of the weather," she warned her. "We'll leave for Denver in the next fifteen minutes to fetch you from the airport. We're so excited to have you home with us at Christmas for a change."

"I'm excited to be coming home too, Mom." Avery got to the gate. She had told her parents she was on a working holiday, but she hadn't told them the nature of her business. "I have to board. I'll call you as soon as the plane has landed."

"Have a good flight, honey, and we'll see you soon. I love you," Judy said excitedly.

"I love you too, Mom." Avery hung up, switched her phone to airplane mode, and put it in her purse before boarding the aircraft.

When she reached her seat, she found that two seats were already occupied: one by a young girl hugging a stuffed rabbit, and the other by the girl's grandmother. The woman was smartly dressed and immaculately groomed, with dark hair streaked with gray and kind blue eyes. For a brief moment, Avery felt like she'd met her before.

The woman moved out of her seat to let Avery through and retook her seat as Avery sat down. The little girl stretched her legs out in front of her. Avery put her purse under the seat in front of her and buckled her seatbelt.

She looked out the window as the plane began to taxi down the runway. She was excited to be spending Christmas at home with her family, but she was also nervous about the task at hand and having to face the man who had broken her heart twelve years ago.

Avery's mind went back over the events of the last week. Her boss was confident the deal for Mistletoe Lodge was going to be easy for her. The owners were drowning in debt, the lodge was in need of a major overhaul, and her boss had found out that she had a history with the Carlisle family.

What he didn't know was that it was not the good kind of history, and the deal was most certainly not as cut and dry as her boss thought.

This wasn't like her other deals, where she kept herself detached from their acquisition. This deal was a lot more complicated because it was personal and although she was getting an all- expense-paid business and holiday trip, this deal was going to cost Avery a lot more than any vacation would.

As the plane started to speed down the runway, the young girl patted her hand and leaned toward her, pulling Avery from her thoughts.

"Are you scared of flying?" she asked Avery as the plane was launched into the air.

Avery turned toward her, glancing down to find she had a white-knuckled death grip on the armrest. She relaxed her hand and smiled at the young girl.

"I don't mind flying. I'm not too fond of the take-off and landing," Avery admitted.

"Would you like to hold Meg?" She held her yellow stuffed rabbit out to Avery. "Whenever I'm afraid, sad, or lonely, I find holding Meg makes me feel safe and happy again."

Avery's heart went out to the child when she saw a shadow of sadness in her big blue eyes. "That's so kind of you." She took the yellow bunny and examined it. "Meg looks like she's a very special bunny and reminds me of the special dolphin I had when I was your age. Her name was Delphine, and she also always made me feel safe."

She handed the bunny back to the child. "And if Meg is anything like Delphine, she can make everyone around you feel that way as long as you're the one holding her."

"Do you think so?" The young girl eyed her thoughtfully for a few seconds. "That would explain why my dad always seems so relaxed when we sit together to watch television or to read a story and I have Meg with me."

Avery's smile broadened at the child's reasoning. "I think for dads, it's a bit different," she explained. "I'm sure holding you would relax your dad because hugs have more power than anyone realizes. Especially when the hug comes from someone you love dearly, and I think Meg just gives a hug a little extra magic."

"Really?" The young girl's eyes filled with interest. "What kind of power?"

"Well, they can make you feel good again after you've been missing someone," Avery told her as an example.

"Yes, you're right!" she said, looking amazed. "Even though I've had the most amazing time with Nana and my aunt these past two weeks, I miss my daddy every day, and I can't wait to hug him again."

"And I bet as soon as you do, everything will feel right again," Avery pointed out.

The young girl nodded in agreement, saying, "I think you're right." She hugged her bunny close to her chest and smiled. "I'll make sure to give my dad a big hug when I see him again."

Avery smiled, feeling a sense of warmth in her heart. She turned her attention back to the window, watching as the plane flew through the clouds. She couldn't help but think about her own family back home and how much she missed them. She couldn't wait to see them again and give them all big hugs

"If I hug Meg, then hug you and Nana in my thoughts, between mine and Meg's hug power, I'll be able to embrace both of you, and you'll both be safe during take-off."

"Exactly!" Avery laughed as the aircraft launched into the air.

"Did you hear that, Nanna?" The young girl turned to her grandmother, who gave Avery a warm smile and mouthed, "Thank you."

"Yes, I did, and I have to agree with...." The child's grandmother looked questioningly at Avery.

"Avery," she said, and the feeling she'd met the woman before returned to her.

Avery gave herself a mental shake to shake off the feeling.

Since her mother told her about the crazy incident with the Zamboni that ruined her holiday plans, Avery felt fate had taken over her festive season.

"I'm Priscilla, and this is my great-granddaughter, Rose." Priscilla introduced them to Avery.

"Hi." Rose gave a little wave and held out her hand. "It's nice to meet you, Avery."

"It's nice to meet you too, Rose." Avery shook Rose's hand and turned her head to see Los Angeles shrink the higher the aircraft climbed.

There was no turning back now. Avery had officially accepted the assignment, which she knew could make or break much more than her career.

Avery hurried through the airport with a yellow stuffed bunny, Meg, under her arm as she made her way to the shuttle. She hoped she hadn't missed it.

On her way to the shuttle, Avery had tried some airport rental companies for a rental car in hopes of avoiding having to take the shuttle.

The airport was in chaos due to the many canceled flights, leaving many passengers stranded. There were no more rental cars, and Avery doubted that a taxi would take her to Frisco in the bad weather gathering outside.

The Mistletoe Lodge shuttle was Avery's only hope of getting to Frisco. Otherwise, she'd be stranded in Denver until the storm passed and the roads reopened.

Avery had just had the most hair-raising flight she'd ever been on. She had no idea how she'd managed to keep it together when her life flashed before her eyes when the pilot literally bounced them to a stop on the runway.

The last thing Avery wanted was to be stranded in Denver. All she wanted to do was get home to her parents and ensure her father was alright. Then she was going to have a long soak in a hot bath. She'd forgotten how cold Colorado was.

Avery scanned the crowd for Rose and Priscilla as she walked to the shuttle. She knew how much Meg the bunny meant to Rose, who must've dropped the toy when she'd disembarked the airplane with her great-grandmother.

Avery had hung back to check her messages, and that's when she found out that her father had a sprained ankle. They had arranged for Avery to get a ride on the Mistletoe Lodge shuttle to Frisco.

When Avery was ready to disembark and reached beneath the seat to get her purse, she found Rose's stuffed bunny.

Avery's heartstrings had pulled tight after seeing the abandoned bunny, and she knew how distraught Rose would be when she couldn't find her special bunny.

Avery had hoped to find Rose and Priscilla at the baggage claim, but they weren't there, and she had been unable to find them anywhere in the airport. With a heavy heart, Avery had to abandon her quest to return Meg, or she would miss the shuttle.

Avery flew out the airport doors when she saw the time. As she rounded the corner that led to the shuttle terminal, Avery froze on the spot and stared in horror at the empty space where the shuttle should be.

"Excuse me." Avery stopped someone wearing an airport security uniform.

"Can I help you, Miss?" The man asked politely.

"Do you know where I can find the Mistletoe Lodge shuttle service?" Avery asked him, hoping she was in the wrong place.

"I'm sorry, but the shuttle left ten minutes ago." He looked at her apologetically.

"Oh no!" Avery's face crumpled in despair, and her shoulders drooped. "What am I going to do now?"

"Perhaps you could try the rental car agencies," The security officer suggested. "But with the weather and the roads closed, it's unlikely that anyone will be able to take you to Frisco tonight."

Avery's heart sank as she realized that she was going to be stranded in Denver, far from her parents and her father's injury. She knew that she would have to wait until the storm passed and the roads reopened before she could finally get home.

"Thank you." Avery gave the security officer a tight smile.

With a heavy heart, she trudged towards the taxi rank, Meg the bunny still clutched under her arm. She knew that it was going to be a long and difficult night, but she was determined to make the best of it. She would find a cab or a hotel, call her parents to check on her father, and hope for the best.

There was no sign of Rose or Priscilla. Avery's heart skipped a beat when she saw a taxi pull up. She took Meg from beneath her arm as she repositioned her luggage to make a dash for the cab.

"What do you think, Meg?" Avery asked the bunny. "Could we persuade the taxi driver to take us to Frisco for a hefty fee?"

She was about to ask the driver about taking her to Frisco when a familiar young voice shouted to her from behind the cab.

"Avery!" Rose called, and Avery stood up, turning toward the sound of Rose's voice.

She stepped back onto the curb as Rose barreled into her, wrapping her little arms tightly around Avery's waist.

"Hey, kiddo, I've been looking for you." Avery dropped down on her haunches and held Meg up to her. Her heart felt even more sore when she saw Rose's puffy, tear-filled eyes. "Look who I found under the seat near my purse. Meg must have jumped out of your backpack and got left behind on the airplane."

"You saved Meg." Rose took her bunny and flung her arms around Avery's neck, nearly knocking her to the ground. "Thank you!"

"Oh, thank goodness you found the bunny," Priscilla said, walking up behind Rose. Her face was flushed from having had to chase after the little girl, and she stopped to catch her breath. "I wasn't sure how I would demand to be let back on the airplane to retrieve a stuffed bunny."

"I couldn't leave Meg behind!" Rose explained to Avery, pulling away, unraveling her arms from around Avery's neck, and wiping the tears from her cheeks. "I asked Nana to please go back and ask the captain to let her find Meg."

"No, of course, you couldn't leave Meg behind," Avery agreed with Rose, giving her a warm smile before standing up. Rose immediately took Avery's hand while she gripped Meg tightly to her chest with the other.

"Meg is the most special bunny in the world."

"But I would've paid to see your great-grandmother having a go at the captain." Avery teased, grinning at Priscilla. "I somehow can't picture you ever losing your cool," she complimented her.

"Trust me, my dear," Priscilla said with a twinkle in her eyes. "I can be quite fierce when defending my loved ones."

"I don't doubt that for a minute," Avery assured her.

"Where are you going, Avery?" Rose asked her.

"Right now, I'm not sure." Avery sighed and watched as the last taxi was taken. "All the rental cars are taken. I've missed my shuttle, and it seems the last taxi is gone too." She pointed to the vehicle pulling away from the space it was parked in.

"Perhaps we can give you a lift," Priscilla offered. "It's the least we can do after you saved me from spending the night in airport jail trying to rescue a yellow stuffed bunny." She smiled teasingly.

"It's kind of you to offer, but I'm going further than Denver, I'm afraid," Avery said, feeling deflated.

"We're also going further than Denver," Rose piped up. "We're going to Frisco!"

Avery's eyes widened in surprise, and she stared at Rose for a few seconds, wondering if she had heard the young girl right or if her tired brain was playing tricks on her.

"Did you say, Frisco?" Avery looked at Pricilla for confirmation.

"Yes, that is where we're headed, so if you're going in that direction, it would be our pleasure to offer you a ride with us," Pricilla told her.

"It just so happens that I'm also on my way to Frisco to spend the holidays with my parents in Frisco," Avery told them.

"Then it's settled," Priscilla said, waving at a man dressed in a black suit and black chauffeur's hat who walked briskly towards them. "Please, can you take our friend's luggage and put it in the trunk? We're going to drop her off in Frisco."

"Of course." The man politely tipped his hat at Avery and took her suitcase from her.

"Now come along, you two." Priscilla linked her arm through Avery's while Rose gripped Avery's hand, and they walked to the town car waiting for them on the curb.

On the journey to Frisco, the snow started to come down with force, and the drive home was slow as the chauffeur expertly handled the big car through the snow.

Rose and Priscilla kept her entertained while they swapped stories about Los Angeles. Rose excitedly told Avery about everything they had seen and done on their holiday.

They were about fifteen miles from Frisco when the driver pulled over to take a call from Priscilla's grandson.

The driver informed them that the pass into Frisco had been closed. No vehicles were getting in or out of Frisco.

"Oh dear," Priscilla said, turning to Avery. "I'm sorry, my dear, but it seems we aren't going to be able to get you to Frisco today."

"Oh no!" Avery breathed.

It was official. Fate really had hijacked her festive season and was busy toying with her.

"Don't worry, you'll come and stay with us until we can get you home." Priscilla comforted Avery by patting her hand. "I know you're eager to see your parents, but I'm sure they'll understand, and I'd rather you be safe with us than get to them in these dangerous weather conditions."

"I don't want to impose," Avery said as a feeling of dread crept up inside her for some reason, which she shook off.

"Not at all," Priscilla said, leaning forward to talk to the driver.

"This is awesome!" Rose's eyes shone with excitement. "You can meet my father, aunt, uncle, and Rory."

"Who's Rory?" Avery swallowed her disappointment in not being able to get home and concentrated on listening to Rose.

"My golden retriever," Rose told her. "He's two, and I've missed him so much."

She reached into her backpack and pulled out a sketchbook. "I'll show you. I drew a picture of him." She flipped through pictures of her book.

Avery was so astounded by Rose's amazing drawings that she forgot to ask Priscilla where she lived and didn't notice the road they turned onto.

CHAPTER 4

Ryder watched as the local vet helped Tinsel, one of the lodge's horses, deliver her foal. He knew his daughter was going to be disappointed that she hadn't been there for the birth, but she knew there was a possibility she might miss it.

As she had been given the duty of naming their new addition to the stables, she left Ryder with two names in case she wasn't there. Ranger if it was a colt, and Willow if it was a filly.

"Oh, my word, he's beautiful!" Emily beamed as she watched the new colt stand up on all fours.

"Welcome to the world, Ranger," Ryder said, giving the colt his name. The vet examined Tinsel and the foal, declaring them both healthy.

"Ranger is an awesome name," Emily commented. "What would the foal be called if it was a girl?"

"Willow," Ryder said, showing Emily the piece of paper with the two names on it.

"Willow is a beautiful name for a filly," she said. "Why can't I think of names like that when it's my turn to name our horses?"

"I don't know, Em," Ryder teased her. "But Tinsel and Popcorn are rather unique names." He laughed at the look his sister gave him.

As the vet left, Ryder couldn't help but worry about the weather. He looked over the snow-covered fields and buildings through the gray shading of the day that reflected off the heavy, dark clouds hanging threateningly over the mountains looming in the distance.

According to the weather report, there was a storm brewing that would hit full force by late afternoon. Local weather stations reported that airports were beginning to close due to the heavy snow that fell early in the morning.

Ryder felt like he had been holding his breath since he stepped out in the deep snow that morning to shovel the lodge's entrance, walkways, and driveway. He hoped that the last of his guests had all made their flights and would hopefully be able to land in Denver.

"I have some good news." Hank walked toward Ryder, pulling his jacket up around his neck as soft white specks of snow started to float down from the sky. "It seems all the guests arriving today have been accounted for at the airport, and the shuttle will be leaving Denver Airport in ten minutes." Hank handed Ryder the message he'd taken from the shuttle driver.

Ryder breathed a relieved sigh. "Thanks, Hank. I needed to hear that." He looked up at the sky as the snow began to fall faster. "Let's just hope the road remains passable for the next two hours to ensure they can get to the lodge." He looked at his wristwatch. "Any news on our homecomers?"

Hank nodded. "According to my friend who works at Denver Airport, their plane was the last to land before flights were rerouted. The car you ordered is already waiting for them."

"Great." Ryder felt a little lighter, but he wouldn't be completely at ease until everyone had arrived safely at the lodge.

"Emily also asked me to tell you she needs you back at the office," Hank said. "If you'll excuse me, I must sort out a leak in cabin five."

"Not again!" Ryder stared at Hank in disbelief. "Didn't you fix that yesterday?"

"I fixed *a* leak at cabin five. This is a different leak, which is why I didn't think it would be a good idea to let guests stay in the cabins we haven't fully fixed up yet."

"I know." Ryder sighed and pinched the bridge of his nose as snowflakes gathered in the brim of his Stetson and collected on his soft leather jacket. "I wasn't expecting to use them, but the news of the festival's revival hit us with that unexpected last-minute influx of guests. We had no options but to use the cabins because we can't afford to turn guests away."

"I know," Hank said. "We'll just have to keep patching things up, that's all."

"Thanks, Hank." Ryder watched him walk away towards cabin five.

He didn't know what they would've done without Hank. He was a Jack of all trades, and his plumbing skills were something that Ryder and Emily relied heavily on. Ryder started to walk back to the lodge. As he got to the front door, the snow picked up its pace and began to fall faster.

"Oh no!" Emily looked worriedly out the glass front doors of the lodge when Ryder stepped inside. "I was hoping the snow would stay away for another two to three hours."

"So did I," Ryder admitted, taking off his hat and jacket to hang them on the hook beside the front door. "But we'll just have to hope for the best." Ryder reassured her. "I just got word that the shuttle is on its way, and the car I ordered for our homecomers is already waiting for them at the airport."

"That's a relief," Emily said, visibly relaxing. "But we still need to keep an eye on the weather and make sure the roads are safe for them to travel on."

"I know," Ryder agreed. "I'll keep an eye on the forecast and make sure to update you and the guests on any changes."

"Thanks, Ryder," Emily said, giving him a small smile. "I don't know what we would do without you."

"You'd manage," Ryder said, returning her smile. "But I'm glad I'm here to help."

"Me too," Emily said. "Now, let's get back to work. We've got a lot to do before the guests arrive."

"Ryder, you didn't dust the snow off before coming inside." Emily's attention was drawn away from the snow to the slushy mess Ryder had made near the front door. "You'll need to get a cloth to clean that up before someone slips."

"Sorry." Ryder looked down at the mess he'd made. "I'll get the mop."

"No, need. I've got this." Nora, the lodge's cook and head housekeeper, appeared like magic.

"Thank you, Nora." Ryder gave her an appreciative smile.

"Honestly, Nora, you have to stop running after him like you do," Emily warned Nora. "You're spoiling him."

"Ryder has been working day and night to get the lodge back in shape," Nora pointed out. "It seems to me like he needs a bit of spoiling."

"At least someone appreciates me." Ryder gave his sister a smug smile and rewarded Nora for her royalty with a peck on the cheek before turning to Emily. "Hank told me you wanted to see me."

"Yes, I do." Emily turned and walked to the office. "We have some details to smooth out for the lodge and the festival."

"Can I grab a coffee first?" Ryder rubbed his hands together. He was cold and needed to warm himself up from the inside. Nothing warmed a person like coffee did. "I need to warm up."

"Why not stand by the fire in the office if you want to warm up?" Emily suggested. "We don't have much time before the guests arrive."

Ryder glanced towards the door. "It's looking like we need to change that statement to *if* the guests arrive."

Emily walked into the office and sat behind the desk, while Ryder sat in front of her.

"Don't be so pessimistic." Emily shook her head and rolled her eyes. "The shuttle driver is on his way with them as we speak."

"And grandmother?" Ryder asked.

"I'm waiting for the driver from the town car service you hired to call me as soon as they leave the airport." Emily fiddled with some papers in a file. "I thought you'd like to know that Small Valley is sending over the two horses we need in the morning due to the snow."

"That's fair enough." Ryder nodded. He couldn't expect his neighbors to drag their horses through a snowstorm. The lodge wouldn't need the horses right away because they were about to be snowed in, which meant no activities until it passed.

"I've filled the final two temporary positions for trail guides." Emily ticked off her list. "Frank Hawthorn is taking the booth." She caught Ryder's eyes as she spoke. "I'm sorry, but I couldn't find out anything about Avery." Her voice had dropped.

Ryder was loath to admit he'd been waiting since he'd opened his eyes this morning for Emily to find out if Avery would be in Frisco for the festive season. Ryder was also surprised by how much he wanted to know.

"Oh, I'd forgotten about that," Ryder lied, quickly moving the conversation away from Avery Hawthorn. "That means all the booths for the festival have been filled."

"Yes, they have." Emily nodded. "I've also arranged for the local school's choir to perform at the opening ceremony, and the mayor has agreed to give the opening speech."

"Sounds like everything's falling into place," Ryder said. "I just hope the storm holds off long enough for everything to go smoothly."

"We'll make it work," Emily said determinedly. "We always do."

"That we do," Ryder said, feeling proud of the work they had put into the lodge and the festival. It had been a long road, but it was all worth it in the end. The lodge and the festival were not only their livelihood but also their passion. They would make sure that this Christmas would be one to remember for their guests and the community.

"Oh, and I've added an extra booth for us," Emily informed him, and before he could say anything about it, she held up her hand, stopping him. "I've thought about it and gone over it a million times. Letting people know about the business we're starting after harvest season next year is a good move."

"Em, I agree, but there is also a downside to marketing too early," Ryder pointed out. "What if we have a bad harvest or our entire crop is destroyed, and we have to put the opening back six months to a year?"

"Then we'll plan how to advance while growing a list of interested contacts." Emily sat back against the chair, folding her arms in front of her, showing him she wouldn't give up on the idea no matter what he said.

"I also fear that knowing our plans with the orchard could spur that corporate hotel and resort chain into getting even more aggressive about obtaining Mistletoe Lodge," Ryder admitted his fears to Emily. "As it is, the mergers and acquisitions company representing them is sending someone to Frisco to make us yet another generous offer before the end of the festive season."

"Let them come." Emily raised her chin defiantly. "We've managed to fight them off this long, and if we can just hold them off for a few more months, we'll be able to get rid of them for good." She cocked her head. "Besides, where's the harm in humoring them and seeing what the person has to say?"

"I have no problem looking over the offer or listening to what they have to say," Ryder told her honestly. "It's what they are seeing and hearing that worries me."

"Then we'll have to be extra careful about what we say around them." Emily cocked her head and narrowed her eyes as she watched Ryder.

"Companies like that don't play by the rules like we're used to, Em," Ryder warned her. "They think nothing of blindsiding us with surprises." Ryder rubbed his face tiredly.

The door creaked open, and the smell of freshly brewed coffee tickled his senses. He turned to see Nora bring in a tray with coffee and freshly baked scones.

"Oh, Nora, you're my savior." Ryder stood up to take the tray from her.

"You skipped breakfast and lunch." Nora scolded him gently. "I thought you could use something to tide you over until dinner."

Ryder put the tray on the desk in front of Emily, and Nora left the room. Ryder had no sooner sat down and picked up one of the scones when the phone rang. Emily answered it while he ate the delicious treat. Ryder picked up his mug of coffee, frowning when he looked over at Emily, who looked like she'd just been shocked.

"Em, what's wrong?" He leaned forward, looking at her worriedly.

"That was Judy Hawthorn," Emily told him. "Frank slipped on black ice on the pavement and sprained his ankle. She wanted to warn us that they may not be able to take the booth. But they're hoping Avery would tend to it for them, but they won't know until they ask her when she arrives home this afternoon."

Ryder was shocked to hear the news that Avery was coming home and spilled his coffee all over the front of the desk and himself. He jumped up when the hot liquid scalded him. Holding his shirt away from his body, Ryder rushed to his apartment attached to the lodge. Inside, he locked the door and pulled off his shirt to tend to the burn.

His hands shook as he found some ointment and put it on the red welt before finding a clean shirt.

As he dressed, he reasoned that while Frisco was a small town, one could go weeks without running into someone. Avery's parents also lived on the opposite side of town from the lodge, making the chances of avoiding each other during her trip home good.

But Ryder knew a meeting between himself and Avery was inevitable, especially if she ran Hawthorn's festival booth. He knew he needed to apologize and explain why he left things the way he did. He would think about how to approach her later, when he had more time alone.

He heard a vehicle arrive and looked out the window to see the shuttle. He pushed thoughts of Avery aside and focused on his guests. He could ponder how to approach Avery later that night.

"What did Gran do now?" Emily asked, clutching an armful of menus as she walked over to the front desk, where Ryder was standing, muttering beneath his breath.

"Apparently, she picked up a stranger in need of a ride to Frisco. The pass into town is closed, so we're putting her guest up in the lodge until the storm passes," Ryder said, irritation lacing his voice.

"Well, it's lucky then that we kept that one room open and ready upstairs," Emily chirped. "Did the driver say who this mystery guest is?"

"No, he was rather vague about it." Ryder frowned. "I'll call him back and find out more."

Before Ryder could dial the driver's number, the town car pulled up outside the lodge. A feeling of dread crept up Ryder's spine, and he shook it off. He'd been feeling uneasy since Emily had told him about Avery. He watched the driver climb out of the car and walk around the back to open the passenger door.

"Gran's home," Emily said excitedly, slapping the menus down on the front desk and making Ryder jump. She then dashed for the front door.

Ryder staved off a shudder and ignored the growing feeling of apprehension that got worse the closer he got to the front door.

CHAPTER 5

Avery's head shot up from looking at Rose's sketchbook when the car came to a stop, and she looked around to get her bearings. She caught her breath when she realized where she was. "You live here?" Avery asked, her eyes wide as she looked questioningly at Priscilla.

"Yes, dear. The lodge belongs to my grandchildren," Priscilla replied.

Before Avery could say more, the back door opened, and the chauffeur helped Priscilla out of the car. Avery's heart sank as she realized why Priscilla had seemed so familiar to her when they'd met on the airplane. They had briefly met twelve years ago.

Avery was about to ask Rose who her father was, but the little girl bounded out of the car so fast that she left her rabbit behind on the car seat. "Well played, fate, well played!" Avery whispered softly, then looked at the yellow rabbit she picked up. "You do know this is all your fault, Meg!" she said accusingly to the rabbit. "If you hadn't fallen out of the backpack, I would've caught the shuttle and would be home by now."

Avery wondered if anyone would notice if she stayed in the car until the storm passed. But Priscilla thwarted that idea. "Avery, dear," Priscilla said as she popped her head into the car. Her hair had flakes of snow sprinkled over it. "Are you okay?"

"I'm fine," Avery squeaked, clearing her throat, knowing she had no option but to slide out of the car. "I'm bracing myself for the cold out there," she lied.

"There's a lovely warm fire in the living room, and Nora, our cook, will bring us all a hot mug of cocoa." Priscilla tempted her with warmth and hot chocolate beverages that Avery knew she couldn't resist. "Now, come meet my grandchildren."

Priscilla gave Avery a knowing smile before walking off, and that's when Avery realized that Priscilla had known who she was from the moment they'd met on the airplane.

"Rosie!" Ryder stooped down and held his arms open for his daughter, who launched herself into his arms.

Ryder's arms closed around her, and he swung her around, hugging her tightly, then kissing her face and hair when he stopped spinning her around. "I've missed you so much."

"I missed you so much too, Daddy." Rose hugged him tightly. "But I feel much better now that I've hugged you."

"Is that so?" Ryder teased her and gave her a tickle. "Because I still need a few more hugs from you before I feel better from missing you so much."

Rose giggled, and just as he was about to let his daughter go, Hank ripped her from his arms, wanting his turn to greet his niece. Rose giggled even more as Hank swung her around, but he soon lost Rose to a possessive Emily, wanting her turn to greet her niece.

"Ryder, be a dear and go welcome my guest to the lodge," Priscilla ordered, giving him a slow smile that made Ryder suspicious. "I think they may be a bit shy." Something twinkled in her eyes.

He knew that twinkle. He thought suspiciously as he watched her greet Emily and Hank. She was up to something. Ryder was sure of it. He turned toward the car and went to get his grandmother's shy guest, whom Ryder hoped wasn't a con artist.

He had often warned his grandmother about talking to strangers, but she would ask how they were expected to become friends if she didn't speak to them.

Ryder sighed and pulled the car door open more forcefully than he should've, nearly pulling his grandmother's guest with it. Their hand got caught in the door, but they managed to yank it free. But they lost their balance. As Ryder reached down to steady the woman, his eyes locked with hers, and Ryder's body went numb with shock. The only thought that filtered through his mind was that his grandmother's guest was no con artist but the woman who had haunted his dreams for the past twelve years.

Avery took a deep breath, readying herself to come face-to-face with a man she'd once vowed she never wanted to see again for the rest of her life.

Her heart started to pound so hard as she reached for the door handle that she was sure everyone outside could hear it.

"Here goes nothing." Avery sighed.

She went to pull the door handle, and she nearly got yanked from the car when the door swung open. Avery's fingers were pulled abruptly from the handle, making her lose her balance. She almost tumbled from the car when a hand reached out to steady her.

"Careful," a deep, familiar voice she had found hard to forget, made her heart stop for a minute. As she turned her head and climbed out of the car, her eyes locked with the one person Avery had hoped to have more time to prepare before meeting—Ryder Carlisle.

"Avery?" he whispered, not believing his eyes.

Avery's face went pale, and her eyes widened in shock. "Ryder?" She whispered back, looking just as stunned as he felt.

They stood there, staring at each other in disbelief, until Priscilla's voice broke the spell. "Avery, dear, don't be shy. Come inside and get warm."

Avery's mind went blank for a minute as she stared at him. He looked exactly the same as she remembered him, just a little more mature.

"You're my grandmother's mystery guest?" Ryder asked, still looking at her as if he couldn't quite believe she was real.

Avery's throat felt dry, and her heart was beating so fast she felt giddy. All rational thought seemed to have left her brain. "I-I was on my way home for the holidays and got stranded by the snowstorm," she stuttered, feeling like a fool.

"I see," Ryder said, still looking at her as if he was trying to read her mind.

Avery felt her cheeks flush with embarrassment. She didn't know what to say or do. All she could think about was wishing she'd stayed hidden in the car.

"Come meet my friend, Aunt Em." Rose's voice caught her attention, and she couldn't have been more thankful for the interruption.

"Avery!" Emily exclaimed excitedly. "Oh, my word!"

"Emily." Avery smiled and was engulfed in her childhood best friend's arms before being dragged into the lodge. She turned as she walked through the door to find Ryder still standing in the snow, staring after her.

Ryder stood watching Rose, Emily, and Avery disappear into the lodge. His and Avery's gazes locked briefly again before she was swallowed by the lodge. Shock resounded through his body. He couldn't believe it.

Avery was here, in Frisco, and at his lodge, of all places. He had no idea what to do or say, but he knew one thing for sure: this festive season just got a lot more stressful and nerve-wracking.

He knew Avery was coming home for the holidays, but Ryder thought he'd have more time to prepare for their meeting. He also hadn't expected to feel that familiar old jolt in his heart and his breath catch in his throat at the sight of her. Ryder was aware that seeing her again was going to be awkward, and he knew that she'd always be his first big love.

But he hadn't expected to feel the burst of emotion he'd felt, making him realize that even time, a loving marriage, and twelve years hadn't dulled his feelings.

They'd just covered them over like a band-aid on a wound that actually needed stitching. After the last time he had to let her go, he felt like there was no surgery in the world that could stop his heart from bleeding.

"Ryder!" Emily stuck her head out the door and called him.

Ryder was jolted from his thoughts. He took a few bags from the trunk to help the driver and walked into the lodge.

As Avery was introduced to Emily's husband, she couldn't help but feel happy for her childhood best friend. Hank seemed to adore Emily. She was only a little in awe of Hank, who was a retired pro hockey player for her favorite team.

While Avery's stomach was in knots over seeing Ryder again, Emily, Rose, Priscilla, and even Hank made her feel happy she'd gotten snowed in with them.

Avery and Emily had been inseparable when they were young, right up until Avery left to go study in Los Angeles and Emily went to study in Denver. At first, they called each other every second day. That became once a week, which slowly dwindled to once a month until their contact stopped. She watched the loving exchange between Emily and her, and her heart squeezed. She was so happy for them.

Rose quickly captured Avery's attention by introducing her to Rory, her two-year-old golden retriever. He was a honey who didn't want Avery to stop petting him, for which she was rewarded with wet dog kisses over her face and arms.

When Ryder walked in carrying Avery's bags, Priscilla asked him to show Avery up to her room. Avery felt a knot form in her stomach as she followed him up the stairs. The small talk between them was awkward and stilted, and Avery couldn't help but feel a sense of discomfort.

As they reached the top of the stairs, Ryder opened the door to her room.

"Here's your room." He pushed open the door and gestured for her to enter.

Avery walked into the room and took in the cozy, warm atmosphere. It was decorated with a Christmas theme and had a small fireplace in the corner. Ryder pointed out a few of the amenities.

"It's lovely. Thank you." Avery avoided eye contact.

Ryder nodded and said, "I'm glad you like it." He paused for a moment before adding, "My family asked if you'd join us for dinner tonight."

She knew that it would be a difficult and awkward evening, but she couldn't be rude and decline.

"I'd like that," Avery lied, hoping her reservation didn't show in her eyes.

"Great, dinner is at six thirty in the main dining room," Ryder informed her. "It's not hard to find." He turned and pointed to the stairs. "Down the stairs and to the right."

"I think I can remember where it is!" Avery gave a nervous laugh.

"If you need anything, you can let the front desk know." Ryder gave her a tight smile. "I'll see you at dinner."

He gave her a nod and left the room, pulling the door closed behind him. Avery let out the breath she realized she'd been holding since walking into the room and felt a sense of relief wash over her. That was until she remembered she'd agreed to have dinner with the Carlisle family and was once again awash with nerves.

Avery glanced at her luggage, which Ryder had neatly placed near the door. She was about to take out some necessary items, thinking she was only going to be there for the night, when she noticed missed messages from her mother.

"Oh, no," Avery muttered.

She hadn't spoken to her mother since the airport, and she must be beside herself with worry. She hit the dial, and her mother answered on the second ring.

"Avery, honey, we've been so worried." Judy's voice resonated with panic and fear. "Where are you?" She spoke so fast, blasting questions at Avery. "Are you alright?"

"I'm fine, Mom," Avery told her. "I got a ride from the airport with Pricilla Carlisle and her great-granddaughter, Rosie."

"Priscilla?" Judy breathed. "She must be back from California."

"Yes, they were on the same flight as me," Avery explained. "I'm at Mistletoe Lodge as we couldn't get into Frisco because of the blizzard."

"I was so worried about that!" Judy exclaimed. "But I'm glad you're safe and not too far from town."

"As soon as the roads opened, Priscilla said she'd let her driver take me into Frisco," Avery told her mother.

"You obviously know that Ryder is back at the lodge." Judy's voice was filled with concern.

"Thank you for telling me Ryder was at the lodge, by the way, mother!" Avery's tone was a mix of surprise and a touch of playful sarcasm. "Why would you keep that from me?" She shook her head. "It would've been nice to know, even if fate didn't intervene and land me at the lodge. I was sure to find out."

"I didn't think it would matter," Judy told her. "Besides, Ryder hardly ever comes into Frisco. We live here, and we've barely seen him a dozen times since he's been back."

"So what?" Avery frowned, rubbing her forehead with the palm of her hand. "Were you hoping we wouldn't run into each other while I was here?"

"No, I was going to tell you when you were here," Judy admitted. "The real reason I didn't tell you when you decided to come home for Christmas was because I didn't want you to change your mind."

"It wouldn't have swayed my decision to come home for Christmas, Mom," Avery assured her. "If I'd known, I would've been better prepared to see him." She sighed. "It was just a shock to see him after all these years."

"I understand, and I'm sorry, honey," Judy apologized. "I'm glad you're safe and sad that you're not here with us as your father and I have been looking forward to you coming home."

"I know, Mom." Avery let out a breath. "But until the weather has cleared, I'm stuck at the lodge, and I don't want you or dad trying to get here to fetch me."

"Don't worry, sweetheart, your father can't drive at the moment, and you know I *never* drive in this weather if it's not for an emergency," Judy assured her. "Call me in the morning."

Avery promised to do so and hung up. She plopped down on the soft bed and stifled a yawn. She was tired as she'd been up most of the previous night being a nervous flier. She looked at the clock on the nightstand and pursed her lips.

Avery had two hours before dinner, which would give her enough time to shower, unpack a few items for her stay at the lodge, and go over some work. She placed her hands on the soft mattress, quelling the urge to curl into a ball and let herself sink into its comfort for an hour's sleep.

Avery sighed, knowing if she did close her eyes for an hour, she'd be all dozy, and she wanted to be alert when she attended dinner with the Carlisle family. Giving herself a mental shake, Avery forced herself off the bed and tended to her luggage before going to shower.

CHAPTER 6

Ryder's mind was a whirlwind of conflicting emotions as he walked away from Avery's room. He hadn't expected her sudden appearance in his life again, and the unexpected rush of memories and feelings from their past had shaken him more than he cared to admit.

He'd spent the past few years pouring his heart into saving the lodge and providing for his family, and he thought he'd moved on from the pain of their broken engagement. Yet, there she was, back in Frisco and now under the same roof.

He needed to clear his head and remind himself that the lodge's guests were his top priority. With a determined breath, he made his way down to the lobby, his thoughts still a jumble of the past and the present.

Just as he was about to approach the front desk to attend to the new guests, a familiar voice called out, "Daddy!"

Ryder turned, and a smile tugged at his lips as Rosie came bounding towards him. Her joy was infectious, and he found himself grinning wider as she threw herself into his arms.

"Daddy, Aunt Em told me the colt was born earlier today!" Rosie exclaimed, her eyes sparkling with excitement.

"Ah, yes, that's right." Ryder chuckled, ruffling her hair. "If you give me a few minutes to help Emily with the new guest arrivals, I'll take you to see him."

"Okay," Rosie said. "I'll help too."

"Thank you, sweetheart, you can take Rory out of the way and take him to the kitchen to see if Nora has a snack for him.

"Sure." Rosie called Rory, and the two rushed toward the kitchen.

Before Ryder could give Avery another thought, he stepped up to the front desk to help his sister get the new arrivals checked in. Twenty minutes later, he went to find Rosie, who was helping Nora bake Christmas cookies in the kitchen.

"There you are." Ryder walked to the counter and stole a cookie that had just been iced.

"Hey, those are for the guests," Nora grumbled.

"I have to test them," Ryder told her.

"You know Nora makes the best cookies, Dad." Rosie laughed at him. "You've eaten them like a million times, so they don't need testing."

"You never know." Ryder grinned, grabbing another cookie. "Are you ready to go say hello to Ranger, the new colt?"

Rosie nodded vigorously, her enthusiasm undeniably infectious as she pulled off the apron, plopped it on a chair, and took Ryder's hand.

"Hold on," Nora said. "I have a few horse nibbles I put aside."

She went to one of the large refrigerators and pulled out a bag with carrots and another with apple slices.

"Thank you, Nora," Rosie said, taking the bags from her. "The horses love these."

Ryder and Rosie left the kitchen hand in hand, and as they were about to head towards the stables, Rosie noticed Avery walking down the stairs. Ryder's heart skipped a beat at the sight of her. She had clearly taken a shower, her hair still damp, and she was wearing a cozy sweater that accentuated her beauty and a pair of jeans with her feet snuggled in fur-lined boots.

Their eyes met, and he felt a swirl of emotions he struggled to contain. Awkwardness, regret, and something he couldn't quite place.

"Avery!" Rosie squealed in delight.

"Hi again," Avery said, offering Rosie a warm smile.

"Hi," Ryder replied, his voice betraying a hint of nervousness he hadn't expected.

Before things could become more awkward, Rosie piped up, her excitement bubbling over. "Avery, you should come with us to see the new colt! I can show you all our other horses." She held up the bags of snacks from Nora. "And we can feed them."

Ryder glanced at Avery, his gaze a mixture of surprise and uncertainty. He hadn't expected Rosie to be so quick to invite Avery along. Ryder's feelings waned between hoping she'd say yes and hoping she'd make an excuse.

Avery's eyes flickered between Ryder and Rosie before she nodded. "I'd love to see the new colt." She looked at Ryder for confirmation. "If that's okay with your dad?"

"Of course," Ryder said, then cleared his throat as his voice sounded a little scratchy.

As they walked towards the stables, Ryder found himself falling into step beside Avery. The silence between them was heavy with unspoken words and memories, and he struggled to find the right thing to say.

"You and Emily always used to be in the stables when you were younger," Ryder finally managed to say, attempting to break the ice.

Avery glanced at him and nodded before once again fixing her gaze on the snowy path ahead. "Yes, we loved to help groom them."

There was so much left unsaid between them, and Ryder suddenly felt the weight of it all. The memories of their past—the hurt he had caused—were haunted by the life they could have had together.

"You and Aunt Em groomed the horses." Rosie looked at Avery with big, curious eyes. "I do that with Aunt Em as well." Her cheeks dimpled. "Aunt Em was the one who taught me to ride a horse." She drew in an excited breath. "When we've finished seeing the colt, I can introduce you to my horse, Star."

"I would love to meet Star," Avery told her as Rosie slipped her other hand into hers.

Ryder swallowed at the sight of his daughter and Avery walking hand-in-hand as Rosie chatted to her about the colt and the other horses in the stables. Avery engaged with Rosie, her smile genuine and warm, and Ryder found himself admiring the ease with which Avery interacted with his daughter.

As they reached the stables, the sweet scent of hay and horses filled the air. Rosie led Avery to the stall where the colt lay, nestled in the hay, his eyes blinking lazily while his mother hovered over him.

"This is Ranger," Avery told her. "And that's his mother, Tinsel. She's one of the lodge's trail ride mares."

"Ranger is adorable," Avery said, her voice soft as she reached out to gently stroke the colt's nose. "And Tinsel is a very proud mother."

"Here, give her an apple slice." Rosie dug one out of the bag for Avery.

"I think Ranger is going to make a fine horse for the lodge," Ryder said, his gaze flickering between Avery, Rosie, and the colt.

The next thirty minutes seemed to blur into a whirl of laughter and horse feeding as Rosie dragged them from stall to stall, introducing Avery to each horse. Ryder and Avery's awkwardness began to fade, replaced by a sense of camaraderie and nostalgia.

"I see the stables haven't changed much except for the horses," Avery commented when they finally left the stables to head back to the lodge for dinner.

The sun had begun to dip below the horizon, casting a warm golden glow over the snowy landscape. Ryder found himself stealing glances at Avery when he thought she wasn't looking. He couldn't deny the pull he still felt towards her, the memories of their shared past, and the chemistry they once had.

"We do have plans to expand as soon as we have the finances," Ryder explained as he glanced around the lodge grounds. "Emily and I want to do quite a bit of expansion and revamping of the place."

Ryder saw Avery's head turn toward the orchard.

"Have you reopened your mother's orchard?" Avery looked at him questioningly.

She gestured towards a fenced area nearby, where rows of young apple trees stood, their branches reaching towards the sky.

"Yes." Ryder nodded, stopping beside her with Rosie hanging onto his hand and his gaze turning to the orchard. "But it's no longer just apples, as I'm now also farming mistletoe."

Avery's eyes widened in surprise. "That's incredible!"

Ryder nodded. A sense of pride evident in his voice. "Yeah, it's been about fourteen months since I started. The mistletoe sales have already been taking off surprisingly well."

Avery looked genuinely impressed. "That's amazing, Ryder. It must have taken a lot of work."

He shrugged modestly. "Yeah, it has its challenges, but I believe in it. It's a way to sustain the lodge and honor its legacy." He gave a soft snort, remembering his mother. "My mother's apples and apple products were well known in Colorado."

"I remember," Avery said. "I'm sure she'd be both pleased and proud."

Ryder nodded in appreciation of her kind words while his heart dropped, wondering if he'd be able to continue the orchard as this season would be the turning point for his family legacy.

"Can we show Avery the orchard?" Rosie looked up at him, hopefully.

"Maybe tomorrow," Ryder promised. "You know how Gran gets if we're late for dinner."

"Aww." Rosie's brow crinkled as she moaned in disappointment.

"We need to keep some fun for tomorrow," Avery whispered conspiratorially to Rosie, making her grin.

Ryder chuckled as he watched the two of them conspire and marveled at how easily Avery had connected with his daughter and how she had become a part of their world in such a short time.

"So, mistletoe and apples," Avery said, her voice lighthearted as they continued their walk back to the lodge. "That's quite the combination."

Ryder nodded, a smile tugging at his lips. "Yeah, it's a bit unconventional, but it seemed like the right way to blend the old and the new. The lodge's history and the fresh start"

Avery glanced at him, her expression thoughtful. "It's a beautiful way to honor the past while building for the future."

Ryder's heart skipped a beat at her words. It was as if she had summed up his entire mission in just one sentence. "Exactly."

By the time they reached the lodge, Ryder's family had already started to gather for dinner.

"Thank you for inviting me to see the colt," Avery said to Rosie.

"You're welcome," Rosie told her. "Tomorrow we can go to the orchard and maybe the lake."

Avery smiled. "That sounds wonderful."

Inside the lodge, the warmth of the fire and the soft glow of the lights welcomed them.

"There the three of you are!" Priscilla walked toward them.

"We took Avery to see the colt and horses," Rosie explained.

"That sounds so exciting!" Priscilla exclaimed. "I bet all that cold and exercise must've worked up an appetite."

"I'm starved!" Rosie exaggerated.

"Then go wash up. Emily and Hank are already waiting for us at the table," Priscilla told them. "You can use the restroom just outside the dining area, Avery."

"Thank you," Avery said with a slight nod before slipping past Priscilla.

"I'll go wash up quickly too," Ryder told his grandmother, who nodded and then turned to head into the dining room while he slipped off to the bathroom that led off his office.

Ryder's mind reeled with the events of the day. His emotions were in turmoil over the unexpected reunion. Avery's presence had unearthed memories and feelings he had thought were long buried. And as he saw Rosie's easy rapport with Avery, he couldn't help but wonder why fate had intersected their paths again and what it could mean for their future.

CHAPTER 7

The dining hall of Mistletoe Lodge was transformed into a cozy haven of warmth and light, with the long wooden table adorned with flickering candles and rich, winter-inspired decorations.

The air was alive with the tantalizing aroma of a delicious winter dinner, a fusion of hearty flavors that spoke of tradition and comfort. Roasted meats, glazed vegetables, and fragrant herbs composed a symphony of tastes that enveloped the senses.

Seated at the table, Avery found herself next to Ryder, the tension from their past still lingering in the air despite their efforts to navigate it. Yet, the jovial atmosphere of the Carlisle family dinner worked its magic, drawing her into the fold and relaxing some of the tension.

Much to Avery's delight, conversation flowed seamlessly around her, the talk revolving around the lodge and the upcoming winter festival that would be held on its picturesque grounds.

Priscilla's eyes twinkled as she addressed Avery. "We're truly delighted you joined us for dinner, dear."

Avery offered a genuine smile. "Thank you for inviting me, Priscilla."

Emily leaned forward, her excitement palpable. "It's so good to see you again."

"Likewise," Avery told her, taking the potatoes from Ryder and nearly dropping them when their fingers brushed.

Hank leaned forward and picked up the bowl of peas to scoop some onto his plate before handing the bowl to Emily and looking at Avery. "You chose the right year to come home for Christmas, Avery." He picked up the gravy boat. "This year we're bringing back the Winter Festival."

"Oh, really?" Avery's eyes widened in excited surprise.

She'd loved the annual Mistletoe Winter Festival as a kid. Her parents would have a booth each year, which she'd help out at in between her and Emily racing around the place.

"Yes, it seemed like the perfect year to bring back the festivities of the festival." Emily passed a bowl onto Priscilla.

Rosie, seated next to Ryder, leaned forward to look at Avery and couldn't contain her enthusiasm. "Avery, you're going to love it!"

"Wow, that's great news," Avery said, putting the bowl she had in her hands on the table. "I used to love the festival as a kid, and like the rest of the town, I was sad when it stopped." She filled her glass with water. "Christmas in Frisco didn't seem the same without the excitement of the festival."

"I know what you mean," Priscilla told her. "Christmas in Frisco lost a bit of sparkle, and the town seemed disjointed."

"Yes, like there was nothing for them to come together for, to share the joy of Christmas," Emily added.

"There was the town market square fair and the lighting of the Christmas tree," Ryder reminded them.

"We know." Hank nodded. "But it wasn't the same." He started to dig into his dinner. "There were no games. There was no coming together to work towards something."

"No spirit," Priscilla said, providing the mixing ingredient for the last ten Frisco Christmases.

"Exactly!" Hank said, pointing his fork. "There was no spirit."

Ryder's gaze locked on Avery's. "That's because the Winter Fair holds a special place in not only the history of Mistletoe Lodge but Frisco as well."

Avery nodded in agreement. "Maybe the fair will bring back some of that Christmas spirit the town has lacked since it was stopped."

"I hope so." Priscilla's eyes held a mixture of fondness and nostalgia. "The festival is a tradition that's been woven into our family legacy ever since my husband's ancestor founded this lodge. My son lost his taste for it when his wife died."

"I think Dad lost a lot when Mom died." Ryder's voice was soft and full of emotion.

Emily's eyes sparkled with determination. "That's why we're not going to have any more losses in this family, and that's why we decided it was time to bring back that magic. To honor the past and breathe life into the present."

Hank's grin was infectious. "And hopefully restore more than just the lodge, but the spirit of Christmas for the town."

Rosie's excitement bubbled over as she told Avery, "There are going to be games, like sack races, sled races, hay rides, and snowman-building competitions."

Ryder chimed in, his voice carrying a mix of nostalgia and anticipation. "We're recreating the charm of the old fair with some modern touches, of course."

Emily's grin widened. "We're going to be kicking the festival off with a Christmas tree lighting on the first evening."

Hank leaned forward. "Picture this: the entire town gathered around the main Christmas tree, which will stand at the end of the stall rows." His eyes gleamed as he got lost in his tale. "The tree stands adorned with all its finery."

"The countdown starts after my grandmother and Ryder have addressed the festival."

"Hey!" Ryder frowned. "Why do I have to do public speaking?" He looked at Priscilla. "I'm sure whatever Gran has to say will be more than sufficient."

"Ryder!" Emily admonished her brother. "Do you mind?" She glared at him. "Hank and I are setting the mood here."

"Sorry!" Ryder pulled a face and turned back to his food.

"Where was I?" Emily looked at Hank.

"You were about to get to the Christmas tree lighting countdown," Hank reminded her.

"The countdown begins when the honored guest," Emily turned and grinned at Avery. "Maybe you, Avery." Her grin grew when she noted Avery's cheeks pinkening.

"Five, four, three, two...." Emily, Hank, and Rosie counted down.

"Avery hits the switch, and the Christmas tree sparkles to life." Emily finished. "It's a magical moment."

"Wow, that was quite a picture you painted." Avery laughed. "I remember when we were kids, Em, you and I so wanted to be the ones pushing that button."

"Yes, and then that one Christmas when the tree lights blew the grid." Emily and Avery laughed at the memory. "We finally got to do it, but without the big ceremony."

"We turned it off and back on again, so each of us got a turn," Avery reminisced.

"I want to have a turn to push the button too," Rosie said, joining in the joviality.

"How about this?" Avery leaned over to look at Rosie. "If I'm asked to push the button, you can come on stage and help me."

"Really?" Rosie's eyes lit up like a Christmas tree at the thought.

"Yes!" Avery nodded and was rewarded with a squeal of delight.

"So, can I take that as a yes? You'll be our honored guest who pushed the button." Emily asked her.

"What about the mayor?" Avery looked at Emily. "Doesn't he usually do that?"

"Oh no, he won't mind," Priscilla assured Avery. "Mayor Green prefers to stay out of the limelight."

Hank's voice held warmth as he moved the conversation away from the tree lighting. "We're organizing various booths—a craft market, local artisans showcasing their talents, and an array of delectable winter treats."

Rosie beamed at Avery. "And guess what? There'll be gingerbread decorating for the kids and ornament crafting."

Ryder's eyes met Avery's again. "It's about creating a sense of togetherness. We're not just reviving the fair; we're bringing back the spirit of community."

As dinner progressed, conversations ebbed and flowed, the family's passion for the Winter Fair evident in every word. Avery found herself once again being drawn deeper into their world as they shared moments from previous fairs. A sense of nostalgia warmed her from the treasured memories of her past with the Carlisle family.

By the time dessert arrived, Avery's tensions had all but gone as laughter filled the table. After dinner, Priscilla insisted they all retire to the family living room to sit around the fire for a cup of cocoa. Avery noticed that Ryder didn't join them and was shocked to feel a pang of disappointment, which soon passed when she and Rosie settled into one of the overstuffed sofas by the crackling fire.

Avery noticed the craft boxes and various ornaments on the coffee table.

"That's for us to make Christmas decorations to add to the Carlisle family collection," Rosie told Avery.

"You still do that?" Avery was surprised to hear they had carried on the tradition.

When Ryder's and Emily's mother died, the Winter Festival wasn't the only thing he stopped. Christmas at the Carlisle family became bleaker each year after that, along with all the Carlisle family Christmas traditions.

Emily once again took Avery on a visual explanatory tour of how they'd revamped the Carlisle family decoration-making tradition.

"We make decorations for all the trees on the property," Emily told her.

"And I chose a tree for the Children's ward at the local hospital," Rose said proudly. "Then we go to the hospital and spend a day with the kids there, making decorations with them too."

"That was Rosie's idea to honor her mother," Ryder's voice came from behind the sofa where Avery and Rosie were sitting.

Avery's heart jolted, and she felt tiny shock waves zing through her system as she turned to see him standing leaning on the back of the sofa.

"We try to create an enchanting wonderland for the kids at the hospital, along with a small Christmas party with gifts," Rosie added.

"That is a wonderful tradition." Avery dragged her eyes away from Ryder to concentrate on Rosie.

Emily's eyes danced with pride as she looked at Rosie. "Rosie here has a natural talent for decorating. She's the creative genius behind a lot of the ornaments."

Rosie beamed with pride, her cheeks flushing with pleasure. "I love making the decorations! And tomorrow, we're making gingerbread houses too!" Her eyes lit up with an idea as she looked at Avery questioningly. "Will you join us?"

"Oh, yes, please, Avery," Emily said, backing up Rosie's invitation. "It would be just like old times when we used to do it as kids."

"I'm not sure how long I'm going to be here tomorrow," Avery told them. "It all depends on the weather." Her heart sank when she saw the disappointment cloud Rosie's and Emily's eyes. "Although I guess I can stay here a little longer, and I do love decorating ornaments, I especially love gingerbread houses."

Rosie's eyes immediately sparkled with delight once again. "We can decorate a house together."

"I'd like that," Avery told her.

A peaceful silence fell over the room as they sipped their cocoa and were drawn in by the fire crackling in the hearth, casting a warm and inviting glow as its flames danced to a beat they couldn't hear.

Ryder broke the silence. "Rosie, honey, it's time for bed."

"Aww, Dad!" Rosie tilted her head back to look up at him. "Just a few more minutes, please."

"You've had an hour longer, sweetheart," Ryder pointed out. "It's time to say goodnight, or you're going to be tired and miss out on all the fun tomorrow."

"Okay," Rosie said, dragging her feet as she hugged everyone in the living room goodnight and left the room with her father.

Not long after Rosie went to bed, Priscilla, Hank, and Emily followed, leaving Avery to enjoy the fire a little longer. As the lodge fell into silence, Avery found she was no longer tired, and the stress of the day had built into a restless energy.

She stood and walked to the large windows that showcased the world outside. The black backdrop of the sky was underlined by the thick blanket of snow covering the ground. The snowfall had ceased temporarily. Avery pulled her coat on as she made her way to the entrance of the lodge, deciding to take a walk to clear her thoughts. She stepped outside into the crisp night air.

Avery loved the serene stillness caused when the snow stopped falling. Like nature was taking a breath and the world lay in frozen anticipation of the next downpour.

The untouched snow crunched beneath her boots as she walked, her mind swirling in contemplation. Avery wasn't sure where she was going. She was deep in thought, her mind ticking over the events of the day while she grappled with her conscience.

The Carlisles were working so hard to save the lodge and had no idea that it was already too late to do so. Guilt washed over Avery as she came to the open area at the back of the lodge, where a handful of fire pits lit the night with their dying flames.

Each pit was surrounded by a circle of benches for the guests to enjoy an evening outside. Just inside the glass back doors was a long table laid out with long sticks and different ingredients for the guests to roast over the fire if they chose to. Avery swallowed, and her eyes misted over at the memories this area held for her.

As small children, Avery and Emily loved sitting around a pit, roasting marshmallows, or coming up with different flavors of s'mores. As teenagers and young adults, Avery and Ryder had made romantic memories around them.

Avery pulled her coat tighter around her as a chill crept up her spine, but this chill was deeper than skin deep. It was the chill of guilt and betrayal. And this wasn't guilt or betrayal from her history with Ryder.

It was over what she'd ultimately come home to Frisco for—to acquire Mistletoe Lodge by any means necessary for her firm's client. She swallowed the burning lump in her throat and fought back the tears.

It wasn't supposed to be this hard! Avery thought. Fate was a cruel master at times, and right now it felt like fate was standing in front of her with a judgmental look on its face.

"Couldn't sleep either?" Ryder's voice, although soft in the quiet night, made her jump with fright, as she'd been so lost in her tortured thoughts that she hadn't heard him approach.

Avery turned to see him standing with his hands shoved into his sheepskin jacket as he stared at her. Her heart picked up speed, and her breath caught in her throat. Ryder Carlisle was still one of the most handsome men, with the most gorgeous smile.

Avery shook her head and hoped her eyes weren't shining with the guilt churning inside her. "It seems like we're both in need of some fresh air."

"I see there are still a few s'mores sticks." Ryder pointed to the table. "Might I tempt you into joining me around the last of the dying fires?"

"You know I can never say no to s'mores." Avery gave a nervous laugh.

Ryder smiled and offered her his arm, which she took, heat rushing up her arm as it linked with his, and her heart sped up even more. It hammered so loudly that Avery hoped Ryder couldn't hear it.

Ryder gallantly chose the perfect stick for her as she gathered the ingredients. They found their way to a stone bench beside the outdoor pit fire, whose flames still danced gracefully against the inky night sky. Avery thought her heart was going to explode out of her chest when he sat close beside her and drew the cozy blanket laid out on the bench over them.

They toasted their marshmallows in silence.

"It's delicious," she murmured, taking an experimental bite of her treat.

Ryder's lips curled into a half-smile. "There's nothing like a s'more on an open fire."

They sat in companionable silence for a while, the crackling fire the only sound that punctuated the quiet while they ate their s'mores, before Avery's curiosity about Ryder's life got the better of her.

"So, tell me about your life in Denver," she began, her tone casual as she turned her attention to Ryder. "My mother told me you were working at an agricultural laboratory as an agricultural scientist."

Ryder nodded, his expression a mixture of fondness and reminiscence. "Yeah, I worked with various crops, finding ways to optimize yields and improve sustainability."

Avery's eyes sparkled with genuine interest. "You were always fascinated with farming."

Ryder stared into the night, his gaze distant. "It was good work and fulfilling. But being back here, at the lodge, starting the orchard—it's a different kind of fulfillment.

It's like breathing life back into something that's been dormant for too long."

Avery's heart skipped a beat, the raw honesty in his words touching something deep within her. "Your orchard and the lodge—it's your way of reviving something meaningful."

Ryder's eyes met hers, a mixture of hope and determination glinting in their depths. "Exactly. We just need to get through this Christmas season. For the first time in years, we're full. And the festival... if it's a success, it could be the turning point we've been waiting for."

As if responding to Ryder's words, delicate snowflakes began to fall once again, drifting down from the night sky. Avery's breath caught in her throat. The beauty of the moment overwhelmed her.

"We should head inside," Ryder suggested, looking up at the sky. "It's going to start coming down hard again."

Avery nodded. A feeling of disappointment about having a companionable moment alone with Ryder surged through her, but she stood, and they started walking back to the lodge. They were a few feet away from the back door when Ryder stooped down, gathered a handful of snow, and pelted it at her. The snowball landed on Avery's shoulder.

Surprise flickered across her face, and her breath caught as some of the cold snow slipped down her neck. Her surprise, however, was quickly replaced by a determined grin.

Caught up in the magic of the soft snow sprinkled over them, Avery gathered snow in her hands, forming a snowball of her own before launching it at Ryder, who was trying to get away from her. What followed was a spirited snowball fight, their laughter echoing in the still night.

Avery had just gathered an armful of snow to make a massive snowball when Ryder tried to playfully tackle her to get rid of it. Laughter rippled through Avery, who, in her haste to avoid him, slipped as Ryder grabbed her.

They tumbled over and fell into the snow in a fit of yelling and laughter. Ryder pushed himself up onto his arms, and their eyes met. As their breaths mingled in the frosty air, time seemed to stand still. Ryder's eyes darkened with emotion, and Avery's heart raced, her pulse echoing in her ears along with the weight of their history and unresolved issues.

Before either of them could move, Emily's voice broke through the moment, pulling them back to reality. "Am I interrupting something?"

Embarrassment tinged Avery's cheeks while Ryder quickly pushed himself up, reaching down to help her to her feet, and even through their gloved hands, Avery felt the electricity his touch caused. A wave of awkwardness hung over Avery and Ryder as they stood staring at Emily like guilty teenagers caught in a passionate embrace.

"I—" Avery started and then cleared her throat. "I was just on my way to bed." She gave Ryder a tight smile before excusing herself and saying goodnight.

As she walked away, she heard Emily say, "Cabin number five's plumbing is acting up again. Hank is already asleep. Could you take a look?"

CHAPTER 8

The early morning at Mistletoe Lodge carried a crispness that hinted at the winter's chill, yet Ryder's steps were light as he emerged from the stables.

He relished the quiet solitude that dawn offered, a time when the world was just stirring from its slumber. His breath misted in the chilly air as he took in the serene landscape that stretched before him.

To his surprise, he wasn't alone for long. He spotted Emily and Avery approaching from a distance as they popped out from the line of pine trees in the Christmas tree grove.

Their figures moved with purpose, indicating they had already been active this morning. He was surprised to see how flushed his sister's cheeks were. Emily rarely embarked on anything that could remotely be called exercise.

He raised an eyebrow as they neared. "Emily, exercising? Now, that's a sight I never thought I'd see."

Emily's brows shot up as she said, defensively, "I exercise!"

"Sure." Ryder nodded. "If you call running away from earthworms while gardening exercise."

"At least I managed to convince her to come with me." Avery chuckled at the banter between the siblings, her breath creating a small cloud in the air. "Although I did have to downgrade my morning jog to a power walk."

"I took Avery through the Christmas tree grove," Emily told him.

"It's a wonderful place to walk and would be a great place for a jogging, cycling, and walking track." She threw the idea out there.

Ryder nodded in agreement. "That is a great idea." He looked at his sister. "Emily wants to put picnic tables between the trees for the guests this summer."

"That's also a great idea," Avery said. "It's so fresh in the grove." Her eyes drifted to the pine trees. "Do you sell the trees at Christmas?"

"Not all of them," Ryder told her. "We donate most of them to hospitals and people who can't afford a tree."

"We have Christmas ornament donation boxes at all the stores in Frisco," Emily added to the conversation. "Your parents have a list of people in need that we give them to."

"Oh!" Avery's eyes widened in surprise. "My parents never mentioned that to me."

"These times are tough for everyone." Ryder's voice dropped. "We do what we can to help."

Just as they were about to continue their conversation, Hank's voice carried from a distance. "Ryder! Can you give me a hand with cabin number five?"

"Coming!" Ryder called.

"Oh no, not again!" Emily rolled her eyes. "I swear we're going to have to move that family elsewhere, Ryder."

"Where do you suggest?" Ryder threw up his hands in exasperation.

"There's always—" Emily's eyes widened with purpose.

"No, that's out of the question," Ryder said, shutting down her suggestion. "Not only has it been shut up for almost eleven years, I don't think Gran would allow it."

"Gran, or you?" Emily frowned.

"Ryder!" Hank yelled again. "This is urgent."

"I have to go." Ryder gave Emily a warning look as he saw the determined one in hers.

Avery and Emily walked off as he went to join Hank.

"So, I believe you had quite the *snowball fight* with Avery, *alone*, last night." Hank grinned teasingly at Ryder as they headed toward the cabin.

"Of course, Emily told you!" Ryder hissed, shaking his head. "That little snitch."

"We have no secrets!" Hank's grin spread as they reached the door to the cabin.

"Oh yeah?" Ryder's brows raised, and he gave Hank a skeptical look. "What about the time you dented Emily's brand-new car before you were married?"

"Shoot, I'd thought you'd forgotten about that!" Hank shook his head and knocked on the door. "Fine, we have one secret."

"Uh-huh." Ryder nodded, knowing otherwise.

"They must've gone out for the day already," Hank stated, using the lodge's spare key to get into the cabin.

While the light was starting to get brighter through the dark tunnel Ryder and his family had been in for the past couple of years, the cabin's plumbing issues cast a persistent shadow.

Hank's steady hands worked with the familiarity of someone who'd done this many times before, and his brow furrowed in concentration. Ryder knelt beside him. His gaze fixed on the leak as he adjusted a wrench.

"You know, Ryder," Hank's voice broke the focused silence, "we're spending an awful lot of time patching up leaks in this cabin."

Ryder's lips twitched into a wry smile. "Tell me about it. It's like this place has a personal vendetta against working plumbing."

Hank chuckled, his eyes crinkling at the corners. "Maybe we shouldn't have rented it out for the season."

Ryder sighed softly, his gaze momentarily distant. "Hank, we didn't have much of a choice. The lodge needs the revenue. You know what's at stake."

Hank nodded, his expression a mix of understanding and resignation. "I know, I know. It's just that every time we fix something, it feels like something else pops up."

Ryder's fingers tightened around the wrench, and his jaw set in determination. "We'll manage, Hank. We always do."

Hank sighed, wiping his hands on a rag. "Maybe we should think about getting a real plumber here. These patches can only do so much."

Ryder's gaze remained fixed on the leak as he replied, "We can't afford a plumber right now, Hank. And besides, I'm sure between the two of us, we'll keep the cabin operational."

Hank's brows furrowed, his concern evident. "Ryder, have you considered relocating the family staying here for the season to another cabin? It might be more comfortable for them."

"There isn't one available, as you know," Ryder reminded him, his grip on the wrench tightening.

"That's not entirely true," Hank pointed out. "There is still one, and maybe it's time to open it up."

Ryder's shoulders tensed, and his eyes narrowed slightly. "Emily's already suggested the same thing." His voice firmed. "The answer is no!"

Hank's sigh was heavy, his tone laden with worry. "Ryder, we're just trying to make things easier for everyone." He stopped what he was doing to look at Ryder. "You've taken a giant step, sweeping away the past and starting the festival again." He took another tool and turned his attention to the leak. "Maybe it's time to air out the ghosts of Mistletoe Cottage as well."

Ryder met Hank's eyes, his expression unyielding. "I know you and Emily mean well. But it's not going to happen." He shook his head stubbornly. "We'll manage, Hank. Somehow."

Hank's gaze held Ryder's for a moment before he nodded, a reluctant acceptance settling in. "Alright, Ryder. If that's what you believe is best."

Ryder's lips softened into a small smile, gratitude shining in his eyes. "Thanks, Hank. And hey, maybe I can start looking for a plumber after all."

Hank's grin was a mixture of relief and reassurance. "Sounds like a plan. Of course, he'll probably suggest the same thing I just did because this cabin needs new pipes and wiring."

As they resumed their work, the cabin's interior echoed with the clinking of tools and the steady rhythm of their efforts. The leak might have disrupted the quiet morning, but the steadfast partnership between Ryder and Hank remained unshaken. In the face of challenges, they were determined to keep Mistletoe Lodge running smoothly, one patched-up leak at a time.

Later that morning, Ryder was on his way to the orchard, his steps carrying a sense of purpose as he looked forward to tending to his apple trees and mistletoe plants. Lost in his thoughts, he spotted Avery heading in the same direction, her presence adding an unexpected spark to his morning.

"Hey!" Ryder called out, his voice warm and welcoming, causing Avery to jump slightly and spin around to face him. "Sorry, I didn't mean to startle you."

She smiled, her expression softening with a touch of amusement. "No, it was me. I was answering messages from work." Avery's fingers deftly tucked her phone into the pocket of her jacket. "I didn't even realize I'd walked this way."

"Well, now that you're here, would you like to see the orchard?" Ryder asked her.

"Sure." Avery's eyes lit up with genuine enthusiasm, and Ryder felt a warmth spread through him at the sight. A smile touched her lips. "I'd love to."

"Great," Ryder said, matching her smile with one of his own. He stepped up next to her, their steps falling into sync as they began to walk toward the orchard. "This way."

As they strolled along the familiar path, Ryder's heart felt lighter in Avery's presence. He couldn't help but steal occasional glances at her, appreciating the way the sunlight played in her hair and the genuine interest that shone in her eyes.

"I'm so glad you finally reopened your mother's orchard," Avery told him. "What made you decide to grow mistletoe?"

"A few reasons," Ryder answered. "There's the benefit of ecosystem enhancement," he told her as they strolled through the apple trees, and he pointed out the mistletoe. "Mistletoe has a symbiotic relationship with trees, providing certain benefits to the tree."

"Oh!" Avery's eyes widened with interest. She looked at the mistletoe attached to the plant. "How does that work, though?" She frowned and drew her head back slightly. "I always thought of mistletoe as more parasitic." She looked at him. "You know, like it sucked the life from the tree."

Ryder's lips curled into a thoughtful smile, glad to share his knowledge. "Well, mistletoe is a parasitic plant that attaches itself to the branches of a host tree, in this case, the apple trees. It's able to extract water and nutrients from the tree's vascular system, but it's not just a one-sided relationship."

Avery's brows lifted in intrigue. Her eyes fixed on Ryder as he spoke. "So the mistletoe gives something back to the tree?"

He gestured toward the mistletoe clusters that adorned some of the apple trees they were passing. "While mistletoe benefits from the nutrients, it also provides the apple tree with protection. Some studies suggest that mistletoe might deter pests from attacking the tree, essentially acting as a sort of guardian."

Avery nodded, absorbing the information with keen interest. "A mutual partnership between the mistletoe and the tree."

"Exactly," Ryder affirmed, pleased by her understanding. "And the mistletoe's green leaves provide shelter for birds and insects, creating a mini-ecosystem within the tree itself."

They continued walking, the orchard unfolding around them in a tranquil display of nature's harmony.

Ryder's gaze settled on the apple trees, his fingers unconsciously brushing against the bark as if in quiet communion with his mother's legacy.

"Speaking of mistletoe," Avery continued, her voice carrying a note of curiosity, "you mentioned there's a big market for it."

Ryder nodded, his eyes returning to her with a spark of enthusiasm. "Yes, especially around the holiday season. People use it for decorations, traditions, and even herbal remedies. It's in high demand."

Avery's smile was genuine, and her eyes reflected her appreciation for the knowledge he was sharing. "It's fascinating how nature can provide so much."

Ryder nodded in agreement, the bond between them deepening as they exchanged thoughts about the delicate balance of the natural world. As they continued their stroll, Ryder found himself opening up more, sharing not only about the orchard but also his own aspirations for Mistletoe Lodge.

"Emily wants to start selling the apples and making apple products like my mother used to," Ryder added after a pause, his voice carrying a mixture of pride and fondness. "She wants to take things a step further with the mistletoe as well. She's been talking about looking into creating herbal remedies with the mistletoe and maybe adding other medicinal plants to be farmed here."

Avery's eyes brightened with interest. Her genuine enthusiasm was contagious. "That sounds like an incredible idea. Apple products have such a wide appeal." She bit her bottom lip thoughtfully. "Emily does have her Pharmaceutical sciences and Biochemistry degrees that will come in handy for various remedies."

"She never really used those degrees." Ryder ran his hand through his hair. "She's already looking into courses for apothecary and homeopathy.
"

"Oh, nice," Avery said, impressed, and then looked around the orchard. "The three of you have really put your all into the lodge."

Ryder nodded, his voice a blend of pride and excitement. "Emily's been experimenting with different ideas. From apple jams and preserves to even baby food. She's determined to bring back that tradition." He laughed. "She's already started dabbling with skin care products and some herbal remedies."

Avery's smile lit up her eyes. "Your family is truly dedicated to keeping the lodge's legacy alive."

Ryder's gaze met hers, warmth and appreciation shining in his eyes. "That's what matters most to us." He looked up at the oldest apple tree on the farm. "Keeping our home so that our children can share in our family's legacy one day."

The quiet sincerity of his words hung in the air, a bridge connecting their past and present, their shared memories, and their aspirations. As they walked on, Ryder couldn't help but feel a sense of gratitude for the unexpected connection that had rekindled between them. The apple trees and mistletoe seemed to stand as witnesses to their conversations, embracing the delicate dance of two souls reconnecting amidst the backdrop of nature's beauty.

They were starting to make their way back when the snow started to fall, but unlike the previous night, nature wasn't sprinkling the earth with snow. She was pouring it out like when a lid falls off a salt shaker and dumps the salt out.

"Oh no." Avery held her hands up as the snow hailed down. "Where on earth did this downpour come from?"

"We're not going to make it back to the lodge." Ryder watched the snowfall get thicker, and his head snapped around to the one place where they could find refuge, and his heart sank. "Come on. I know where we can hold up until this blows over."

Without thinking, Ryder took Avery's hand, and they ran toward Mistletoe Cottage. It was the place where his parents had lived and where he and Emily had grown up. The cottage had been closed when his mother died, and his father moved into the apartment attached to the lodge. The apartment that Ryder now lived in.

"Mistletoe Cottage!" Avery breathed as they stopped under the patio roof.

Ryder pulled out the bunch of lodge keys he always carried with him. His freezing fingers were fumbling as he looked for the key. His heart was beating wildly in his chest from a mixture of the run, holding Avery's hand, and entering the cottage. A place he hadn't set foot in since his mother died.

CHAPTER 9

The snowfall had turned into a swirling dance of white as Avery and Ryder sought refuge within the embrace of Mistletoe Cottage. The wooden structure stood nestled amidst the wintry landscape, its quaint charm a testament to years gone by.

As they stepped through the threshold, the air seemed to carry a sense of hushed nostalgia, whispering the secrets of the past.

Avery's heart beat a little faster as she took in her surroundings. It had been fifteen years since she had set foot in Mistletoe Cottage. This was the place where her dreams and plans had once woven together with Ryder's, a shared future that now existed only in the faded memories of her youth.

The cottage bore the essence of history, with each piece of furniture and every corner holding stories of laughter, love, and heartache. The living room exuded warmth. Its walls were adorned with wooden panels that seemed to embrace you.

A worn but cozy couch sat facing a fireplace, its mantle adorned with knick-knacks and framed photographs.

Ryder busied himself, collecting firewood and kindling from a nearby stack. The crackling of the fire, once ignited, filled the room with its comforting embrace. Avery's gaze wandered, her eyes catching the glimmer of something on a shelf.

She stepped closer, her fingers reaching out to touch the edges of a framed photograph. It was a picture of her and Ryder, their younger selves smiling out from the captured moment.

Her heart constricted as she traced the outline of their faces, the familiarity of his smile a bittersweet reminder of what they had once been. This cottage was meant to be theirs, a shared haven where they would build their lives together.

But the universe had other plans, and on what should have been the happiest day of her life, the wedding day, it had all fallen apart.

Avery's eyes blurred with unshed tears as her gaze swept over the room. This was where she had gotten ready for the wedding. The morning light had filtered through the curtains, painting the room with a soft glow as she stood in her wedding dress, full of hopes and dreams. All it took was a knock on the door, which she instinctively wanted to shout out to Emily not to answer, as warning bells had resounded in her head.

Before Emily had walked into the room where Avery's mom had just put a veil on her head, Avery knew what was in the letter clasped in Emily's hand. All it took to change the course of Avery's life and have her young dreams shattered was a letter.

Her steps carried her further into the cottage as she swiped the tears away. Her memories intertwined with the reality before her. She entered a room that had once been Emily's, only to find it transformed. A hospital bed dominated the space, a silent witness to the pain that Ryder's family had endured.

She stood there, her throat tight with emotions that threatened to engulf her. She was nearly driven to her knees by the weight of her guilt at her childish rage which had kept her from seeing Angela Carlisle, Ryder's mother, when she'd gotten sick. Avery's chest tightened as she felt like a weight was being pressed against it. She blamed Angela and Ryder's father, David, for Ryder's decision not to go through with the wedding.

Avery had been so blinded by hurt and anger that she'd pushed the Carlisle's to the back of her mind and frozen them out of her heart.

Ryder's voice broke through the silence, his words infused with an attempt to keep the atmosphere light. "I found some cocoa," he said, holding up a tin with a small smile. "I thought we could warm up a bit."

Avery quickly swept away the tears before she turned to look at him, her heart aching with the weight of the past. She managed a faint smile, appreciating his effort to ease the tension. "Cocoa sounds perfect."

As he moved to prepare the cocoa, Avery's gaze settled on the room once more. She thought of Ryder's mother, whose presence was still felt within these walls. Avery took a deep breath to steady her throbbing emotions and made her way back to the living room. Taking a seat on the sofa and soaking up the heat of the roaring fire Ryder had made.

A few minutes later, Ryder returned with two steaming mugs of cocoa, breaking her reverie. He handed her a mug and took a seat beside her. His eyes reflected a mixture of emotions. Avery curled her hands around the mug, allowing the warmth of it to seep into her cold fingers.

"Thank you," she said softly, offering him a small, genuine smile.

"You're welcome," Ryder replied, his gaze holding hers for a moment before he looked around the room. "This place holds a lot of memories."

Avery nodded, her throat tight as she took a sip of the cocoa. Memories flooded her mind—the laughter, the plans they'd made, and the love that had once bound them. And then there was the pain of that fateful day—the wedding they'd never had, as Ryder left her and she'd taken off for Los Angeles without a backward glance.

Ryder's gaze was on the fire, and his voice was a mixture of reflection and acceptance. "My mother loved this place. She always said it was our family's heart."

Avery's heart ached, the sincerity in his words piercing through her. She had loved this place too and had envisioned it as her home with Ryder. But it was a dream that had slipped through her fingers like grains of sand. Now all that remained were the echoes of what could have been and the heartache and tragedy of a family watching a loved one fade away.

They sat in silence as the snow piled up outside the cottage, surrounding them as if holding them hostage while forcing them to face the ghosts of their past.

"Your mother loved to tell the story of how the farm came to be known as Mistletoe Farm." Avery took a sip of the sweet, warm beverage as she stared into the fire, trying not to let her proximity to Ryder affect her senses. "I loved that story."

"My mother used to read it to us each Christmas." Ryder's smile turned nostalgic.

"Is the book still here?" Avery's eyes widened with an idea. "I'd love to hear it again."

"Seriously?" Ryder frowned, and Avery nodded. "Okay, I'll find it."

He stood and disappeared down the hallway. Avery looked at the fire, remembering the big sign board that used to stand at the entrance to Mistletoe Lodge. It spun a tale that combined the legend of Mistletoe with that of Mistletoe Lodge.

She smiled, remembering the sign, and made a mental note not to tell Ryder it would be a great idea to put the sign back up. Her mind pictured the sign that once held fascination for her and the many people who'd entered Mistletoe Lodge. Even if you'd done so a million times, a person would still find themselves reading the board.

In Norse legend, mistletoe, once a symbol of loss, was transformed into a symbol of hope, connection, and the enduring power of love to conquer darkness. A tale of tragedy was turned into a celebration of love's resilience.

The moment you pass through the gates of Mistletoe Lodge, think of it as passing beneath mistletoe. From the tragedy of great loss, Mistletoe Lodge arose as a symbol of love, family, unity, friendship, and a beacon of hope for those lost in the darkness of pain, anger, sorrow, and despair.

"Found it!' Ryder walked through carrying a leather-bound journal and plopped beside Avery on the sofa, flipping through the aged pages. "Are you sure you want to do this?"

"Of course," Avery said, nodding.

"You do know that there's a legend attached to reading this, and that's why my mother used to read it to us every Christmas!" Ryder warned, making Avery laugh.

"Yes, I understand the cost of reading the book." Avery put her empty mug on the side table and made herself comfortable before reciting the legend. "As mistletoe is a symbol of unity, all those who read from or listen to the words written by the hand of Fiona Carlisle, the first wife of Mistletoe Lodge, will forever be bound by a love that transcends time."

"Good memory," Ryder grinned. "Do you think you can write that down for me?" he teased. "I could never remember it."

"Can you please just read the story?" Avery laughed and shook her head.

Ryder found the page, and Avery sat back, listening to his deep tones as he read:

The story of Mistletoe Lodge by Fiona Carlisle

In *this startlingly beautiful land, embraced by rolling hills and whispered tales, lived a rancher named Angus Carlisle. He, along with his beloved wife Fiona, tended the earth and nurtured the land's spirit. They were deeply in love with each other and the life they were cultivating.*

But fate dealt a bitter hand when their newborn daughter, Eleanor, was lost amidst a feud with their neighbor over a prized bull. Grief and sorrow shadowed their once-fertile fields. And as with everything negative emotions touch, their once joyful life started to turn into one of turbulent battles, diseased cattle, and failing crops as a feud sprung up between neighbors.

The only spark of good and light to be had in the following years was the birth of their son, Angus junior. But that light was overshadowed as the feud deepened. It led to a tragedy Angus could never have foreseen, resulting in his untimely end.

The ranch's future was uncertain, its soil tainted by sorrow and strife. In the face of this heartache, Fiona made a decision that would forever change the destiny of their land.

With courage in her heart, Fiona transformed their ranch into a place of unity and healing. She sold the cattle that had once been their livelihood, and, in a poignant tribute to her husband's memory, she built the lodge and renamed the land "Mistletoe Lodge." The name carried a promise—to mend the fractures of the past and bring peace, love, and joy to those who walked its grounds.

In the shadow of a grand vision, Fiona initiated the Winter Festival—a gathering that embraced the spirit of unity and celebration. Just as mistletoe symbolizes love and connection, the festival kindled bonds between neighbors and strangers alike. It was a beacon of light in the heart of winter, a reminder that even in the chilliest times, warmth and togetherness could thrive. Beneath the bitter snow of winter lay the promise of spring and the warmth of summer.

And so, Mistletoe Lodge became a haven where families gathered, couples celebrated love, and friendships flourished beneath the watchful eye of mistletoe. Fiona's legacy echoed in every corner, a testament to the enduring power of love to mend the deepest divides.

In Norse legend, mistletoe, once a symbol of loss, was transformed into a symbol of hope, connection, and the enduring power of love to conquer darkness. A tale of tragedy was turned into a celebration of love's resilience.

As you enter Mistletoe Lodge, remember the legend that shaped its name—a story of healing, unity, and the radiant hope that even in the face of sorrow, a legacy of love can flourish.

Avery sat staring at the book in Ryder's hand as he snapped it shut. How many times as children had she and Emily sat gathered in front of this fireplace listening to the soft tones of Angela reading it to them? Guilt, remorse, and pain shot through Avery's heart once again, and her eyes filled with tears.

"Avery." Ryder's voice drew her back to the present. "Are you okay?"

He put the journal on the coffee table and sat back, looking at her with worried eyes.

She took a deep breath, her gaze meeting Ryder's. "I'm so sorry I wasn't there for your mother. I should have come home. I should have been here."

Ryder's eyes were filled with compassion. "Avery, there would've been nothing you could've done." He reached out and took her hand. "You sent a lovely letter."

He swallowed. "I was here when Emily read it to her. She lit up as she listened to it." He held her gaze. "My mother understood your reasons." He looked at their clasped hands. "She asked me to one day give you a message."

"Are you serious or just making this up to make me feel better?" Avery looked at him suspiciously.

"No." Ryder shook his head. "I think she thought you'd say that."

He got up and walked out of the room, returning a few minutes later with an envelope with the Mistletoe Lodge logo on it—the same type of envelope that his father delivered to her on their wedding day.

"I never thought we'd ever see each other again." Ryder cleared his throat as she sat down again, looking at the envelope in his hand. "I kept this with me until the day she died." His voice got throatier, and his eyes misted over as he turned to her. "I put it in the side drawer next to the hospital bed she was confined to in her last few months."

"Ryder, I'm so sorry about your mother." Avery's heart bled for him and for his family, and it filled with acid at the thought of how petty she'd been. "I blamed her for —" She finally said what she'd kept in her heart all these years. "Two days before the wedding, she came to me and told me that I should think hard before getting married." She played with her fingers. "Your mother tried to convince me to back out of it because we were both so young and had our whole promising lives before us." She sucked in a shaky breath. "She told me that if we were meant to be, we'd find our way back to each other when the time was right."

"What?" Ryder's brows drew together, and he looked at her in confusion. "You never told me this."

Avery lifted her head and looked at him in surprise. "I thought you knew."

"No," Ryder said, shaking his head.

"I thought that's why you left me on the day that was supposed to be our wedding day." Avery looked at him curiously. "I thought maybe she'd told you the same thing, and you decided she was right."

"No!" Ryder shook his head. "It wasn't my mother. It was—" He broke off and turned toward the fire before looking at her again. "It doesn't matter now."

"Yes, it does!" Avery unfolded her legs, which were curled up on the sofa. "For fifteen years I've blamed your mother for you running off, and now I find out you didn't even know she'd spoken to me!"

"Avery, maybe it's best to let it go," Ryder advised. "I've really enjoyed the time we've been spending together now that all that awkwardness has gone." He cleared his throat. "Maybe it's best to leave the past where it is." Ryder moved uncomfortably on the cushion.

"What are you keeping from me?" Avery's eyes narrowed.

"It's not important now," Ryder hedged. "We both moved on and look at you." He smiled proudly at her. "You've shone in your career."

"Oh no, you don't!" Avery wouldn't let it go that easily. "For fifteen years, I thought it was your mother that finally got to you and talked you out of marrying me." Her eyes blazed. "I was humiliated." She shook her head as the old feelings from that day stirred up. "I couldn't even face all those guests waiting for us." She swallowed down the burning lump in her throat. "I ran home, packed a bag, and got on the first flight to Los Angeles." She blew out a breath as emotions tumbled through her. "I didn't even change out of my wedding dress."

"Don't you want to read my mom's letter?" Ryder made one last effort to change the subject and move away from that fateful day.

"Not until you tell me what happened," Avery demanded. "All your note said was that I deserved to live the big life I was meant to, not be limited by the confines of small-town Frisco."

Ryder blew out a breath and ran a hand over his eyes. "Fine." He sat back against the cushions. "I got the same talk as you did. Almost word for word." He admitted but didn't look at her.

"From your father, or was it your grandmother?" Avery asked.

"It wasn't any of them either." Ryder's voice dropped.

Alarm bells started to echo through Avery's head, and she felt shock start to pulse inside her as a cold feeling slithered up her spine, and she knew before he told her she wasn't going to like the answer.

"It was your mother." Ryder pinched the bridge of his nose. "I swore to her that I'd never tell you about our conversation." He swallowed, and when he turned to look at her, she saw the haunted look in his eyes. "I wished every day after that day that you'd rock up on the doorstep of my dorm and tell me you wanted me more than your career."

Avery sat staring at him in shock. Her mind whirled as a roar resounded in her ears at the revelation. Their mothers had conspired against them? It wasn't just his family but also hers that had ripped them apart! She gave herself a mental shake, not wanting to believe what she was hearing, but a small part of her did.

Flashes of the months leading up to the wedding sped through her mind. Her mother dropped little hints about how marriage was a huge commitment and if Avery was sure about giving up on going to UCLA.

The fire crackled, its warmth a counterpoint to the coldness that had settled within Avery's heart. Ryder's words were echoing through her mind, which was now clouded with confusion, while her heart felt the punch of betrayal from someone she trusted the most in the world.

CHAPTER 10

The fire crackled in the hearth, casting a warm and flickering glow across the room as Ryder and Avery sat facing each other. The air was heavy with the weight of the past, and yet there was a palpable sense of determination as they finally began to address the unresolved issues that had haunted them for years.

Ryder cleared his throat, his gaze steady as he began to speak. "That day, Avery—the day of our supposed wedding—it was one of the hardest days of my life."

Avery said nothing as she sat watching him intently.

He took a deep breath, his fingers tracing an absent pattern on his jeans. "Walking away from you, leaving you standing there at the altar... it tore me apart. But I thought it was the right thing to do. Your mother's words—they had so much weight for me. The closer we got to the moment when you'd walk down the aisle, the heavier that weight got."

Avery's voice was void of emotion, her eyes never leaving his face. "I want to say I understand, but even now, knowing what I do, I can't—I don't." Her face crinkled, her shoulders lifted, and she shook her head. "Your mother, my mother, and you had no right to decide what was best for me!"

Her eyes grew stormy and haunted with past shadows of hurt and pain.

"You're right." Ryder nodded, his gaze distant as he re-lived that painful moment.

"My father always says that there's no point going over what you should've done, but reflect on what you could've done to make sure you do that if ever faced with a similar situation," Avery quoted her father. "But right now, I'm thinking about what you *should've* done back then." He watched her jaw clench as she closed her eyes, trying to compose herself. "You should've spoken to me!" Avery exclaimed, her hurt, anger, and frustration evident in her tone as the words tumbled out.

"You're right again!" Ryder's heart felt bruised all over again as they rehashed that painful day.

"Actually, *I* should've spoken to you as well and told you what your mother had said to me." Avery took her share of the blame. "Maybe then we could've had this conversation then, and things would've worked out differently."

"You think I didn't think that afterward?" Ryder's voice was filled with pain and remorse. "For years after I walked away, a part of me hoped, Avery." His voice wobbled with emotion, and he paused to get it in check. "A part of me hoped that you would come after me, that you would refuse to give up on us or at least demand an explanation in person." He swallowed, suddenly realizing how stupid that sounded now that he said it out loud. "I thought that maybe you would track me down and that you would tell me that you wanted to be with me more than anything." He gave himself a mocking laugh. "I rehearsed the conversation we'd have in my head." He pinched the bridge of his nose again. "I would tell you how you had so much more to accomplish in life. Your dreams were always bigger than mine."

Avery's eyebrows lifted in surprise. "You wanted me to find you? You wanted me to fight for us."

Ryder's lips quirked into a bittersweet smile. "Yes. I wanted you to choose me, Avery. I wanted you to make that decision on your own, without any influence or pressure. I wanted to know that you were with me because you wanted to be, not because you felt obligated."

"Then why didn't *you* come speak to me on our wedding day instead of sending a note?" Avery's voice rose slightly and echoed her anger. "We could've figured this out together." She blew out a breath. "Even if we still parted ways, at least I wouldn't have left hating you for hurting me and crying alone on an airplane still in my wedding dress."

"You went to Los Angeles in your wedding dress?" Ryder looked at her in amazement.

"I didn't care what I was wearing then." Avery rubbed her forehead. "My heart was broken, and all I wanted to do was put as much distance between myself and this town as possible." She looked into the fire.

"My hometown was filled with memories of my life up to that point." Her eyes grew distant. "Memories that were shattered by the earthquake caused by my fracturing heart"

"Avery—" Ryder reached out for her hand, but she pulled it away and moved further to her corner of the sofa. "I thought I was doing the right thing." He gave a snort. "A gallant thing."

"What's gallant about leaving me stranded with a whole town full of guests waiting to see us get married, only to have you run out on me?" Avery's words were pulled from her heart. "For months afterward, I went through the days in a dazed routine." She licked her lips. "My world was so turned around, and to make it worse, it was turned around in a strange town that you could probably fit Frisco into one of its neighborhoods."

"I know." Ryder's voice was soft as he watched his fingers trace a pattern on his jeans, and his confession tumbled from his lips. "Six months after our breakup, I went to Los Angeles to find you."

"You did what?" Avery breathed in surprise.

"I finally managed to get Emily to tell me how to find you." Ryder's eyes met hers. "I went and stayed with my grandmother's sister, and she drove me to UCLA."

"That's when I saw how happy you were." Ryder swallowed, remembering how he'd seen her standing and talking to a group of people.

"Happy?" Avery looked at him in disbelief. "It took me three years to be able to date again after our breakup."

"You were laughing, and I was close enough to hear you and your friend planning a trip to Hawaii," Ryder told her.

"I was going with Heather on a trip for her archeology paper," Avery told him. "You were there that day?"

"Yes!" Ryder nodded. "I couldn't bear not to see you, and I wanted to know for sure that I'd made the right choice." He rubbed his temples and squeezed his eyes shut. "Actually, to tell you the truth, I had no idea why I went. I was torn between throwing myself on your mercy and begging you to forgive me." He gave another mocking laugh. "I missed you so much that I was even willing to find a college to study at in California so we could be together."

"Are you being serious?" Avery looked at him, amazed. "You were in Los Angeles. Right there, and you never approached me?"

"When I heard you planning that trip with your friend and saw how excited you were, I knew I'd made the right choice, and I also knew that if I had approached you, I'd never have had the strength to let you go again." He looked at the ceiling.

"So, you didn't just walk away from me once." Avery's voice dropped to a hoarse whisper. 'You walked away from me twice."

"I thought I was doing the right thing." Ryder knew how hollow that excuse sounded to his own ears.

"The right thing for you, maybe." Avery's eyes dulled with hurt, anger, and betrayal. "No one has the right to say what's best for me but me."

"Sometimes it takes an onlooker to point out that we're not on the right track," Ryder quoted his grandmother. "We tend to see only what we want to see, while an onlooker sees a bigger picture and isn't blinded by shortsightedness."

They fell into a tense silence, each lost in their own tortured thoughts. Ryder was reeling from knowing that his mother had gone to try and talk Avery out of marrying him, and now he'd never know or get the chance to ask her why she'd done that. Ryder could only imagine how Avery must be feeling after finding out it was her mother who had gotten to Ryder.

He turned to see Avery's face set, and the tortured look in her eyes tore at his heart. Ryder reached over and took her hand, and this time she let him.

"I'm sorry, Avery." Ryder's apology came from his heart, recited by his soul. "My heart felt like it had been smashed with a hammer and shattered into a million pieces that day." He swallowed, and his thumb gently stroked her hand. "Even now, those pieces have never been put back together, and I feel the sting of the shards whenever a memory of you pops up."

"Thank you." Avery turned her head and gave him a sad smile. "I'm sorry that my mother thought she could interfere with our lives." She shook her head and frowned. "I would never have thought she'd do anything like that."

"I can say the same thing about my mother," Ryder pointed out. "Being a parent myself, I think I can understand why they thought they were protecting us."

"That was protecting us?" Avery's voice grew bitter. "That was manipulating us and pushing us down a path they wanted us to go."

"No, Avery." Ryder's heart slammed against his ribs when he saw the anger in her eyes. "I'm sure that's not what they were doing."

"It sure feels like that." Avery blew out another breath and glanced at the envelope now lying on the sofa between them. "Will you read that to me?"

Ryder's eyes followed hers, and he nodded. Letting go of her hand, he picked up the envelope and opened it, pulling out the letter from his mother to Avery.

Dear Avery

It's been a long time since I've seen you, and I don't blame you for not wanting to talk to me. Over the years, your mother has kept me updated about your life. You and Emily were always at each other's houses, and you felt like a second daughter to me. So, when your mother's eyes would fill with pride at your accomplishments, my heart would swell with it too.

I know you think your mother and I had no right to meddle with your and Ryder's lives, but one day you'll be a parent and you'll understand. Hopefully, then, you'll find it in your heart to forgive us and know that we only wanted what was best for the both of you.

The two of you were so besotted with each other that you were blind to the future. A future that held so much more in store for both of you than being tied down and restricted by marriage. Both your mother and I are from broken homes. Our parents were also childhood sweethearts who cut off their future by choosing to get married too young.

We both saw firsthand how that could destroy two people. Two people who were once madly in love ended up hating each other and blaming each other for never having lived their dreams. Your mother and I never wanted that for you and Ryder.

Avery, you are such a special woman, and I know in my heart that everything will work out the way it should when the time is right.

If one day yours and Ryder's paths cross again, be gentle with him. He was broken for a long time after he left you, and he still is ten years later. I know that you'll find your way back to each other because if your love is real and true, it will always find a way.

Love

Angela

Ryder's voice had grown hoarse near the end of it, and when he looked up, tears streamed down Avery's cheeks.

"I only just realized that your mother died before you met your wife, and she never got to know Rosie." Avery sniffed and wiped the tears from her cheeks. "I should've come to see her."

Avery dissolved into a flood of tears. Ryder's heart burst with compassion as he felt her pain and slid over to her, putting his arm around her and pulling her to him, letting her sob as he held her and fought back his own tears.

"I'm sorry." Avery pulled away from him and sat up. "I didn't mean to go all weepy on you."

"It's been an emotional day," Ryder said, getting up to go find a tissue for her.

He found a box on the mantle and handed it to her as his phone rang.

"Hello," Ryder answered a little abruptly, unable to hide the spark of annoyance at having this moment with Avery interrupted, as it was a moment they had needed for a long time.

"Ryder, where are you?" Emily sounded frantic. "Is Avery with you, as we can't find her?"

"Yes, we were at the orchard when the snow started to come down, and we've taken shelter at the cottage," Ryder informed her, and Emily fell silent for a good few seconds, making him wonder if she was still on the line. "Emily?"

"Did you say you were at the cottage?" Emily asked for verification, and he could hear the astonishment in her tone. "Mistletoe Cottage?"

"Yes, Emily, Mistletoe Cottage," Ryder confirmed, and he glanced around the room. Suddenly he felt like a dark cloud had lifted from around his heart, and before he could give himself time to think, he blurted out, "I think you might have been right." His eyes met Avery's. "Maybe we should move the guests from number five here."

Again, silence fell on the other side of the call before his sister's voice echoed excitedly, "Are you serious?"

"Yes, I'm serious." Ryder sighed, and his eyes did a more thorough scan of the room. "Although we're going to need to get a cleaning crew in here and modernize it as best we can."

"We have to move the hospital bed that's in my room as well." Emily spoke softly.

"I know!" Ryder nodded. "We can discuss it as soon as the snow stops and we can get back to the lodge."

"Have you looked outside?" Emily asked him. "I don't think the snow is going to let up any time soon."

"We're going to starve!" Ryder said as his stomach growled at him.

"I can send Hank to you with some food on the snowmobile," Emily offered. "But he won't be able to bring either of you back as it's not a two-seater."

"Is it safe for him to do that?" Ryder asked.

"I'm sure he'll be okay," Emily said. "He is a pro hockey player and part of the volunteer mountain search and rescue team."

"True," Ryder said. "Then if he can, please. We're both starving."

"I'll get him to bring you some supplies." Emily promised. "Chat later and —" She paused.

"And?" Ryder asked, his eyes narrowing.

"Maybe this is fate's way of getting the two of you to finally talk things through." Emily spoke quickly. "Okay, then bye."

She hung up before Ryder could say anything else, and he stood staring at the phone, knowing she was right. His mother's words from the letter echoed through his head.

I know that you'll find your way back to each other because if your love is real and true, it always finds a way.

CHAPTER 11

The snow had woven a cocoon around Mistletoe Cottage, trapping Avery and Ryder within its walls. After the hearty meal that Hank had brought them, they found themselves sitting across from each other on the worn-out sofa, caught between the weight of the past and the uncertainties of the present.

Avery's fingers absently traced the rim of her empty mug, her gaze fixed on the dancing flames in the fireplace. The crackling firelight painted flickering shadows across the room, and its warmth seemed to echo the slowly thawing atmosphere between her and Ryder. Though the physical chill was still palpable outside, within the cottage, the frostiness between them was slowly melting away.

"So, tell me a bit about you." Ryder finally broke the silence, his voice careful and measured. "How are you doing in Los Angeles?"

Avery nodded, her eyes still fixed on the fire. Well, it's not Frisco." She laughed. "There's so much going on there all the time. But it's been my home for the past fifteen years, and I've made some good friends." She took a sip of her coffee. "And I have a great job."

Ryder leaned back, studying her intently. "You're in marketing, right?" He squinted at her. "At least that's what you said you wanted to do."

Avery nodded again, her answers remaining elusive. "Close enough."

"As long as you're doing something you love." Ryder smiled. "And Los Angeles certainly is a place with a *lot* more creative opportunities than Frisco."

She glanced at him, her heart jolting as a surge of guilt washed over her. "Yes, I guess so." Avery couldn't meet his eyes. "I'm up for a promotion to VP of my department."

"That's amazing, Avery." Ryder spoke softly.

"It's a big step up and something I've been working hard to accomplish." She looked at the fire, tried to keep her voice as steady as she could, and hoped her guilt wasn't shining in her eyes. "But it's tied to the success of the current project I'm working on."

Ryder's brows furrowed. "Is it a hard project?"

"At first, I thought it wouldn't be." Avery swallowed and looked down at the mug in her hands. "I thought that what I was working on would help, and I would be doing a good thing." She cleared her throat. "But then I found out it was a lot more complicated, and I may have to pivot so all parties get what they want and no one gets hurt."

"Wow, that sounds like quite the project and a huge burden for you to carry alone," Ryder said. "I know I'm not an expert in your field, but sometimes an extra pair of ears can help a lot."

"Thank you." Avery gave him a grateful smile, her guilt growing by the minute. "Tell me more about the lodge." She turned, lifting one leg onto the sofa and resting her arm on the back of it so she could see him. "How did you end up back here?"

Ryder leaned forward, his elbows resting on his knees. "When Dad passed away three years ago, he left the lodge to Emily and me. Emily had moved back here a year before he died to look after him. That's when she got a huge shock at just how badly the lodge had been doing for a few years. It was a mess, financially and otherwise." He shook his head and stared into the fire. "I moved back a month after he died to help Emily, Hank, and my grandmother with the lodge."

Avery's eyes softened with empathy. "That must've been really tough on both of you."

"It was," Ryder admitted with a sigh. "We struggled to keep it afloat." He looked at her, his eyes dark with emotion and determination. "This place is our family's legacy." He drew in a breath. "We've been fighting to keep it going and hanging onto it by the tips of our fingers."

Avery nodded in understanding, feeling the weight of his words while guilt pounded through her and she felt like she was spying on them.

"Even with the struggle and all the stress, this place has been good for Rosie," Ryder continued, his voice cracking slightly, "and me." He swallowed, his gaze growing distant as he stared into the fire. "My wife... she was in an accident. A drunk driver. She didn't make it."

Avery's heart clenched, her gaze locking onto his somber eyes as he turned to look at her. "I'm so sorry, Ryder."

He nodded, a small, sad smile touching his lips. "Life has a way of throwing curveballs when you least expect it. But Rosie and I found a way to keep moving forward."

Avery's fingers tightened around her mug, and her voice was gentle. "That must've been so hard for you to have been left with a young child as well."

Ryder's eyes held a mix of pain and resilience. "We moved back here, to Frisco, from Denver. It was the best decision we ever made. Being here, working on the lodge, and being closer to family helped us heal. For me, for

Rosie—it was like finding some semblance of normalcy again."

Avery felt a lump in her throat as Ryder opened up to her, sharing a side of him she hadn't seen before. "Rosie seems to be thriving." She took a sip of her rapidly cooling coffee. "From what I've seen, she's happy, healthy, friendly, and well adjusted."

Ryder's eyes softened as he spoke of his daughter. "She's a resilient kid. She's grown so much over the years, and she's my world. Being a single parent has its challenges, but we've found our rhythm."

Avery nodded, her heart aching for the pain he must have endured. "Again, from what I've seen, you're an amazing father, and from the conversations I've had with Rosie, you're her world too."

Ryder shrugged, a mix of humility and pride in his gaze. "I try to be the best dad I can." He laughed softly. "Parenting doesn't come with a manual. It's this whole series of trial and error." He raised his eyebrows. "My grandmother says as long as she's alive, happy, and healthy, you know you're doing a good job."

"Based on that, I say you're a first-rate dad," Avery assured him, and they both laughed.

Silence settled between them as they both sank into their own thoughts. Avery's fingers toyed with her mug, and her thoughts were a swirl of guilt and a search for ways to turn her assignment around. She'd meant what she'd said to Ryder about having to change her plans and strategy for her current project.

The spots of swirling snow tormented by the wind mirrored Avery's troubled thoughts, just as the snow outside seemed to mirror the sense of stillness within the cottage. After just a night and a day at the lodge, she knew there was no way she'd move forward with the acquisition. She also knew that if she didn't find another solution for her firm's client, they'd just send someone else to do it.

Then there was the financial situation the lodge was in, and no matter what Ryder and Emily thought, a good season and the festival were not going to save the lodge. It might put the wolves off for a while, but they'd be back before long.

Avery wanted to help, and to do so meant she needed to try and find a cash injection for them that wouldn't mean they'd have to give up their family legacy. She gave herself a mental shake to clear the problems from her mind, as there was nothing she could do while they were stuck in the cottage. She forced herself to concentrate on the present.

"I'm glad you found a way to heal," Avery finally said, her voice soft yet sincere.

Ryder's gaze met hers, gratitude evident in his eyes. "Thank you. And I'm glad you've found your path too, even if it's a thousand miles away from Frisco."

Avery's smile was bittersweet. "Yes, it's been a journey. But I've learned that sometimes the hardest decisions lead to unexpected growth." She put her mug on the side table. "It is good to be back in Colorado, even if I have been trapped by the snow, and it appears that nature doesn't want me to get to Frisco." She shivered. "I've missed the snowy winters."

Ryder nodded, his fingers tracing the patterns on the cushion. "I'd like to experience a warm Christmas some time."

"For people like us who grew up with white Christmases, it's quite a weird experience," Avery explained. "My first Christmas in Los Angeles, I bought a can of fake snow to decorate my apartment windows with." She grinned, remembering her flat mate's look of sheer disgust. "I would leave all the windows and balcony doors open in the evenings to experience the cool air and make the fake snow seem real."

As the fire crackled in the hearth, casting dancing shadows across the room, Avery and Ryder continued to share fragments of their stories. The heaviness of unspoken truths and the weight of past regrets were gradually lifting, replaced by a sense of connection they hadn't felt in years. They were two souls still navigating the complexities of their lives, yet finding solace in each other's company within the walls of Mistletoe Cottage.

The snowstorm outside showed no signs of relenting, and the future remained uncertain. Avery hoped she'd be able to find a solution to help both Ryder and her client. But for that moment, in that cozy cottage nestled in the heart of Frisco, Avery and Ryder were finding a way to mend the pieces of their fractured pasts. The future would be a problem for tomorrow when nature no longer held them hostage with a snow storm.

Ryder glanced at his wristwatch, and his eyes widened in surprise. "Wow, it's late."

He looked at her, and she could see that his feelings mirrored her own. They were enjoying each other's company for the first time in fifteen years, and the walls between them were starting to tumble down. Neither of them wanted the evening to end, but tomorrow was another day, and they both needed to navigate it with clear, alert minds.

"Yes, we should get some sleep," Avery said, looking at the fire. "I think I'll stay on the sofa if that's okay." She pointed to the fire. "It's so warm in the living room."

"I was thinking the same thing," Ryder admitted. "I'll get a mattress from one of the single beds and sleep on the floor in here too, if that's okay?"

"Yes." Avery grinned. "Like camping out in the living room."

Ryder got up, and Avery got up and went to gather blankets and pillows. Fifteen minutes later, Avery lay snuggled under a soft blanket on the sofa, and Ryder was stretched out on a mattress on the floor. The lights had been turned off, and only the golden orange glow of the fire lit the room.

"Ryder?" Avery's voice was soft.

"Yes?" Ryder answered, turning on his side to look at her.

"I'm glad we got snowed in." Avery smiled and saw his eyes flicker with a mix of emotions she couldn't quite put her finger on.

"Me too." Ryder smiled, stifling a yawn. "I think this was long overdue for us."

"I agree," Avery said and paused for a few beats before asking, "Have you really not set foot in the cottage for ten years?"

"Yes." He sighed and flipped onto his back, placing his hands beneath his head. "None of my family has. Cleaners come here once a week."

"I'm glad you've decided to open it up," Avery told him. "This cottage was always filled with love and warmth." She glanced around the room. "It needs to be filled with that again."

"You're right," Ryder agreed with her, and she could hear his words drifting as his eyes shut.

A few minutes later, she knew he was asleep from the soft rhythm of his breathing. Avery tossed and turned for ten minutes before falling into a fitful slumber. Her mind worked in the background to find a solution for the lodge and her client. It was in the early hours of the morning when Avery was jolted awake after having bizarre dreams, but as her eyes opened, the solution struck her.

Avery sat up and found her phone, but there was no signal. She looked at the time. Los Angeles was an hour behind Frisco. It was nearly five in the morning, and she needed to get to her laptop to put some figures together and a proposal together before nine. Avery was about to put her phone down when she noticed a message from the previous morning that she hadn't seen. It was from her boss.

Avery, we need your report and a new proposal for the lodge by the close of business tomorrow.

Avery's eyes widened. *Oh no!* She hadn't even had a chance to go over anything since arriving in Colorado. She looked out the window and noticed the snow had let up. Avery glanced over and saw that Ryder was still fast asleep. She didn't want to wake him, but she also needed to get back to the lodge. Avery decided to put some coffee on and then check if it was safe outside to wander back to the lodge on her own.

While she was making coffee and heating up some of the leftover food from the previous night, her phone got a signal, and another message came through. Avery picked up her phone, and her blood ran cold. The message was from her rival for the VP position at work, Larry Grimes.

Avery, our client is worried about the acquisition of the lodge, and my uncle has asked me to join you in Colorado to ensure it goes smoothly. I'll be there as soon as the airports open. - Larry

This wasn't good! Avery's heart hammered against her rib cage, and she nearly jumped out of her skin when Ryder came through to the kitchen.

"Good morning." Ryder smiled. "The smell of food and coffee woke me."

"I was going to wake you with a steaming mug." Avery quickly switched off her screen. "If you don't mind, I need to get back to my room." She swallowed. "I have some urgent business that needs my attention."

"Sure." Ryder gave her a tight smile. "Let me finish my coffee, and we can go."

"I can help tidy up quickly," Avery said.

"No need," Ryder assured her. "I'll send the cleaning crew up later."

After they finished their coffee and the last of the left-over food, they started their walk through the thick snow back to the lodge. As they neared the door, Avery's conscience got the better of her.

"Ryder—" Avery stopped them a few feet from the door. "I need to tell you something."

"Okay!" Ryder frowned.

But before she could say anything more, the door to the lodge flew open, and Emily charged toward them.

"Can we meet later this afternoon?" Avery said quickly before Emily reached them. "There's something I really need to talk to you about."

"Sure," Ryder said, his voice clouding with worry. "Is everything alright?"

"I'm hoping it will be," Avery told him cryptically. "Can we meet at six this evening?"

"Sure, come to my office," Ryder told her before they were engulfed in Emily's embrace.

CHAPTER 12

The soft sunlight filtered through the trees, casting a warm, golden hue over the winter wonderland that surrounded him. Ryder took a deep breath, feeling a sense of calm wash over him. It was moments like these that reminded him of the beauty and tranquility that this place held, even amidst the challenges it presented.

Emily emerged from the cottage, her gaze meeting Ryder's as she joined him on the porch. They exchanged a smile, their bond as siblings stronger than ever. The memories of their shared past had woven a tapestry of experiences that no amount of time could unravel.

"Remember the winter Mom was sick?" Emily's voice held a hint of nostalgia as she leaned against the wooden railing.

Ryder's gaze softened, his thoughts echoing her sentiment. "How could I forget? That was a tough time for all of us."

A shadow of sadness passed over Emily's features as she continued. "She was so strong, so full of life, even in the face of illness. I miss her, Ryder."

"I do too." Ryder's voice was gentle, and his heart was heavy with the weight of the memories. "She loved this place. It was her sanctuary, a haven where she could escape from the pain and worry, if only for a little while."

A soft sigh escaped Emily's lips. "She wouldn't have wanted Dad to shut down the cottage, you know? Or cancel the Festival."

Ryder nodded. His mind drifted back a few years as he recalled his parents' relationship.

"You're right. She believed in the magic of this place and in the joy it brought to families during the Festival. Dad... he just shut down emotionally after she passed away. It was like a part of him died with her." Ryder leaned against a pillar.

Emily's gaze met his, understanding passing between them. "That's why he let the lodge slip in his last years. He lost the enthusiasm, the drive to keep it going."

Ryder sighed, the weight of their conversation settling on him. "Yeah, I think he couldn't bear the thought of carrying on without her."

Silence enveloped them for a moment, the memories of their parents and the cottage intertwining in their thoughts. Then Emily's voice broke the silence.

"We're not going to lose this place, are we, Ryder?" Emily's eyes were filled with worry as she looked at him. "We can't lose because that would be like losing all our memories with it."

A determined glint shone in Ryder's eyes as he turned to his sister. "I promise you, little sister, I'm going to do everything in my power to ensure that doesn't happen."

"You mean *we're* going to do everything in *our* power to stop that from happening?" Emily corrected him. "We're in this together, remember!"

"I know!" Ryder nodded. "And the first thing we need to do together is get this cottage in order."

A small smile played on Emily's lips. "I know, and I'm so excited about the changes we want to make this summer. Converting the cottage into a family cabin with three bedrooms, renting it out to others while keeping its spirit alive,"

Ryder's smile matched his sister's enthusiasm. "It's a good plan. But for now, we need to concentrate on making it livable for the season and move the family from number five in here."

"I'll make sure they have a few complimentary morning muffin baskets delivered to the house for the next few days to apologize for the troubles they've endured in number five," Emily told him.

"Good idea," Ryder agreed.

As they turned to head back inside the cottage, Ryder couldn't help but feel a sense of purpose and a renewed determination to keep the lodge thriving. Emily's optimism was infectious, and he knew they were on the right path.

Inside, as they stood in the cozy living room, Emily turned to Ryder, her expression a mix of playfulness and seriousness. "You know, we're going to have to move Mom's hospital bed."

"I know!" Ryder took a deep breath. "The cleaning crew is coming in in a few hours, and Hank has gone to get some bunk beds and a single bed from storage."

"I think mom would've wanted us to donate it to someone who needs the bed but can't afford it," Emily suggested.

"Do you think Gran would know of anyone?" Ryder looked questioningly at his sister.

"We could ask, and I could put some feelers out at the local hospital," Emily offered.

"Another good idea." Ryder grinned. "You're bubbling over with them today."

"I'm just so excited that you've finally decided to do something with this place." She stopped talking for a few minutes as they walked through the bedrooms, taking stock. "You know that Dad left it to you, right?"

"I do!" Ryder sighed. "But I would rather it be used as part of the lodge now." He glanced around, and memories of the past intertwined with the ones from the previous night. "I think it will see family, fun, and laughter again from all the families that come to the lodge on vacation."

"That's a lovely thought," Emily said with a whimsical smile, her eyes landing on the leather-bound journal as they walked back into the living room. "You found Fiona Carlisle's journal?"

Before Ryder could answer, Emily dashed across the living room to get it. She plopped on the well-worn sofa, frowned, stuck her hand between the cushions, and pulled out an envelope.

"What's this?" Emily turned it over to see Avery's name on it. "It's a letter to Avery in Mom's handwriting."

She started to open it, and Ryder flew across the room but got to her too late, as she'd already pulled the letter out and had started to read. Ryder rolled his eyes and shook his head.

"You know reading someone else's mail is a crime!" Ryder reminded her.

"There was no postage stamp or address on the envelope," Emily pointed out absently as she finished reading the letter, her eyes shining with tears as she lifted her emotion-filled eyes to his. "Ryder, it was Mom and Judy that broke the two of you up?"

"It wasn't as simple as that, Em," Ryder told her, sitting next to her and snatching the letter from her. He folded it and put it back in the envelope. "At the end of the day, I was the one who made the decision to walk away."

"What did Mom tell you that would've made you do that?" Emily asked him.

"It wasn't Mom who spoke to me," Ryder explained to Emily.

By the time he'd finished telling her the story and about his conversation with Avery the previous night, his sister's eyes shone with angry tears.

"That's why Avery became so cold to Mom right before the wedding!' Emily exclaimed. "She never said a word to me about it."

"I don't think she told anyone," Ryder said, pulling his ankle over his knee, his jeans stretching over his leg muscles.

"If the two of you had talked to each other back then—" Emily shook her head.

"We'd probably still be where we are today," Ryder finished for her. "Maybe Mom and Judy were right. Avery and I would probably have ended up hating each other even more. At least with what happened to us, we got a chance to work things out."

"And you think if you had been married, the two of you would be divorced with irreconcilable differences?" Emily guessed. "But you don't know that for sure, and neither did Mom or Judy." Her eyes blazed once again. "No one could've known that."

"As a parent, part of me understands that Mom and Judy did what they thought was best for us and were protecting our hearts and souls." Ryder shrugged.

"And?" Emily's eyes narrowed.

"And what?" Ryder frowned at his sister.

"What else happened between you and Avery?" Emily asked impatiently. "How did you leave things?" Ryder could see the wheels turning in her head. "And what does she want to speak to you about at six?"

"Ah, I forgot you have super hearing." Ryder raised an eyebrow at her. "Well, when you want to, that is."

"Stop hedging!" Emily swatted him on the arm.

"As I told you, we spoke, and we found out things. I feel we resolved a lot of the mess that was left between us." Ryder's lips curved into a thoughtful smile. "We still have a way to go, but at least our failed relationship isn't a bone of contention between us anymore."

"And what are the two of you going to discuss in top secret at six?" Emily pushed for an answer.

"I really don't know," Ryder answered honestly. "All she said was that she had something to tell me, and it was important."

"You don't have a secret love child I don't know about, do you?" Emily's head was pushed back as she eyed him suspiciously.

"No, definitely not," Ryder assured her. "And I honestly don't know what she wants to tell me."

"You do know that now I have to eavesdrop on your meeting, right?" Emily warned him.

"I would expect nothing less." Ryder laughed.

Emily's gaze glinted with worry. "Do you still have feelings for her?"

Ryder's expression softened, his memories of Avery resurfacing. "I'll always have feelings for Avery. She was my first big love, Em. It's hard to completely let go of something like that."

"I know, Ryder. Just remember, moving forward doesn't mean erasing the past." Emily's smile held a hint of understanding. "And, because of your heart, big brother, Avery's life is in Los Angeles now, and giving it to her again could mean losing it again as she takes it with her to California."

"I'm fine, Em," Ryder promised her. "I have no expectations about my relationship with Avery, and I know her life is no longer in Frisco."

"As long as you do!" Emily didn't look convinced. "I'm glad the two of you sorted things out." Her look became pensive.

"What's wrong?" Ryder raised his eyebrows, knowing that look on his sister's face meant she was either about to meddle in someone else's life or she was worried about something.

"It must've been a huge shock for Avery to find out it was her mother that ultimately ruined her wedding." Emily's voice was low. "I wonder how she's going to be when she goes home to face her mother."

"I'm sure Avery will work it out, Em," Ryder told her with a warning look in his eyes. "Please don't interfere in this."

"Avery's my friend," Emily reminded him. "I'm already involved in this, especially as I was the one who had to console her on the day that she was supposed to get married but had her heart broken instead." Her eyes narrowed angrily. "I was the one torn between loyalty to a cad of a brother who'd just broken my best friend's heart and my best friend."

"I'm sorry, Em," Ryder said, giving her a tight smile. "I know I left you in a horrible situation that day."

"Thank you," Emily said. "This is the first time you've apologized for leaving me to clean up the mess *you* made that day."

"I know, and I should've done it a lot sooner," Ryder acknowledged. "I didn't even think about how hard it would've been for you to have been caught between two people you loved."

"It was like being torn in two," Emily admitted. "Although the bigger part was with Avery, as I couldn't believe you'd do that to her."

"You didn't speak to me for over a year," Ryder reminded her.

"You're lucky it was only a year," Emily told him. "And Mom threatened not to invite me to Christmas again if I refused to talk to you."

"Ah, so that's why you started speaking to me again!" Ryder gave a snort. "I am sorry I did that to you and Avery, Em." He looked at his hands and sighed. "I was devastated and thought I was doing what was right, and in order to do that, I had to just leave and not look back."

He swallowed. "Because if I'd stopped for even a second, I wouldn't have been able to leave at all."

"I'm trying to understand, and I think maybe I do," Emily told him. "But the whole situation was so messed up."

"I know," Ryder agreed. "But hopefully now both myself and Avery can move on."

"I don't think it's that simple for her," Emily pointed out. "She thought it was our parents that ruined her life, but now she's found out that hers were involved too."

"Yeah!" Ryder ran his hand through his hair. "I guess that's not going to make for a happy Christmas reunion this year."

"It's not just what they did, but they've also kept it from her for fifteen years!" Emily noted. "You know what Gran always says about secrets. It doesn't matter how deep you bury them. They always rise to the surface."

"Maybe I shouldn't have told her." Ryder now felt awful after hearing his sister out.

"No, don't do that, big brother." Emily shook her head and looked at him. "You and Avery needed this, and you need the truth aired out so now the wound can finally heal."

"I know, but what wounds is it now going to inflict on others?" Ryder asked worriedly.

"I'm sure they'll work it out," Emily said, sounding confident. "And you can't meddle there either, just like you warned me not to."

"I know." Ryder blew out a breath and nodded before standing. "I think we should get back and organize for the cabin to be cleaned and let cabin 5 know they're moving."

Emily let him help her up. The weight of the past seemed to lift as they prepared to leave the cottage, replaced by the promise of the future they were determined to shape. The snow-covered landscape outside mirrored the pristine canvas they had before them, ready to be painted with new memories and experiences.

And as they stepped out into the winter air, Ryder couldn't help but feel a sense of hope that they could save Mistletoe Lodge so their children could carry on the Carlisle family legacy in Frisco.

CHAPTER 13

The snow-covered landscape outside seemed to merge with the sense of anticipation that filled Avery's heart. She sat at the desk in her cozy room at Mistletoe Lodge, her laptop open in front of her. It was a rare moment of quiet amidst the holiday rush, and she was using it to work on a project for her firm's client, the Pembrook Hotel, Resorts, and Spa Group.

Avery's fingers danced over the keyboard as she sorted through properties that matched the client's criteria. She was looking for a place similar to Mistletoe Lodge, and her search led her to a property called Slopes Hotel. Nestled between Frisco and Breckenridge, it seemed to check all the boxes.

The hotel had the same kind of picturesque setting as Mistletoe, with stunning views of the surrounding landscape. It was larger, had more amenities, and had been a competitor to Mistletoe in the past.

A cruel blizzard last winter had devastated part of the hotel, and its owner, Malcolm Morris, couldn't afford to rebuild. As a result, the property was up for sale, and by the look of the listing date, it had only just come on the market. She read through the details, and excitement bubbled up within her.

This could be the perfect alternative to Mistletoe Lodge for her client, and Avery knew just how to spin it in a proposal to get the Pembrook Group interested in it. Hopefully interested enough to no longer want to acquire Mistletoe Lodge. Especially as the group was losing patience with Mistletoe Lodge and wanted to start setting up their new mountain resort and spa early the following year.

Slopes would be more than perfect for that. Her heart hammering in her chest, she grabbed her phone. Avery dialed her boss's number and leaned back in the chair as she waited for him to pick up. When he answered, she wasted no time in explaining the new property she had found.

"Hi, Harry, it's Avery. I've come across a property called Slopes Hotel that I think could be an even better fit than Mistletoe Lodge for the Pembrook Group's requirements. It's in a fantastic location, similar to Mistletoe Lodge, and it's on the market at a steal."

Her boss's voice crackled through the line. "Are the owners of Mistletoe Lodge giving you problems?" Harry enquired.

"No, I haven't had a chance to discuss the proposal with them yet, Harry," Avery told him honestly. "And to be honest, I don't think they're going to go down without a fight." She frowned and tapped her pen on the desk. "And as they have the support of Frisco and most of the small towns supporting Mistletoe Lodge, Pembrook could find themselves having their permits stalled."

"I thought that might be the case," Harry grumbled. "I know these small towns and how they gather together." He sighed. "I thought maybe as a local you'd be able to sway them."

"I will still do my best to do that, Harry, if Pembrook isn't interested in the Slopes Hotel," Avery promised. "But the property is already a hotel, and Malcolm Morris, the owner of Slopes, is having financial difficulties and needs to sell."

"Mm," Harry said. "Okay, get me all the details and draft a proposal. Let's see if it's a viable option."

"Absolutely, I'm on it," Avery replied, grinning as she scanned the proposal she'd already drafted for Harry along with all the necessary information he'd need. "Okay, done. I've just sent it through to you."

"Oh!" Harry breathed, and she heard her email ding on his computer. "Give me a minute." He paused for a while. "Can I call you back?"

"Sure," Avery said.

"Give me an hour," Harry said. "I remember this hotel, and it was their first option, but Malcolm Morris wasn't willing to sell."

"I've set up a meeting with him for tomorrow morning at eleven, so I'll need an answer before then." Avery knew she was pushing it, but she had to get Pembrook Group to no longer be interested in Mistletoe Lodge.

"I think you may have won the jackpot with this, Avery," Harry told her. "But I'll have to call Pembrook Group, and I'll let you know what they say."

"Great," Avery said, scouring her email and glancing at her wrist watch. "Let me know as soon as you can."

"I will," Harry promised, and he hung up.

Avery stared out the window for a few seconds, and her heart felt a little lighter. She was not looking forward to the conversation with Ryder and Emily about why she'd actually come home for Christmas. But hopefully, if her plans pan out, she'd be able to let them know she'd gotten Pembrook interested in another property and a plan to save Mistletoe Lodge.

Her eyes once again scoured her inbox impatiently.

"Come on, please answer my email or my message." Avery looked at her phone. "Argh. I hate having to wait."

She noticed the time and found she only had another hour before she was to meet with Ryder. Avery was going to have to put that meeting off until the next day and ask to include Emily in it. She clicked on the second proposal she'd been working on that day, which she'd sent to another client of hers, and went over it for the umpteenth time.

She was closing down the file when her heart slammed into her ribs once again as her phone rang. Avery grabbed it and froze, her breath catching in her throat—it was her mother. She let out a breath as the conversation she'd had with Ryder the previous day flashed through her mind.

Avery knew she should take the call, as her mother would probably be wondering why she hadn't called all day. But Avery wasn't ready to talk to her mother after finding out she'd played a big part in her breakup with Ryder fifteen years ago.

She swallowed and knew if she didn't answer it, her mother would probably risk driving in the bad weather to come find her. So, she hit answer and tried to keep her anger at her mother from her voice.

"Hello," Avery said a little stiffly.

"Hello, sweetheart." Judy's soft voice rang through the receiver. "You haven't answered any of my messages and calls all day." She moaned. "I was getting so worried that if you hadn't answered this call, I was going to risk driving to the lodge."

"Sorry, I've been busy." Avery tried not to snap. "I was going to call you later," she lied.

"I just wanted to make sure you were alright and let you know that your father's recovering nicely," Judy told her. "How are things at the lodge?"

"It's been great. The Carlisle's have been very accommodating." Avery cleared her throat, and while she was talking, she noticed the email she'd been waiting for appear in her inbox. "I'm sorry, Mom, but I have to go.

An email I've been waiting for from work has arrived, and I have to attend to it right away."

"Goodness, Avery, are you still working?" Judy sounded astonished. "I thought you were here on vacation."

"The only reason I was able to change my vacation at such short notice was if I took an assignment," Avery explained. "Unfortunately, I still have to work until I've closed this deal."

"I understand," Judy sighed. "And your father and I are so grateful you were able to do this for us."

"I know Mom," Avery said, her anger toward her mother dissipating. "Now I must go, but I'll call you tomorrow."

"Okay, sweetheart, have a great night." Judy blew kisses through the phone.

As soon as Avery hung up, she opened the email from the CEO of the Holland Corporation, and her heart soared.

Hi Avery

It's good to hear from you, and thank you for the proposal you've sent to me.

I'm interested in delving deeper into this.

Can we meet in the next few days?

Avery's fingers flew over the keyboard as she punched in a response and hit send, then breathed a sigh of relief. Her heart raced as she leaned back in her chair, fingers drumming on the desk. It had been a grueling day, but the prospect of what this proposal could lead to filled her with excitement.

She knew that she'd probably only get responses the next day, so Avery decided to go downstairs and find Ryder to push their meeting to the following afternoon. After that, Avery was going to take a much-needed break. The awful guilt that had been weighing heavily on her shoulders since she arrived at the lodge had lifted a little.

Closing her laptop with a satisfied smile, Avery stood up and stretched. The rollercoaster of emotions that had defined her day seemed to culminate in this moment, which hopefully would be triumphant for her and the lodge. She grabbed her jacket, slipped on her faux-fur-lined boots, and headed for the reception area to find Ryder.

Avery's steps were light as she descended the stairs of Mistletoe Lodge, her mind still abuzz with the excitement of her recent achievements. As she reached the landing, she spotted Rosie heading in the opposite direction with an apron in her hands.

"Hey, Avery!" Rosie's cheerful voice echoed through the hallway. "You're just the person I was looking for."

Avery paused, turning to face Rosie with a curious smile. "Oh, that's funny because I was just about to come looking for you."

"I was going to ask you if you wanted to bake Christmas cookies with our Chef, Nora, and me." Rosie invited Avery.

Avery's eyebrows lifted, and she pursed her lips. "I'd love to." She told Rosie. "But first, I have to find your father."

Rosie's grin widened. "I can help you find him."

"Great!" Avery said, gesturing with his hands animatedly.

"Follow me." Rosie beckoned with her hand, turning to walk past the front desk and down the small hallway that led off it to the office. She knocked on the door before pushing it open. "Dad."

"Hey honey," Ryder called from the other side, making Avery's heart skip a few beats.

"Avery's here to see you," Rosie said, pushing the door open and stepping into the office with Avery following her.

"Hi," Avery said, giving a small wave and swallowing as his eyes met hers and his smile widened. "I need to push our meeting to tomorrow afternoon."

"Meeting?" Ryder's brow furrowed. "I thought it was just an informal chat about something you wanted to tell me."

"Yes, well, it's both a meeting and a chat." Avery left out the informal because it was about business and about her confessing why she was there.

"Sure." Ryder nodded. "Tomorrow afternoon should be fine."

"Do you think you could ask Emily to join us at, say, two?" Avery asked.

"Okay!" Ryder's brow knitted a little tighter. "Can you give me a hint as to what it's about?"

Rosie, growing impatient with the adult conversation, interrupted, "I'm going to the kitchen, and I'll meet you there." She told Avery as she skipped out the door, calling over her shoulder. "Don't be too long, Avery."

Avery grinned as she watched Rosie leave. "I'll be right there."

Avery shook her head as her eyes held his. "All I can say is that it could be really beneficial for you, Emily, and the lodge."

Ryder steepled his fingers in front of him as he watched her intently. "Well, now you've piqued my curiosity."

Avery laughed softly. "I guess you'll have to wait until tomorrow to find out." She pointed to the door. "I better go meet Rosie. We're baking Christmas cookies."

"Enjoy," Ryder said as she nodded and left his office, hoping he didn't notice how wobbly her legs were.

As she entered the lodge's bustling kitchen, the warmth and the enticing aroma of baking cookies enveloped her. Nora, the lodge's chef, greeted Avery with a bright smile.

"Avery, honey, how are you?" Nora stretched out her arms to engulf Avery in a warm hug. "It's been forever since I've seen you."

"I know, Nora." Avery smiled as Nora let her go and stepped around the large center island.

"Young Rosie here tells me you're joining us to make Christmas cookies." Nora busied herself gathering ingredients.

Rosie was already donning an apron, her eyes dancing with excitement. "Avery, here's an apron for you."

Avery accepted the apron and tied it around her waist, a feeling of nostalgia washing over her. She hadn't done anything like this in years. The three of them gathered around the kitchen island, ingredients and baking tools at the ready.

Nora handed each of them a bowl of cookie dough, and soon they were all laughing and chatting as they rolled out the dough and cut out festive shapes that Nora put on baking trays and popped into the oven.

While those cookies were baking, they made more batches until the first batch was ready and cooled enough for them to ice. As they decorated the cookies with icing and sprinkles, Avery found herself sneaking quite a few of the cookies with Rosie.

Avery, Rosie, and Nora worked together, their laughter and camaraderie creating an atmosphere of pure joy. Mixing dough, cutting out shapes, and applying colorful icing turned into a symphony of fun, with each of them contributing their creativity to the festive baked goods.

As they focused on their culinary masterpiece, Ryder appeared in the doorway, his amused smile a clear indication that he couldn't resist joining in the holiday festivities. Rosie was the first to spot him.

"Dad!" Rosie's eyes lit up. "Just in time to join us."

Ryder's eyes twinkled as he entered the kitchen, his gaze locking onto Avery's for a fleeting moment before he greeted Nora. "You all seem to be having a blast."

Nora grinned mischievously. "Well, if you want to join the cookie-making party, you'll have to earn your place."

Ryder's brows lifted in mock surprise. "Oh, really? And how do I do that?"

Nora handed him an apron and a rolling pin. "You get to roll out the dough."

Ryder chuckled and tied the apron around his waist with a good-natured grin on his face. As he set to work rolling out the dough, the kitchen erupted with laughter and playful banter. He wasn't exactly an expert in the cookie-making department, but his enthusiasm was infectious, and soon everyone was laughing along.

But then, with a mischievous gleam in his eye, Ryder grabbed a handful of flour and dramatically blew it towards Rosie. She let out a mock gasp, her eyes widening in playful shock.

"Oh, it's on now!" Rosie's eyes narrowed with purpose.

In an instant, flour was flying through the air once again, creating a whimsical winter scene in the midst of the warm kitchen. Laughter filled every corner as they engaged in the flour fight with abandon. They were all soon coated in a fine dusting of white.

Avery found herself in the middle of the chaos, laughing so hard that her sides ached. She and Ryder exchanged flour-filled glances, and for a brief moment, it was as if they were transported back in time. To the days when they used to have flour fights and cooking or icing competitions at Mistletoe Cottage.

And then, unexpectedly, Avery's foot slipped on some flour on the floor, and she found herself in Ryder's arms, pulled close to his warm, hard chest. Her heart was beating so hard against her ribs that she wasn't sure if it was her heart or his; she could feel pounding between them.

Their eyes collided once again, and it was as if time stood still and they were pulled into a bubble where only they existed. Avery's breath caught in her throat as his strong arms held her, and she could feel his breath mingle with hers. But Nora's voice snapped them back to reality, bursting their bubble.

"The last batch of cookies is ready for icing, everyone!" Nora hurried to the oven as the timer dinged.

With flour-covered hands and aprons, they gathered around the island once more, ready to put the finishing touches on their creations. As Avery dipped her brush into a pot of vibrant icing, she stole a glance at Ryder. There was something different in the air between them—a newfound ease that hadn't been there before.

As they worked side by side, their hands occasionally brushed against each other's, sending her pulse racing and her breath catching each time as the butterflies tickled the inside of her stomach. As the final cookie was iced, Avery and Ryder exchanged a triumphant high-five, their laughter ringing out in harmony.

As their fingers met, electricity shot through Avery's arm, and their eyes met once again but were soon torn apart when Rosie jumped in for a high five as well.

Avery and Ryder took their places, with Rosie in between them, to survey their finished cookies, a sense of accomplishment shining in their eyes. The kitchen was a joyful mess, with flour and icing covering every surface.

"All right everyone, now each grab a cleaning utensil and let's clean up this mess," Nora commanded.

Sometime later, when the kitchen was clean, Priscilla called them for dinner, insisting that Avery join them once again. After dinner, they all retired to the living room, where Avery got stuck into helping make Christmas ornaments. The time flew by, and before she knew it, everyone was retiring to bed.

Feeling restless once again, Avery went for a walk in the crisp night air, once again finding herself at the fire pits. As she stood warming her hands, the crunch of boots on snow caught her attention. She turned to find Ryder coming up behind her with his hands held behind his back, grinning.

"I was hoping I'd find you out here," Ryder said.

"I needed some air," Avery told him, wondering what he was hiding behind his back. "What are you hiding?"

Ryder's smile grew as he pulled his hands in front of him and held up marshmallow roasting sticks and the ingredients to make s'mores.

"I thought we could make some s'mores." Ryder guided her to one of the benches.

"You know I never say no to s'mores!" Avery grinned while sitting beside him.

Her heart went wild as he snuggled close to her and pulled the blanket over their legs. While they were getting their s'mores ready, Avery tilted her head to look up at the sparkling, clear night sky and caught a shooting star darting across it.

"Did you make a wish?" Ryder's voice was deep and throaty.

"You know I can't tell you." Avery smiled at him. "But yes, I did."

"Well, I can tell you my wish," Ryder told her. "Because it's already started to come true."

Their eyes locked and held as the fire crackled softly beside them. Their lips were drawn toward each other, but before they could touch, the sound of someone clearing their throats had them jumping apart.

"Hi!" Emily stood, giving them a wave, with Hank towering behind her. "We thought we'd join you."

Hank held up the s'mores sticks. "It's my cheat night from my diet."

Soon the four of them were engaged in light conversation, reminiscing over Christmas's past, their laughter ringing through the night.

CHAPTER 14

As dawn broke over the snow-covered landscape, Ryder found himself rising with a sense of anticipation. The early morning light filtered through the windows of his cozy room, gently rousing him from his slumber. For the past four days, he'd been feeling a remarkable shift in his mood, an unexpected lightness in his step, and a lifting of the burdens he'd been carrying for years.

He'd tried to attribute it to the festive spirit of the season, but deep down, he knew it had more to do with a certain someone's return to his life.

With renewed vigor, Ryder hurried through his morning routine. He could hardly wait to join Emily, Hank, and Avery in their Festival preparations. Ryder had just finished the paperwork he had to see to in his office and was in a hurry to get his coat when he bumped into his grandmother, who was passing by in the hallway.

Priscilla looked at him with a knowing glint in her eyes. "You seem unusually cheerful, Ryder. It's quite a change from the past few years."

Ryder's lips curved into a half-smile as he shrugged his shoulders, trying to appear nonchalant. "Well, Grandma, we've got a lot to look forward to with the Festival preparations. The lodge is at capacity for the season, and things are looking up for us." He kissed her forehead. "I feel I can let a bit of Christmas cheer fill me up."

She raised an eyebrow and tilted her head. "Is that the only reason, dear? Or could there be something—or someone—else adding a little sparkle to your demeanor?"

Ryder's heart skipped a beat, and he could feel heat creeping up his neck. He opened his mouth to respond, but his grandmother was already walking away, chuckling, leaving him both flustered and amused by her uncanny ability to read him.

Grabbing his jacket and Stetson, he headed out the front door of the lodge, his heart light as he anticipated joining the others. He stepped outside, taking in the fresh mountain air, and his gaze settled on the area to the left of the lodge entrance, near the tranquil lake. It was there that the Festival would come to life, with booths and activities filling the space with holiday magic.

As he walked, his thoughts drifted back over the past four days. Avery's presence had ignited a transformation within him that he hadn't anticipated. He had been cautious, hesitant to let himself acknowledge the emotions that were bubbling up. But as he reflected on the genuine moments they had shared and all they'd managed to clear up, he couldn't deny that his heart felt lighter than it had in years.

It was time to admit the truth to himself, even if he wasn't ready to voice it aloud. He still had feelings for Avery, feelings he had thought were buried in the past. Yet here she was, and those feelings had resurfaced, stronger than ever. He had to remind himself that Avery was here only temporarily and that she would be returning to Los Angeles after Christmas. Ryder knew he couldn't let himself fall into old patterns, into a love that would ultimately fly away at the end of Christmas.

But as he approached the area where the Festival preparations were in full swing, his heart raced with anticipation. He could feel the tug of their shared history, the connection that had remained even through years of distance and heartache.

It was a dance of emotions that he was determined to navigate carefully to ensure that their newfound camaraderie remained platonic. Ryder didn't want to repeat the mistakes of the past, and this time when Avery left, hopefully she'd do so with a full heart.

He smiled, thinking that maybe she'd come home more often now that the shadows of their past had been swept away. As he joined the group and their laughter and chatter enveloped him, Ryder found himself exchanging a bright smile with Emily, whose sparkle was also back.

They set to work, marking off spaces for the booths, discussing layout ideas, and putting their collective creativity to good use.

The conversation flowed a lot easier between Ryder and Avery. He caught himself stealing glances at her, admiring the way she got so involved with every project she took on. A few times their eyes met and held, making his breath catch in his throat and his arms itch to encircle her waist to pull her to him for a kiss.

His lips yearned to feel hers against them again, but he shook off the feeling and broke eye contact before he did something foolish. Ryder reminded himself over and over again while they worked side by side that Avery was in Frisco on vacation. Their lives were in two different states now.

During a short break, Avery stepped away to take a call, leaving Hank, Emily, and Ryder to continue their work.

Emily turned to Ryder with a worried look in her eyes. "You know she's leaving after New Year's Day?" She gave his arm a gentle squeeze. "I know the two of you have cleared away all the debris of your past, but be careful, big brother." She looked to where Avery was talking on her phone. "This time it will be her walking away and leaving you here with a broken heart."

"I know," Ryder assured her. "We're..." His voice trailed off. "I'm not quite sure where we are right now."

He ran his hand through his hair. "I'm just glad that we are moving back towards being good friends."

"Good," Emily said. "Because I don't want to have to be mad at my best friend for breaking my big brother's heart." She smiled. "I'm enjoying having her back because I've missed my best friend."

"Of course." Ryder nodded. "It's so nice to see your sparkle back, Em." He kissed her brow. "Don't worry, Avery and I are good." He smiled and held up his hands. "But *just friends* is good."

"Let's keep it like that!" Emily gave him a hug and went off to join Rosie, who was throwing a stick for Rory.

"A bit of advice, bro," Hank said, having stood to one side and listened to the exchange between Emily and Ryder.

"Sure!" Ryder looked at him curiously.

"Friends don't give friends lingering smoldering looks or go on late-night romantic dates around a fire," Hank told him. "And for the record—" He patted Ryder on the back. "I didn't believe a word of what you said to Emily about you and Avery just being friends."

Hank chuckled, gave Ryder another pat on the shoulder, and went to join Emily and Rosie in throwing and fetching with Rory as Avery walked back toward him.

"Sorry about that." Avery shoved her phone into her jeans pocket. "Work!"

"I thought you were on vacation." Ryder's eyebrows rose.

"The only way I could change my vacation time to come to Frisco was to take on a new project," Avery explained. "Until I have the deal done, I have to work."

"How long is that going to take?" Ryder asked her curiously.

"Hopefully not too long," Avery said with a smile, her eyes lit with excitement. "Especially now that my new proposal for the deal has been approved." She glanced at her wristwatch. "Speaking of business, I have to go. I have a video meeting in twenty minutes."

"Sure," Ryder said. "You go. We'll finish up here." He smiled, trying to ignore the disappointment. "Thank you for all your help today."

"It's a pleasure." Avery's smile widened. "I enjoyed it."

"Do you still want to meet this afternoon?" Ryder asked, trying to keep her from leaving for another few minutes.

"I'll have to get back to you," Avery told him, pulling a sorry face. "I'm sorry for moving it. I just need to get some details together before we meet."

Ryder's frown deepened. "What are you up to, Avery Hawthorn?"

"You'll see." Avery winked mischievously before turning and rushing off.

Ryder stood watching her go, a mix of emotions flowing through him while the butterflies in his stomach had been stirred up and were causing havoc in his stomach.

"Dad!" Rosie called him out of his reverie. "Come play with us."

She squealed in delight as Hank rushed toward her, and she dodged him to run off while Emily scooped up a huge mound of snow to fashion a snow bomb. Ryder laughed as he watched Rory, Rosie's Golden Retriever, bark and prance as they had fun in the snow.

"I'm on my—" Ryder's words were cut off when Emily's snow bomb hit him on the side of the face and slid down his neck. "Why you...."

Ryder's laughter rang out as Emily and Rosie squealed when he scooped up snow and ran after them. Laughter echoed through the crisp winter air as they engaged in impromptu snowball fights. The snow flew in every direction as the four of them plus Rory were lost in the joy of the moment, their playful shouts mingling with the sound of snowballs hitting their intended targets.

Ryder was mid-laughter, preparing to launch another snowball at Emily, when the unmistakable sound of helicopter blades cut through the playful cacophony.

The group froze, their gazes lifting to the sky as
the source of the noise became clear—a helicopter
descending toward the designated festival parking area.

As the helicopter's sleek form came into view,
they watched in awe as it expertly maneuvered its
descent. The churning of snow beneath the powerful
downdraft sent flurries swirling around them, adding
to the surreal nature of the moment.

With practiced ease, the helicopter touched
down on the snow-covered ground, its blades creating a
mesmerizing whirlwind of snowflakes. The noise of its
blade throbbing through the valley and echoing off the
trees that swayed behind it.

Wide-eyed and fascinated, Emily, Hank, and R
yder exchanged glances, their snowball fight
momentarily forgotten as they tried to make sense of
the unexpected arrival. The helicopter settled, but the
blades stayed swirling above as the door swung open,
and a figure emerged—a familiar, petite, red-headed
woman bounded out the door. Even from this distance,
they could see the smile on her face.

The woman leaned into the helicopter to retrieve a backpack and Stetson, her movements efficient and practiced. With a friendly wave to the pilot, she closed the door behind her, her gloved hand twisting the handle before she released it.

The helicopter's engines roared to life once again as the woman pulled away from it. With a powerful surge, it lifted off the ground, ascending back into the sky with a sense of graceful power.

Now standing alone in the cleared space, the red-headed woman watched the bird gain some height before it flew off in the direction it had come from. She straightened and slapped her Stetson atop her head, its brim casting a shadow over her features.

The four of them watched as her eyes scanned the surroundings before settling on them. A big smile lined her face as she saw them, and she waved before rushing toward them.

"Is that Heather?" Emily gaped and looked at her brother. "Did you know she was coming?"

"No!" Ryder shook his head, not taking his eyes off the young woman hurtling toward them.

"She's still full of that boundless energy I see," Hank commented.

"Yup!" Ryder and Emily said it together with a nod.

Rosie stepped up next to Ryder and took his hand. Daddy, is that Heather?"

"Yup!" Ryder said it again and sighed resignedly. "Grandmother's going to be delighted."

"Hello, hello!" Heather beamed, her cheeks pink from the chilly air. Dropping her pack carelessly in the snow, she bounced into Ryder's arms, planting a kiss on his cheek. "Hey Ry, it's good to see you."

Ryder was nearly knocked off his feet from the impact and didn't get a word in as Heather bounded to her next victim to embrace in her exuberance. She'd always reminded him of Tigger, and he pictured her with a tail bouncing everywhere.

"Emmy!" Heather wrapped her arms around Emily, and as small as she was, she lifted Emily off her feet as she squeezed. "I've missed you soooo much."

"Hey, Heather," Emily squeaked, finding it hard to breathe in Heather's surprising strong embrace.

"Rosie?" Heather dumped Emily back onto her feet and turned to Rosie, who took a step behind Ryder. "My word!" She observed Rosie. "How you've grown in two years."

"Hi," Rosie said shyly, cowering behind Ryder, not wanting to be squeezed to death by the energetic strawberry.

Heather turned her attention to Hank, whose eyes narrowed at her warningly, but that didn't deter Heather. She gave him a cheeky grin and went in for a hug.

"You're still making grand entrances, I see, Heather," Ryder said.

"Gran always says a lady must make an entrance to be noticed," Heather mocked, her green eyes sparkling with laughter. "I heard the festival was back on, so I thought I'd come lend a hand."

"Aren't you supposed to be counting polar bears in the Arctic?" Emily asked.

"Tagging," Heather corrected her. "Tagging polar bears."

"You were tagging polar bears?" Rosie's curiosity outweighed her shyness as she looked at Heather.

"I did," Heather confirmed. "Do you want to see some pictures?" She pulled her phone from her bomber jacket pocket to show a fascinated Rosie.

"Oh, wow!" Rosie's eyes were huge. "Look, Daddy." She pointed to a picture of Heather sitting next to a polar bear that had obviously been tranquilized.

"Yeah, Heather does a lot of dangerous stuff like that," Ryder said.

"I want to go work with polar bears too," Rosie told him.

"Heather doesn't only work with polar bears, sweetheart," Ryder explained. "She's a wildlife vet, which means she works with all sorts of wild animals."

"That's so cool," Rosie said, staring at Heather in awe.

"If you're trying to scare her away from being like Heather," Hank laughed, patting Ryder's shoulder. "You're not doing a good job of it."

"What's wrong with being like me?" Heather asked, pocketing her phone and picking up her well-worn backpack.

"Nothing," Emily assured her, rolling her eyes at Ryder. "Just Ryder being a protective father."

"Ah!" Heather nodded. "So, how's the preparation going?" She looked at Ryder and Emily.

"Thanks to the weather, we've only just been able to get started," Emily told her.

"So that means you could use an extra hand around here?" Heather grinned at Ryder.

"You're always welcome at the lodge, Heather," Ryder said through gritted teeth, his shoulders tensing up. "This is your home too."

"Are you still mad at me for voting to sell this old place?" Heather's eyes held a glint of teasing as she goaded him.

"For the purpose of keeping the peace for the festive season, I'm going to ignore what you just said," Ryder informed her stiffly. "We're done here for the day."

"Come on, Heather, let's get you settled." Emily linked her arm through Heather's. "I'm sure Grandmother's going to be thrilled to see you. You're going to have to stay in her cottage with her as we're filled to capacity."

"Not a problem," Heather said as they started to walk to the lodge. "It will be like the good old days."

"Daddy, can I go with them?" Rosie asked, and he nodded.

Rosie called Rory and skipped off after Heather and Emily, who stopped to wait for her to catch up.

"Why do you let Heather goad you like that?" Hank asked Ryder when they were alone. "You know she does it to get a rise from you."

Well, she knows how to get under my skin like a bur beneath a horse's saddle," Ryder hissed, his hands curled into fists at his side as he reigned in his anger. "Emily and I wanted to buy her shares in the lodge, but she wouldn't sell them." He shook his head, his eyes narrowing as the three of them disappeared in the distance. "Once she knew a big resort chain wanted to *acquire* the lodge, she did everything in her power to get us to let it go."

"Yeah, but she knew the lodge was bleeding money and in need of a huge financial outlay to fix it up," Hank reminded him. "I'm sure Heather thought she was helping and trying to lift the burden of this place off your and Em's shoulders."

"It's not a burden. It's our legacy!" Ryder hissed. "Heather doesn't get it like we do."

"Heather's always been a rolling stone," Hank pointed out. "Nature's her home, and the animals she's fighting to save from extinction are her legacy." He gave Ryder an understanding smile. "She grew up feeling like she was always on the outside of your family, looking in. Heather's parents were killed when she was four. All she had was your grandmother."

"She had us too," Ryder said. "We always included Heather in everything."

"Yes, but at the end of the day, you and Em went home as a full family unit. She had two missing." Hank sighed and looked around the area. "Besides, we really could use the extra hands because we have a lot to do in four days." He raised his eyebrows. "And Heather is a hard worker and surprisingly strong for such a tiny thing."

"I guess," Ryder agreed. "I just hope she doesn't fill Rosie's head with crazy ideas." He shook his head, and he and Hank started to make their way back to the lodge. "You know how exuberant Heather can get." He pulled his coat up as the snow started to fall again. "Next thing I know, Rosie wants to go on a lion-taming safari with the energetic strawberry."

"Where did she get that nickname from?" Hank glanced at Ryder. "I always thought her hair was more ginger than strawberry."

"It was red like a strawberry when she was young," Ryder told him as they reached the lodge. He looked up in time to see his grandmother's face light up as she walked out of the dining room and saw Heather. "At least she's made my grandmother's day."

"Don't worry, Ryder," Hank teased. "Your grandmother loves you all the same."

"Funny!" Ryder glared at him before they stepped into the lobby and got pulled into the happy family reunion.

CHAPTER 15

Avery sat at the desk in her room at the lodge, her laptop propped up in front of her. The screen displayed a video call interface. The participants in the call were her boss, Harry, Sly Pembrook of the Pembrook Corporation and Malcolm Morris, the owner of the Slopes Hotel. The meeting concluded with a happy Malcolm as he signed off, leaving Avery and Harry alone with Sly Pembrook.

Sly, the CEO of the Pembrook Group, had a reputation for his shrewd business decisions and calculated moves. However, this time, his tone held a warmth that caught Avery off guard.

"Avery, my dear," he began, his voice surprisingly genial, "I must congratulate you on your work with the Slopes Hotel. You've managed to secure us a valuable acquisition."

Avery felt a surge of pride at Sly's words. The past few days had been a whirlwind of negotiations and presentations, and it seemed her efforts had paid off. She exchanged a quick glance with Harry, who wore a knowing smile.

"Thank you, Sly," Avery responded, her professional demeanor firmly in place. "I'm grateful for the opportunity to contribute to the company's success."

Sly's smile widened. "In fact, Avery, I wanted to personally express my gratitude. Your dedication and keen eye have not gone unnoticed. Once Harry assumes his new position, I would be more than pleased for you to take the lead on managing the Slopes Hotel account."

Avery's heart raced. The prospect of handling such a significant account was both thrilling and daunting. She had worked hard to prove herself, and it seemed her efforts were finally paying off.

"I appreciate your confidence in me, Sly," she replied. "I won't let you down."

Sly nodded approvingly. "I have no doubt about that, Avery. Keep up the excellent work." With a final nod, he ended the call, leaving Avery alone with Harry.

"Well done, Avery," Harry said with a genuine smile. "You've certainly made your mark."

"Thank you, Harry." Avery returned the smile, her mind still processing the weight of Sly's words. "It means a lot coming from both you and Sly."

Harry's tone grew more serious. "Avery, I have some news for you as well. The promotion we discussed is looking more and more likely to happen. The board is impressed with your performance and the results you've brought in."

Avery's heart swelled with a mix of excitement and gratitude. She had been working tirelessly to prove herself, and it seemed that her dedication was finally paying off.

"Thank you, Harry," she said, her voice tinged with emotion. "I'm truly honored."

"Keep up the momentum, and I have no doubt you'll be stepping into your new role soon," Harry assured her. "You've got a bright future ahead with Grimes Mergers and Acquisitions, Avery."

With those encouraging words, Harry ended the call, leaving Avery alone in her room. She leaned back in her chair, taking a deep breath as a sense of accomplishment washed over her. Avery breathed a sigh of relief that Mistletoe Lodge was no longer the target of the Pembrook Group.

While Avery had managed to divert that company's attention from the lodge, it didn't stop whoever else came for it next, like the bank that held the mortgage for the property.

Avery checked her phone and emails once more before she closed her laptop, but there was none. She had been hoping to hear back from the Holland Corporation. Avery picked up her phone and composed a message to the CEO of the Holland Corporation:

Let me know if you can still meet today.
Avery

After sending the message, Avery stood up from her desk and stretched. She needed a change of scenery and a breath of fresh air, but before she did that, she needed to postpone the meeting with Ryder and Emily. Avery's heart twinged, knowing it wasn't going to be an easy conversation about her being the one sent to acquire the lodge.

Hopefully, the fact that she'd managed to prevent the acquisition would soften the blow. She swallowed, knowing that even though she'd managed to do that and hopefully had more good news for them, Avery had still betrayed and lied to them.

Slipping on her coat and boots, she left her room and headed downstairs. As she entered the lodge's common area, she was taken aback by an unexpected sight. Heather Jessop, Ryder and Emily's cousin, stood there with a smile on her face.

Avery and Heather had never quite seen eye to eye. Heather's perceived jealousy of her close relationship with Emily fueled Avery's feelings of tension between them.

Suppressing her surprise, Avery forced a smile onto her face. "Heather," she greeted, her tone as pleasant as she could muster. "What a surprise."

"Hey, Avery," Heather replied, her expression surprisingly friendly as she stepped forward and enveloped Avery in a hug.

"Oh!" Avery exclaimed, a bit shocked by the gesture. "We're hugging."

"How are you?" Heather asked, and her eyes held none of the usual malice she used to look at Avery with.

"I'm good." Avery's brow crinkled as she looked at Heather suspiciously, not too sure how to take her. "How are you?
"

Heather's smile widened, and Avery couldn't shake the feeling that there was something different about her.

"I'm great," Heather told her.

"My mother tells me you're a wildlife veterinarian." Avery felt compelled to indulge in the required amount of small talk so as not to appear rude.

"I am!" Heather's eyes sparkled. "I work with Veterinarians Without Borders."

"Oh!" Avery's brows shot up. She'd heard about that organization. "That must take you all over the world."

"Yeah, I've had some exciting adventures," Heather confirmed. "I believe you're living in Los Angeles." Her eyes widened with excitement. "I love Los Angeles."

"That's because it's always buzzing and busy." Ryder's voice came from behind Avery, making her heart skip a beat. "Just like you."

Avery turned toward him, and when their eyes met, her heart sped up even more as a smile spread across his lips.

"I can't help it. I like to be busy," Heather told them.

"Have you finished your business for the day?" Ryder addressed Avery.

"Yup," Avery nodded. "Only I'm going to have to put our meeting off again."

"No problem," Ryder told her. "In fact, that fits in well with Emily's plans."

"She wants us to all help fix up some of the old booths," Heather added before Ryder could.

"That sounds like—" Avery raised her eyebrows and grinned. "Fun?"

"It's going to be," Rosie promised, skipping into the reception area from the dining room with Rory by her side.

"When does she want us to start?" Avery looked at Ryder.

"Now!" Ryder shrugged.

"Why don't the three of you go and start?" Priscilla instructed as she followed Rosie. "Avery needs to have something to eat."

"I'm fine," Avery said.

"Oh, I insist," Priscilla said with a smile, her eyes letting Avery know she wanted some alone time with her, making alarm bells start to ring in her brain.

"When Gran insists, you know she's not going to let you go anywhere," Heather warned. "We'll see you in the barn."

With that, Heather shunted Rosie and Ryder off as Priscilla linked her arm through Avery's and walked her into the living room.

"I'd like a word with you please, Avery." Priscilla confirmed Avery's suspicions. "But you also need to eat. Nora told me you didn't have breakfast or lunch."

"I got busy," Avery told her. "You don't have to worry about me. I sometimes forget to eat."

"That's not good, my dear," Priscilla said.

She guided Avery to a small, secluded table near the large window that had views of the majestic Tenmile Mountain Range with their mirrored reflection trapped beneath the iced-over Mistletoe Lake. They took a seat opposite each other, and Priscilla beckoned a server over to them.

"Avery, what are you going to eat?" Priscilla handed her the menu from the table.

The server put two bottles of water and some glassware on the table.

"I'll have a grilled sandwich." Avery smiled at the server. "With cheese and tomatoes."

"Okay." The server nodded and looked at Priscilla. "Would you like something?"

"Just some tea, please, Terri," Priscilla replied, looking at Avery. "What would you like to drink, dear?"

"I'll have some tea as well, please," Avery addressed Terri, who nodded and left them.

"Now, Avery, I have a confession to make," Priscilla surprised her by saying.

"Okay!" Avery's eyes narrowed curiously.

"My grandson left this on his desk in the office." Priscilla pulled the letter from Ryder's mother to Avery from her jacket pocket and put it on the table between them. "And Emily tells me that you and Ryder have managed to talk through all your emotional baggage."

"We have," Avery confirmed, feeling a little exposed by having her personal business known to the residents of the lodge.

"That's good," Priscilla said, nodding. "First, I want to say that I didn't know that my daughter-in-law or your mother had anything to do with yours and Ryder's break-up."

"How could you have known?" Avery asked. "You weren't living at the lodge then." She frowned.

"No, I left years before that." Priscilla glanced out the window. "My late husband and I separated. So, I took Heather, and we moved to Los Angeles to live with my sister."

"The sister you were visiting recently," Avery guessed.

"Correct." Priscilla nodded. "It turned out to be a fortuitous visit as well." She pulled a rolled-up document from her pocket. "I'm still the executor of the Mistletoe Trust and the matriarch of this family," she informed Avery, and something glinted in her eyes that made the alarm bells jangle in Avery's head again. "While I might be retired, I still oversee all the lodge's legal business."

"You're an attorney?" Avery looked at her, impressed.

"Yes, my dear." Priscilla smiled. "My sister and I inherited my father's law firm in Los Angeles." Her smile widened as she watched Avery intently. "You may even have heard of it."

"There are many law firms in Los Angeles," Avery reminded her, opening the bottle of water and pouring some of it into the glass.

"Oh, I think you'll know this one. There aren't many people who haven't heard of it." Priscilla's eyes shone as she watched Avery take a sip of water. "Venter and Associates."

The name dropped like a bomb on the table, and Avery nearly spewed her mouthful of water all over the place as she choked in shock.

"Goodness, dear." Priscilla handed her a napkin. "Are you okay?"

"You're P. Venter?" Avery coughed and took the napkin, wiping her face and the mess she'd made.

"Yes," Priscilla confirmed, unrolling the document, stretching it out, and putting it between them on the table. "You can imagine my surprise when one of my legal team members called me a few days ago to let me know about this document."

Words failed Avery as she stared at the document in front of her. It was the acquisition agreement Avery had Grime Mergers and Acquisitions draw up for Mistletoe Lodge.

She leaned her elbows on the table. "The acquisition wasn't what surprised me. I knew that grimy Sly Pembrook was after the lodge. He's been after it since my son started to let the place slide into ruin." She tapped the name on the document. "But this surprised me."

"I can explain." Avery said, noting the name she was pointing to was Avery's.

Priscilla held up her hand to stop Avery. "I did my homework, Avery, dear." She sat back, and something hit Avery.

"Oh, no!" Avery gasped, her heart dropping in her chest. "I didn't think Ryder and Emily would've seen this document yet."

"They haven't." Priscilla shook her head.

Something else dawned on Avery. "Why am I getting the feeling our meeting on the airplane wasn't a chance meeting?"

"Because it wasn't." Priscilla gave her a smug smile. "Being a Venter has its perks."

"Like finding out what flight I was on and manipulating your way into the seats next to me?" Avery guessed.

"Something like that," Priscilla confirmed. "I was going to pay you a visit, but then fate intervened and changed the course of my plan." She gestured with her hands. "And here we are."

"Okay!" Avery still wasn't certain what Priscilla was trying to accomplish. "What were you hoping to accomplish by cornering me on the flight?"

"Oh, I wasn't cornering you on the flight," Priscilla assured her. "I was going to offer you a lift back to Frisco so we could talk in my car."

"That's why you hadn't left by the time I got to the taxi rank." Avery's eyes narrowed accusingly. "Did you leave Meg the bunny behind on purpose?"

"No." Priscilla shook her head. "That was once again just a twist of fate." She grinned. "But I did get the bus to Frisco to leave early."

"What!" Avery spluttered.

"I know the owners of the shuttle," Priscilla explained.

"Of course you do." Avery sighed, unable to believe she'd been duped by Priscilla. "Wow!" She looked at the woman in disbelief. "Where are you going to bribe the taxi driver as well if he'd agreed to take me home?"

"I'm sorry, my dear." Priscilla sighed. "I had no option. Especially with yours and Ryder's history." She paused as Terri came back with their beverages and Avery's grilled sandwich. "Sly Pembrook has come at us from all sides, and when I saw your name on that acquisition document, I thought he'd finally found his perfect weapon."

"You thought I took the deal to get back at Ryder?" Avery's eyes widened in disbelief as she gaped at Priscilla.

"Hell hath no fury as a woman scorned, my dear," Priscilla recited the proverb, adapted from a line in William Congreve's play, *The Mourning Bride*.

"Are you serious?" Avery couldn't believe she'd think that of her. "I took the project for two reasons. The first one being that it was the only way I could get home for Christmas, and the second one being that I could ensure that Ryder and Emily got the best possible deal." Her eyes narrowed, and she couldn't help feeling a little insulted by what Priscilla had insinuated. "I know how Pembrook works, and I would *never* let my personal life filter into my work ethics."

"I know that—" Priscilla's gaze remained steady, and she seemed unfazed by Avery's taking offense to what she'd said. "Now."

"For the record, I've been wanting to meet with Ryder and Emily to confess the reason I came home this Christmas to them." Avery decided to let Priscilla know what she was up to. "As the lodge's legal counsel, I'm sure you'll find out soon anyway."

"Avery, I wasn't attacking you, dear," Priscilla interrupted Avery. "I've been watching you these past few days, and I was pleasantly surprised to find you weren't motivated by spite." She held up her hand when Avery tried to talk. "Please let me finish."

Avery nodded and took a bite of the delicious grilled sandwich to stop herself from demanding Pricilla let Avery have her say first.

"I also think you're not in favor of the acquisition," Priscilla commented.

"No, I'm not!" Avery put her sandwich on the plate and wiped her mouth and hands. "As I was about to tell you, Grimes Mergers and Acquisition will soon be sending Mistletoe Lodge a letter rescinding the acquisition." She saw Priscilla's brows raise in surprise. "I managed to secure Pembrook a property more suited to their requirements."

"Oh?" Priscilla's eyes lit with interest. "May I ask what property?"

"The Slopes Hotel," Avery told her.

"Malcom Morris won't be too pleased," Priscilla said.

"Actually, he was delighted," Avery told her. "It turns out he was desperate to sell after the damage the hotel sustained last year."

"Huh!" Priscilla pulled an amazed face. "I don't like the man, but I do hope you got him a decent deal."

"I did!" Avery nodded. "There's something else you should know, though." She picked up her coffee. "But I ask that you allow me to discuss it with Ryder and Emily."

"Okay." Priscilla's brows furrowed.

As Avery finished her food, she explained what she'd done to Priscilla, who listened intently and made a few suggestions. Forty minutes later, they were leaving the living room when Avery looked at Priscilla.

"There's something I don't understand," Avery said before they left the dining room.

"And what would that be, dear?" Priscilla looked at her inquiringly.

"You're a Venter. You could've bailed the lodge out of trouble," Avery pointed out.

"My grandchildren won't let me," Priscilla told her. "I've even offered them some of their inheritance to help bail them out, but Ryder and Emily were determined to do this on their own." She shook her head. "When I saw that document from your firm, I was going to go over their heads and bail the lodge out anyway." She looked at Avery. "As soon as the roads cleared and I could get into Frisco, I was going to buy the lodge's debt."

"Oh!" Avery's eyes widened. "That would've put a dent in Pembrook' s plan."

"Exactly." Priscilla grinned. "That old fool should've known he'd never best me or take something from my grandchildren."

"Wow, you really do know how to go all out to win!" Avery gave a small laugh, getting the sense that Priscilla and Sly Pembrook had quite the feud going.

"I do," Priscilla admitted.

"Well, then I'm glad I didn't have to go up against you." Avery breathed a sigh of relief.

"Now, Avery, dear." Priscilla linked her arm through Avery's. "As soon as you hear from your contact, come to me, and as we agreed, we'll speak to my grandchildren together."

"Of course," Avery promised. "But if that doesn't work out, you may still need to buy the lodge's debt because, I can assure you, once the Pembrook Group starts converting the slopes—"

"It will awaken the other large chains in competition with them, who'll go all out looking for places like the lodge that are in a weak state to snap up at any means possible," Priscilla added. "I understand. Pembrook is chumming the waters for the rest of the sharks."

"Exactly," Avery agreed with her. "And the next time, I won't be here to prevent it."

"I'm glad we caught the same flight to Denver, Avery." Priscilla gave her a conspiratory wink. "Oh, and honey, may I offer you some advice about your mother?"

"I'm really trying not to think about what my mother did," Avery told her. "I don't want to ruin Christmas."

"I'm sure your mother and Ryder's were only looking out for the two of you," Priscilla told her. "I know it's going to be hard and that you're feeling the worst kind of betrayal right now." She rubbed Avery's arm comfortingly. "All I'm saying is that you take a breath, think over what you're going to say carefully, and then try to respond and not react to whatever she says."

"Thank you, Priscilla." Avery smiled gratefully at her. "I'll try my best to keep a level head."

"Good. Listen with your mind and not your heart. The mind is logical and the heart emotional." The young woman at the front desk caught Priscilla's attention. "Excuse me."

Avery nodded and watched Priscilla walk away before pulling on her jacket and heading toward the barn to help with the booths. Her mind was filled with the conversation she'd had with Priscilla over a late lunch.

CHAPTER 16

Ryder woke up that morning with a heavy feeling in his chest. He had stayed up late the previous night, working on booths and hayride carts with Avery, Hank, Emily, and Heather. After they were done, Emily had suggested they make cocoa and s'mores and sit by the firepit beneath the star-studded sky.

It was the perfect way to end the day, yet it had left him more emotionally tangled with Avery than ever. Especially after Hank, Emily, and Heather had gone to bed and left them alone.

Ryder and Avery stayed outside for another magical hour after that. He drew in a breath, lifting his arms behind his head as he closed his eyes and pictured the scene. The crackling fire had cast a warm glow on Avery's face, and her laughter mingled with the soft rustle of the wind. They talked about everything and nothing, sharing stories and jokes, yet Ryder couldn't shake the awareness that he was playing with fire.

He had spent so much time convincing himself that he could be friends with Avery. But being so close to her and feeling the pull of her laughter and the sparkle in her eyes, it was like trying to hold back the tide with his bare hands. It had taken all the willpower he'd had not to pull her into his arms and kiss her until the world around them faded away.

He swallowed as he remembered when they were still together how perfectly she'd seemed to fit into his arms, as if the two of them had been perfectly made for each other.

He let out another breath, opened his eyes, and then lay in bed, staring at the ceiling, replaying their conversations in his mind. There was an undeniable chemistry between them—a connection that went beyond friendship.

Ryder was sure that Avery felt it too, as he could see it in her eyes every time their eyes locked. There was a force drawing them together, like two magnets not being able to stop the attraction.

Ryder sighed. He knew he had to tread carefully. Avery was leaving after the New Year, and he didn't want to complicate things further. He didn't want her to leave Frisco with her heart in pieces again, having seen enough of how tangled emotions could lead to heartache, and he was determined not to let that happen again. Not to Avery or himself.

With another sigh, he swung his legs out of bed and got up. The lodge was already bustling with activity as everyone prepared for the upcoming festival. After his late night, he'd slept in later than he usually did as he had a long day ahead, and he hoped that throwing himself into work would help distract him from the whirlwind of emotions inside him.

His heart hung heavier in his chest when he checked his phone for the weather report and found that the roads into Frisco were open, and he knew Avery would be leaving. His movements got more hurried as he quickly went through his morning routine, hoping he could get Avery to have breakfast with him before she left.

As he entered the lodge's entrance, his heart did a strange flip when he saw Avery standing there, her bags packed, waiting for a taxi. He blinked, momentarily taken aback by the sight of her, and then did a dip, realizing she was ready to leave for Frisco.

He watched as Rosie clung to Avery with tears in her eyes. They had become fast friends over the past few days, and Ryder could see the genuine affection between them.

"Can't you stay and get your parents to come stay here too?" Rosie asked her.

"Oh, sweetie, there's no room for anyone else at the lodge," Avery pointed out with a warm smile.

"They can have my room, and I'll sleep in my father's room," Rosie offered.

"That's very kind of you," Avery told her with another hug. "But we don't live far from here, and I'll be back tomorrow to help with the final preparations for the festival." Avery promised Rosie.

"For the whole day?" Rosie asked hopefully.

"Yes, from early in the morning until we've finished getting everything done." Avery kissed Rosie's cheek and ruffled her hair.

Avery hugged Hank, then Emily, and even Heather looked saddened to see Avery go. Nora hurried from the kitchen with a tin wrapped in a festive bow.

"I'm so glad I caught you," Nora beamed, handing Avery the tin before hugging her. "Those are for your parents. They are my ginger Christmas cookies your parents love."

"Thank you, Nora." Avery took the tin. "I'm sure they'd be so pleased to get these. My father brings them to Los Angeles each year."

"I know," Nora told her. "I sent extra because I know they're your favorites too."

The last person beside Ryder to say goodbye was his grandmother.

"It's been so lovely having you here, Avery dear," Priscilla said, stepping toward her, giving her a hug, and then taking her hands. Their voices dropped to a low whisper. He saw Avery nod and smile. "Send your parents my regards, and I hope your father's foot gets better soon."

"Thank you, Priscilla," Avery said before turning toward him.

Ryder's breath caught in his throat as his heart stopped for a few seconds when her lips curved into a smile. He felt a tug inside him—a sense of longing he tried to suppress.

He had no right to feel this way and had to keep reminding himself about Avery's imminent departure. The moment felt charged, with emotions simmering beneath the surface, but before he could say anything, Avery's taxi arrived.

"I'll help you with your luggage," Ryder offered before anyone else could.

He walked over to her, his heart feeling heavier with each step.

"Thank you," Avery replied, her own smile a touch wistful.

Ryder walked her to the taxi, the awkwardness of the situation palpable. He wished he could tell her to stay and spend more time at the lodge, but he knew it was unreasonable. She had come here to see her parents and felt that nature had held her snowbound hostage for long enough.

"Thanks again for everything, Ryder," Avery said, her voice carrying a mixture of gratitude and something else he couldn't quite place. "I would've been stranded in a hotel room in Denver for the past few days if it wasn't for your family."

"You're welcome," Ryder replied, his gaze lingering on her. "And thank you for all your help around here."

She nodded, and there was a brief silence, a weight hanging between them that Ryder didn't quite understand. But then the moment shifted, and Avery's eyes seemed to hold a different kind of spark.

"Would you be interested in having dinner tonight?" Ryder blurted out before he could second-guess himself. "There's a new Italian restaurant in Frisco, and I heard the food is amazing."

Avery blinked, surprise flickering across her features, and then a slow smile spread across her lips. "I'd love to."

Relief flooded through Ryder. "Great. How about I pick you up at six?"

"Sounds perfect," Avery agreed.

They exchanged a quick hug, and for a moment, it was as if the world around them faded. There was an undeniable connection between them, and Ryder's heart raced in his chest. But then the taxi honked, and reality crashed back in.

"Have a safe trip," Ryder said, his voice softer than he intended.

"Thank you," Avery replied, her gaze lingering on him.

Then, with one last smile, she turned and climbed into the backseat of the taxi, and Ryder closed the door. He watched the cab drive away, a mixture of emotions swirling inside him. He turned back to the lodge, taking a deep breath.

There was a lot to do, and the festival was opening in just two days. He had to focus on that—making sure everything was perfect for the event.

As he threw himself into work, his mind kept drifting back to Avery. He was determined to keep his emotions in check to navigate this new friendship without getting hurt. But with each passing moment, he couldn't help but wonder if he was fighting a losing battle.

As Avery's taxi headed down the road towards her childhood home, her mind and emotions were in turmoil. The past four days had been a whirlwind packed with unexpected twists and turns. She glanced out of the window, taking in the breathtaking scenery of the snow-covered landscape. It was incredible how everything could change in such a short span of time.

Her thoughts inevitably drifted back to Ryder. The intensity of their connection had caught her off guard. She had come here to acquire the lodge from Ryder and his family and spend the first Christmas in fifteen years in Frisco with her parents. It was supposed to be a cut-and-dry deal ending with a cozy Christmas at home. Avery hadn't expected to get entangled in a web of emotions she thought she had left behind in her past.

Every glance and every brush against each other had ignited something within her that she'd been trying so hard to suppress. But her feelings for him were undeniable, and it left her in a state of both longing and confusion.

Thinking about Ryder led her down another path of reflection—learning about her mother's betrayal and the role she had played in Avery's breakup with Ryder fifteen years ago. The anger burned inside her, not only because of the betrayal itself but also because her mother had never confessed her actions to her. Avery felt the betrayal cut through her, as her mother knew how devastated she'd been when Ryder left her at the altar.

Still, she'd said nothing and had kept quiet about it for fifteen years, making Avery question the foundation of trust they had. Avery bit her lip and took a deep breath, trying to put out the blaze that burned through her.

Priscilla's words echoed in her mind. The wisdom of Ryder's grandmother had struck a chord with her, and the anger started to cool. Avery didn't want to ruin her first Christmas home in fifteen years with the weight of her mother's actions. Her father was already dealing with enough, with the broken foot and the store to fix up.

Avery knew she had to be there for her parents, to offer them the love and support they needed right now. What had happened had happened fifteen years ago and could wait until she was back in Los Angeles to deal with it. At least that way she could have the conversation over a video call, and she'd have a lot of distance between her and her mother to give Avery space to get over it.

As the taxi pulled up in front of her family's two-story house, a modern-day-style family home with all the markings of comfort and warmth, she was happy with her decision. When she noticed the outside was decked out in holiday decorations, her rage faded and was replaced by a smile.

As she stepped out of the car, the sight of it filled her heart with a sense of belonging and nostalgia that nearly overwhelmed her. She turned and glanced around the neighborhood, which was alive with the spirit of the season. Each house and lawn competed with the others in a display of lights and ornaments.

Her parents were waiting on the porch, her mother rushing towards her with open arms while her father carefully navigated the path on his crutches. Avery's heart swelled nearly to the point of bursting as she embraced her mother.

She felt the familiar scent and warmth envelop her, and the tension of her unresolved feelings with her mother eased. Avery knew at that moment just how much she'd missed being home for the holiday season and how good it was to be here.

"Welcome home, sweetheart," her mother said, tears glistening in her eyes as they pulled away from the hug.

"Thank you, Mom," Avery replied, her voice slightly choked.

Her father reached them, a soft smile on his face despite the crutches he leaned on. "It's good to have you back, Avery."

Avery's eyes welled up with tears as she looked at her parents. It was a simple statement, but it held so much meaning. She was back home, back where she belonged, and nothing else seemed to matter at that moment.

"I've missed you both," Avery admitted. "I've counted down the days until the festive season."

"We've missed you too," Judy said, her grip on Avery's hand firm.

"We're so glad you could make it home." Jim tried to help Avery with her luggage, but she swatted his hand away. "I would've hated to have to wait another year to visit."

"Dad, I've got my luggage," Avery told him as he tried again to help her with her bags. "I was making contingency plans in case I couldn't make it home for Christmas." She assured them as they made their way to the front door. "I was going to make sure I could at least get home for New Year's if I couldn't make it from Christmas."

"And you only just made it too," Jim reminded her.

"Yes." Avery laughed. "It's been quite a journey to get here."

"But you are, and that's all that matters now." Judy stroked Avery's arm.

As they entered the house, Avery felt a sense of peace settle over her. She had decided to set aside her grievances for now and focus on being present with her family during this festive time. The evening ahead held the promise of more emotions and uncertainties, especially with her upcoming dinner with Ryder. But for now, as she looked at her parents and the warm lights of her childhood home sparkling with the joy of Christmas, Avery was determined to savor every moment of the holiday season.

As Ryder pulled up in front of Avery's house, he couldn't help but feel a mix of anticipation and nerves. He turned off the engine and took a moment to collect himself. He wanted this evening to go well. It was a chance to spend time with Avery outside the lodge, away from any lingering, haunting memories of their broken past. Tonight wasn't about yesterday; it was about the here and now—good friends enjoying each other's company and soaking up the spirit of Christmas.

He stepped out of the car and walked up the front path to the porch. The house was adorned with festive lights, and the air was filled with the scent of pine. It was clear that Avery's family still embraced the holiday spirit, and he couldn't help but smile at the bright twinkling ornaments that adorned the house and garden.

He rang the doorbell, and within a few moments it flew open to reveal Judy, with Jim hobbling after her on crutches.

"Hello, Ryder." Judy welcomed him with a warm smile.

"Hi!" Ryder greeted them both
.

"Ryder, good to see you," Jim replied, his voice warm and genuine. "Come on in; it's freezing out there."

Ryder turned and looked pointedly at the garden, saying, "You've really outdone yourself with the decorations this year."

Jim chuckled. "Well, you know how much we love Christmas around here. And this year, as we're in Frisco for Christmas, I'm taking back my best Christmas Decorations for the neighborhood."

"I think that trophy is definitely yours again this year, Jim." Ryder nodded and stepped inside the warm house.

The scent of fresh baked goods made his stomach churn, reminding him he hadn't eaten since breakfast.

Before he could continue the conversation, Ryder's attention was immediately drawn to Avery as she descended the stairs with an air of elegance. He couldn't help but admire how beautiful she looked in her outfit, and his heart skipped a beat at the sight of her.

"Hi, Ryder," Avery said, her voice a mix of excitement and warmth.

"Hey," Ryder replied, his eyes never leaving hers. "You look absolutely stunning."

Avery's cheeks turned a light shade of pink, and she gave a shy smile. "Thank you. You clean up pretty well yourself."

Ryder chuckled, feeling a wave of relief wash over him. "I try my best." He fiddled with his jacket before offering her his arm. "Shall we?"

Avery nodded, slipping her hand through his arm, and they walked towards the car together. The streets of Frisco were alive with the festive spirit, and as they drove past houses adorned with colorful lights and decorations, as they neared the restaurant, Avery's attention was caught by the street market that filled the town square.

"Oh, I'm so glad the market's still there." Avery turned and looked at him. "Maybe if it's still open after dinner, we could take a stroll through it? I still have a few gifts left to buy."

"Of course," Ryder agreed.

They arrived at the restaurant, and Ryder parked in a spot conveniently located between the restaurant and the market. When they walked into the restaurant, he couldn't help but notice the heads turning toward him. Ryder and Avery knew most of the people there. They hadn't seen Avery in fifteen years, so making their way to their table took longer than normal as she was stopped and greeted by some of the locals.

By the time they got to their table, the aroma of Italian cuisine that wafted through the air had played havoc with his hunger pangs. He only hoped that the buzzing of soft conversation had dulled the noise so Avery wouldn't hear it.

The evening unfolded with hardly any awkwardness while Ryder and Avery fell into an easy, flowing stream of conversation. They talked about their work, Los Angeles, and a host of other topics.

As they finished their meal and lingered over dessert, Ryder realized that he was enjoying himself more than he had in a long time. They left the restaurant, and Ryder was glad that the market was still open to prolong their evening as they strolled among the booths.

They ended the evening with a decadent hot chocolate while sitting close to each other on a bench that looked over the town square and the last lingering customers browsing the market.

"Thank you, Ryder," Avery said, her hands curled around her cup. "I've had a wonderful evening."

"I have too," Ryder admitted. "I hope we get to do it again before you go home to Los Angeles."

"I'd like that." Avery turned, and their eyes locked.

Once again, Ryder felt himself being drawn to her as the world around them shrank, their lips moving closer together until the twinkling lights turned into sparks as their lips finally touched. Ryder didn't know how long they remained lost in each other until the cold finally drew them apart as a sprinkling of snow spilled over them.

They laughed, lifting their heads to the heavens as the sprinkling started to get heavier.

"We should get going," Avery said, standing up and throwing their used cups away before they made a dash for Ryder's pickup truck.

They drove back to Avery's house in silence as Ryder concentrated on the road ahead. The snow had picked up pace, and the world around them turned into a tunnel of snow raining around them. By the time they got to Avery's house, it was coming down so hard that Ryder feared he wouldn't be able to drive home.

"You can't drive home in this." Avery's words echoed his thoughts as he walked her to the door.

"I'm sure I'll be fine," Ryder lied.

"No, you won't, young man." Jim's voice brooked no argument. "You'll stay with us tonight."

"I've already started making up the guest bedroom," Judy told Ryder. "It's our turn to look after you."

"Thank you." Ryder smiled gratefully and glanced at the road. "I think you're right about not driving home tonight."

"You should call someone at the lodge and let them know," Judy advised him before walking up the stairs to finish getting his room ready.

"Come in, you two." Jim stepped to the side after realizing he was blocking the door as he balanced on his crutches. "Take off your coats and go get warm by the fire."

"Thanks, Dad." Avery kissed his weathered cheek as he closed the door behind him.

After calling his sister, Ryder found Avery curled up on the sofa in front of the fire.

"My mother poured us some warm cider," Avery said, pointing to his mug.

"Thank you," Ryder said, taking a seat next to her. "Where are your parents?"

"It's way past their bedtime." Avery smiled. "They said to tell you goodnight."

Ryder took a sip of the warm cider and felt the fire thaw him out.

"It was nice of them to let me stay over." Ryder made small talk, unsure how to approach what had happened at the market.

"Of course," Avery breathed. "There's no way I would've let you drive in that downpour either."

They fell silent for a few moments, both watching the fire do its mesmerizing dance as it spread its warmth through the room.

"Ryder," Avery said at the same time he said, "Avery."

"You go," Ryder said.

"I just wanted to say that this has been an amazing evening." Avery cleared her throat, and her eyes held his. "While I'm not sure where this can go or even if it will go anywhere, I'm not going to lie and say that I didn't enjoy our kiss."

"Oh, thank goodness." Ryder breathed a sigh of relief and grinned, putting the cider on a coaster on the coffee table before pulling her close to him. His lips were moving towards hers. "Because I was going to say the same thing." His voice was soft and hoarse. "If you hadn't agreed, I was going to do this again to prove how right it felt."

Avery's arms snaked around his neck as their lips melted into each other.

CHAPTER 17

Early morning sunlight streamed through the trees, casting a golden hue over the Mistletoe Lodge's grounds, where the festive events of the day were about to unfold. Avery bustled around the hardware booth, arranging an assortment of tools and gadgets. The excitement in the air was palpable, and it was hard to believe that the past week had gone by so quickly.

The memory of the previous day's joys and activities danced through Avery's mind as she worked. The night after her dinner with Ryder, he asked her out again, but she had to refuse in order to help her parents fix up their hardware store so they could reopen after the accident.

It had been a welcome surprise when Hank, Emily, Heather, Rosie, and Ryder turned up ready to help. What would've taken Avery and her mother three days to do with her father out of action took them a couple of hours with their help.

A smile touched Avery's lips, and her heart thudded, remembering the secret caresses and stolen kisses from Ryder amid the chaos and hard work. Avery and Ryder had offered to get everyone hot chocolate from the booth in the town square market.

Before going back to the hardware store, they'd had some more stolen moments together. They'd lingered and shared some roasted chestnuts on the bench where they'd sat the night before.

Then there was last night, after a day filled with last-minute festival preparations, when Avery and Ryder slipped away to the Christmas Tree Grove, enjoying a serene picnic beneath the stars. Those moments had been precious, filling Avery with a sense of happiness that she hadn't felt in a long time.

She swallowed and took a breath, reminding herself that she couldn't fall in love with Ryder again. They lived in two different states now, and unlike when they were younger, they'd now put down roots. And Avery wasn't sure how she'd handle a long-distance relationship.

As she arranged a set of gleaming wrenches, Avery's eyes scanned the festival, and her smile grew. Through the bustle of the set-up for the festival, two shadows still hungover Avery's head. When she thought about them, she felt the vice of tension gripping her. The lodge's financial state was still a huge worry, and she knew it wouldn't be too long before another company was on the Carlisle's doorstep to acquire it.

Avery pulled out her phone and checked her messages and email once again—the CEO of Holland Corporation still hadn't gotten back to her. It wasn't like him to take three days to get back to her. She sighed and shoved her phone back into her pocket. Today was a day for celebrating the opening of the Winter Festival and enjoying the magic of Christmas, which was only five days away.

She shrugged off her frustration and annoyance with Holland Corporation and was just rearranging a display when her mother and father approached the booth. Avery swallowed and refused to let the anger she felt at her mother's secret betrayal surface.

That was for after New Year's and when she was back in Los Angeles. Thinking about going back to Los Angeles made her heart ache, but before she could ponder over it, Hank, Ryder, and Rosie approached. Ryder was carrying a comfortable chair, Hank had a footstool, and Rosie carried a warm blanket.

The sight of Ryder was an instant mood lifter, dispelling her worries even if just for a moment, and her smile appeared on her face, lighting up her eyes.

"Morning," Ryder greeted, and he moved around to the side of the booth where Avery was standing.

Her heart went wild as she could feel his warmth. He was so close to her while he positioned the chair.

"Good morning," Avery replied with a smile. "What are you doing with that?"

"Ryder has brought it for Jim," Hank said as they arrived at the booth.

"Thank you, Ryder and Hank," Jim said to both men, a warm smile clinking the lines around his eyes. "It's much appreciated."

"Of course, Jim," Hank replied before Ryder could. "We don't want you to miss out on the festivities."

"Well, I'm not going to be winning the sack race." Jim made them all laugh. "But at least it will be good to be able to join in, as it's been a long time since we've had a winter festival here."

"Too long," Emily agreed, joining them with a tray filled with steaming mugs and muffins. "I brought some coffee."

"Thank you, honey," Judy said gratefully. "That will be most welcome once we get Jim settled."

Ryder and Hank set up the chair and footrest in a position where Jim could help with the booth, and Rosie tucked him in with the blanket.

"There you go, all warm and cozy." Rosie grinned.

"Why thank you, Rosie!" Jim said. "My leg won't ache from the cold now."

"You're very welcome," Rosie told him, then turned to Avery. "Avery, I hope you don't mind, but I've signed us up for the sack race and the snowman competition! You're on my team!"

Rosie's eagerness made Avery laugh. "Sounds like a plan. I'm in."

"Awesome!" Rosie's grin widened. "We're going to rock these events."

"I don't know how many I can do, though," Avery warned Rosie. "I have to help my parents with the booth."

"Oh, don't worry about that, honey," Jim told her. "Your mother and I are quite capable of running the booth." He waved a hand around. "You've worked so hard since you arrived home that you deserve to have some fun and enjoy the fruits of your work."

"Agreed," Judy said, backing her husband up. "Besides, you make the most beautiful snowmen, and I'm sure that the two of you are going to win."

"Three!" Ryder held up his hand. "There has to be three to a team."

"Yeah, and Hank, myself, and Heather are going to make the biggest and baddest snowman ever," Emily bragged, and everyone laughed at her competitiveness.

"Oh, Em, don't delude yourself, little sister." Ryder put his arm around her shoulders. "Avery's home this winter, so you know you don't stand a chance."

"Mm." Emily rubbed her chin, and her eyes narrowed. "We used to win those competitions together when we were younger," she reminded Avery. "Any chance I can talk you into defecting to my team?"

"No Way, Aunt Em," Rosie said with a shake of her head. "You can't go stealing other people's team members, and besides, I booked Avery first."

"She has a point," Avery pointed out with a laugh.

"Fine, but Rosie, you and Avery are on my team for the gingerbread decorating contest," Emily told them.

"Deal!" Rosie and Avery spoke at the same time.

"Good, that's settled then," Emily beamed. Then she looked at Avery and Judy. "Would you two ladies be interested in helping judge the pie-baking contest?"

"If my father can handle the booth on his own," Avery turned to look at her father questioningly.

"Of course." Jim waved a hand in the air. "It's my leg that's broken, not my brain."

"Great," Avery said. "Then I'm in." She looked at her mother. "Mom?"

"I'm afraid I can't," Judy told them. "I've promised Nora I'd be her baking partner for the competition."

"Oh!" Emily and Avery spoke at once.

"Yes, she called me last night to ask me when she found out that Catherine Simms had entered." Judy shook her head. "Catherine, as you both know, is a baker."

"Well, she does own the bakery, Mom," Avery pointed out.

"Yes, but somehow it doesn't seem fair to go up against a baker," Judy said.

"Her daughter, Glory, is in the gingerbread house decorating contest," Rosie informed them. "Glory wins all those icing-type things every year."

"Well, not this year," Emily declared, looking at Avery for confirmation. "What do you say, Avery?" She raised an eyebrow. "Do you think we still have what it takes to win this?"

"Absolutely," Avery said with a vigorous nod, grinning at Rosie. "We're going to show Glory that there's a new icing team in town."

The group laughed, and all too soon they split up to go their own way and make sure everything was ready for the opening of the festival.

The day started with a bang and ended with Rosie and Avery lighting the huge Mistletoe Christmas tree that greeted guests at the entrance to the lodge. The next five days went by in a whirl of laughter, games, and hard work as sales at the hardware booth were surprisingly good.

People came from far and wide to the festival that was turning out to be a huge success, making Ryder and Emily realize how much people had missed it.

Avery heard the two of them discussing making it an annual event once again. That both delighted and frightened Avery, who still hadn't heard back from Holland Trading after a week.

Avery shook her annoyance with the man off and let her mind drift back over the events of the last week. A smile lifting her mouth. Avery, Ryder, and Rosie came in third for the snowman building contest, with Emily, Hank, and Heather coming in second behind their icing rival Glory and her two older brothers.

The battle for the gingerbread house decorating competition was fierce, but Emily, Avery, and Rosie won, much to Rosie's delight.

Emily, Heather, Avery, and Rosie got to judge both the chili-making and pie-baking contests. Nora, Priscilla, and Judy were not happy when Mrs. Gardner won the pie baking contest with her warm cherry pie with a caramel crust. Hank and Ryder's Hot Hanks chili came in second to Nora's and Jim's Jim Noire chili. Rosie and Avery came in third in the sack race but won the egg race.

Avery couldn't remember having so many consecutive days of fun in a long time, and all too soon the end of the festival loomed. Including the current day, there were only three days left of the seven days, which ended with the Christmas Eve dance.

Her heart jolted when she thought about the dance. It was a formal function, and Avery didn't have any formal clothes with her as she wasn't expecting to be going to a dance. She swallowed her nerves and refused to think about her wish that Ryder would ask her to the dance.

Avery reminded herself for the millionth time that she was going back to Los Angeles after New Year's. That getting involved with Ryder, even in the casual capacity in which they'd been flirting and having stolen moments, would lead to nothing but heartache. She was so deep in thought that she nearly jumped out of her skin when the object of her thoughts tapped her on the shoulder.

"Oh, sorry!" Ryder's eyes widened at her reaction to his touch. "I didn't mean to frighten you."

"Sorry." Avery breathed, her hand over her heart as it hammered against her chest. "I was deep in thought. I didn't hear you approaching."

"Are you okay?" Ryder's brow drew into a worried frown.

"Yes, I'm fine," Avery lied. "I was just thinking about how fast the days have gone by since I arrived in Frisco."

Avery saw his eyes darken and knew he'd been thinking about that too, and they stood in silence for a few seconds.

"Time flies by, doesn't it?" Ryder's voice broke through the calm morning air, his gaze fixed intently on Avery.

Avery nodded. "Yes, it's hard to believe how quickly the days have gone by." She looked around the festival. "I can hardly believe there are only two more days left of the festival."

The days had been a whirlwind of festivities, laughter, and unexpected moments. Avery knew she was fighting a losing battle with her feelings for Ryder as their eyes locked.

Ryder's lips curled into a warm smile. "It's been amazing having you here. The festival just wouldn't have been the same without you."

Avery's heart skipped a beat at his words. "Thank you, Ryder. I'm glad I could be a part of it." She gave a soft laugh. "It seems Frank's grandchildren may have done me a favor by running his Zamboni into my dad's shop."

"I know it's a terrible thing to say." Ryder's smile broadened, and his voice became hoarse with emotion. "And I hope you don't take this the wrong way because it was terrible what happened to your parents store, but I'm glad it brought you home."

Their gazes held for a moment longer, unspoken words passing between them. Avery could feel the pull of their history, the memories they had shared, and the emotions that had once bound them together.

Ryder took a step closer, his eyes holding a mix of playfulness and sincerity. "You know, there's one event left to look forward to."

Avery's heart gave a small leap. "Oh yeah, and what would that be?" she challenged him teasingly.

"The Winter Festival Dance." Ryder moved a few steps closer to her.

They were alone in the hardware booth, and she swallowed, feeling him brush up against her.

"Oh, right!" Avery cleared her throat and tried her best to maintain her calm playfulness.

Ryder's eyes darkened as he leaned in slightly. His face was close to hers. "I was hoping that you'd attend the dance with me."

Her heart skipped a beat, and her breath caught in her throat. The thought of spending an enchanting evening with Ryder made her pulse race with excitement.

Avery's lips curled into a sultry smile, but a thought struck her, dampening her excitement a little. "I'd love to, Ryder," she told him, frowning. "But I didn't pack anything suitable for a dance like that."

Ryder's smile remained, his eyes glinting with a hint of mischief. "Ah, then you're in luck." He winked. "Because Emily and Heather were moaning about the same thing."

"Oh, were they now?" Avery nodded, her eyes narrowing curiously.

"Yes, and it so happens that they've decided to plan a shopping trip to Silverthorne tomorrow to find dresses for the dance." His smile turned into a smug grin. "I overheard them mention inviting you to join them."

Avery's eyes widened in response, as she hadn't anticipated a shopping day and it would be nice to go to Silverthorne again. It would also be nice to spend the day with Emily, even if it meant Heather would be tagging along. At least Heather seemed to have grown up and changed.

"That sounds tempting," Avery admitted, tapping her chin thoughtfully. "But I have the booth to worry about, as it's also the last day of the festival."

"I've thought about that already," Ryder assured her. "Between myself and Hank, we'll watch the booth for you when your parents aren't here."

"Speaking of parents," Avery said, looking around the festival. "I haven't seen Priscilla today."

"Oh, she left for Denver early this morning," Ryder told her. "She got a call late yesterday afternoon. Some urgent business to do with the law firm came up, and she had to go into Denver to attend to it."

"Denver?" Avery's brows drew together in confusion. "I thought her family's law firm was in Los Angeles."

"It is." Ryder nodded. "But Priscilla has a small branch in Denver."

Ryder took a step closer, his gaze unwavering, making Avery's heart flutter even more.

Avery swallowed. His closeness was making her thoughts turn to mush. "Priscilla didn't say what the business was about."

"No." Ryder shook his head. "Now, enough about my grandmother." He took her hands in his. "You haven't answered my question."

Avery took a breath and held her voice as steady as she could to maintain her excitement. "Yes, I'd love to go to the dance with you."

Ryder brought her hand to his lips and kissed it. "Good, I'll pick you up at seven."

"You don't have to drive all the way to Frisco," Avery objected. "I'll meet you here."

"Oh, that's the other thing I overheard Emily and Heather talking about," Ryder admitted sheepishly. "They want to invite you to get dressed here with them tomorrow."

"Oh!" Avery's eyes widened once again. "That actually sounds fun."

"Don't sound so surprised." Ryder laughed. "You and Emily used to always get ready for dances and outings together."

"I know, but we were kids then," Avery reminded him with a soft laugh.

"What about being kids?" Emily's voice cut through their conversation, making Ryder take a few steps away from Avery as he turned to look at his sister.

"I was just telling Avery about your plans to go to Silverthorne tomorrow," Ryder told her, clearing his throat.

"Why do you have to always steal my thunder?" Emily grumbled, glaring at her brother. "I suppose you told her about staying here tomorrow as well?"

"No." Avery laughed at the siblings. "He did mention me getting ready here with you for the dance, though."

"Thanks, *brother*!" Emily jokingly stuck her tongue out at Ryder.

Ryder laughed before excusing himself and leaving the two of them alone.

"So, what do you say, Avery?" Emily asked as soon as Ryder was out of earshot. "Do you want to come to Silverthorne tomorrow?"

"I would love to," Avery said, accepting the invitation. "I haven't been there for years, and it will be nice spending the day with you there." Her smile grew nostalgic. "Just like old times."

"Yes, but with Heather!" Emily rolled her eyes. "I tried to talk her out of coming, as I wanted to spend time together. Just the two of us, because we haven't managed to get much of that while you've been home."

"I know," Avery agreed. "I was just thinking about that."

"We could always ditch Heather and leave extra early!" Emily's eyes widened at her brilliant plan.

"No, that wouldn't be very nice," Avery pointed out. "Plus, she's grown up a lot and doesn't seem so bratty."

"No, now she's just braggy!" Emily shuddered. "But I suppose you're right." She frowned. "Although, speaking of Heather..." She looked around the festival. "I haven't seen her since before my gran left this morning."

"Oh!" Avery said. "Well, maybe she went with Priscilla?"

"Maybe." Emily's frown deepened as she glanced around again. "I'll call my grandmother later and find out."

"What time are we leaving tomorrow?" Avery asked, her excitement about spending the day with her childhood best friend growing.

"Around seven," Emily said. "We can have breakfast at one of the restaurants before shopping."

"Sounds like a great plan," Avery told her. "I'm looking forward to it."

"Great!" Emily smiled. "And are you going to get ready with us at the lodge tomorrow afternoon?"

"I think I can do that," Avery said, nodding. "We haven't done that since—"

It suddenly hit Avery that the last time was when she'd gotten ready with Emily at Mistletoe Lodge, and her heart thudded—her wedding day.

"For a long time." Emily gave her a knowing smile as she finished Avery's sentence. "It's going to be fun, and you can stay over for the night as well." Her eyes brooked no argument on the point. "Well, unless you want to drive to your parents' home." She pulled a face. "Sorry, I forgot that they'd probably want to come to the dance."

"Oh, no," Avery said, shaking her head. "My mom is sad that they won't be able to make it." She shoved her hands in her back pockets as she stood speaking to Emily. "But my dad wouldn't be comfortable with his broken ankle, and he's been pushing things as it is by insisting on being here every day."

"I know. I did mention to him yesterday that he should be resting," Emily told her. "But he said that he didn't want to miss a day of the festival." She grinned. "He said something about it being a historical moment, the reopening of the Mistletoe Lodge Winter Festival."

"Yes, I think everyone in Frisco and all the surrounding towns thinks the same," Avery informed her.

"I can't believe what a success it's been." Emily sighed in contentment. "A lot of hard work, but so worth it."

"I have to agree." Avery glanced around the busy booth's and smiled as she saw the hayride cart pull into its starting point. "I see Hank and Rosie are really enjoying taking people through the Christmas Tree Grove Winter Wonderland."

"Oh, yes." Emily rolled her eyes again and shook her head. "The two of them worked hard on putting the forest together." She laughed.

"They did an amazing job of it," Avery said. "It was so sweet how they wouldn't let any of us see it until it was done."

"They let Heather help." Emily's eyes narrowed.

"Yes, but you and Ryder were busy with the rest of the festival preparations. You didn't need more on your plate, so I think Heather was only trying to help." Avery teased her. "Not to steal your place as Rosie's favorite aunt."

"Oh, that would never happen." Emily waved the thought of. "Rosie and I are tight." She grinned.

"Exactly!" Avery agreed. "Besides, Heather is only exciting for a few moments until the excitement of her adventures wears off." She grinned mischievously as Emily took the bait. "Once she's told all her stories, she's really not that cool anymore."

"Now you think Heather's cool?" Emily looked at her in disbelief. "I think what she does is really great." She shrugged. "But she's no Indiana Jones."

"I think they're two different types of adventurers." Avery frowned and laughed when Emily glared at her. "But I understand what you meant."

"So did my brother ask you to go to the dance with him?" Emily suddenly asked, leaning back and folding her arms. Her brows raised knowingly as she gave Avery a smug smile.

CHAPTER 18

As the winter sun began its descent, casting a warm golden glow across the Mistletoe Lodge's grounds, Ryder found himself completing his final run of the day, steering the hayride cart through the enchanting winter wonderland forest.

It was hard to believe that the festival was already coming to a close with only two days left. Ryder had initially harbored doubts about the festival, especially about securing funds from his grandmother for the expenses.

Guilt washed over him as he'd not told his sister how he'd managed to finance the festival, and his grandmother had agreed to keep that knowledge between them. However, as he navigated the winding path and saw the smiles on the faces of the visitors, all his reservations seemed to melt away.

Safely parking the hayride cart, Ryder took a moment to reflect on the past few days. Despite his reservations, the festival had become an undeniable success. He had been concerned about the financial burden, yet now he realized it had been more than worth it.

His gaze shifted to where Avery's parents' booth was set up. Avery was engaged in conversation with a customer, her laughter ringing through the air. Ryder watched her for a moment and felt a jolt zap through him that he knew was more than admiration. It was also a lot more than a casual flirtation or friendship. He ran a hand through his hair and took a breath, knowing he was in trouble.

Ryder hopped off the cart and busied himself with the horses. Once the stablehand had come to take them, he managed to push the cart into the barn. The physical labor helped keep his mind off his emotional turmoil. But as he walked out of the barn, his gaze was once again immediately drawn to Avery as she interacted with a customer.

"Oh, Ryder, boy," Ryder muttered to himself. "You're not falling for Avery again." He sighed as he watched her deftly gift-wrap an item. "You never stopped loving her."

He fiddled with his Stetson before plopping it on his head and finding himself making his way over to her booth. Ryder waited patiently as she finished assisting a customer.

His heart did a few flips when she turned her attention to him; a warm smile lit up her features. "Hey there," she greeted. "How are the hayrides going?"

"Done for the day." Ryder breathed a sigh of relief. "It's fun for the first three to four times," he told her. "Then it starts to get monotonous."

"But it's so worth seeing the smiles on the kids' faces." Avery grinned. "I can hear their squeals of delight as they go through the Christmas tree grove."

"Yeah, you should hear how loud their squeals are when you're driving the cart." Ryder laughed. "Luckily,

Popcorn is a docile horse that doesn't spook easily, or the hayride would turn into a hay-ho ride."

Avery laughed, and he could see her picturing Ryder trying to control a runaway horse cart with kids and their parents hanging on for dear life.

"You're picturing it right now, aren't you?" Ryder accused teasingly, his eyes narrowing.

"It does make for a funny picture," Avery admitted. "Frightening too, though, and that wouldn't be good publicity for the lodge or the festival."

"No, not at all!" Ryder's eyes widened in horror. They were silent for a few seconds before Ryder asked. "How are sales going?"

Avery's smile grew, her eyes sparkling. "Surprisingly well, actually. It seems like tools and gadgets are a hit and a popular Christmas present for men and women alike."

Ryder chuckled. "Who would've thought?"

"I know, right?" Avery said animatedly.

Just as he was about to continue their conversation, another customer approached the booth, and Avery excused herself to help them. Ryder took a step back, content to watch her work. He couldn't help but admire her dedication and the genuine care she showed to each customer.

When Avery was free once more, Ryder leaned against the booth and smiled at her. "Would you like to have dinner with me tonight?"

Avery's eyes lit up with surprise and delight. "I'd love to."

As another customer approached, Ryder stepped aside to wait for her to finish before continuing with his dinner invitation. "Great. Let's say around seven?"

Avery nodded, her smile still in place. "Sounds like a plan." She looked at her wristwatch. "My parents should be back by then to take over the evening shift."

As the customer left, Ryder took a step closer and spoke softly. "Meet me in cabin number five."

With a nod of confirmation, Avery returned to her duties, and Ryder lingered for a few moments before heading off to make preparations for their evening. His eyes scanned the festival, wondering where his sister was, so he could ask if she'd mind watching Rosie. Normally his grandmother would take her if he had plans for the evening, but she'd messaged to say she and Heather were staying in Denver and wouldn't be back until the next afternoon.

Ryder saw Hank helping one of the booth occupants and walked over to him.

"Hey, Hank," Ryder called, getting his brother-in-law's attention. "Have you seen Emily?"

"Yes, she's gone to the office to call your grandmother as her phone died and she needs to charge it," Hank huffed as he moved a large statue of an elephant. "You could give me a hand here!"

"Oh, sure," Ryder said, helping Hank move the granite elephant.

"Thanks," Hank said, straightening and wiping his hand on a rag.

"Thanks gentlemen." Mrs. Potter smiled warmly at them. "You saved me from getting a hernia trying to move that monstrosity."

"Where is your grandson, Mrs. Potter?" Hank asked her.

Before she started talking again, Ryder quickly excused himself, not wanting to get trapped by the opening Hank had given Mrs. Potter to brag about her grandchildren. She had fifteen of them, and once she got started talking about them, a person got their entire histories.

Ryder walked to the lodge to find his sister. His mind was preoccupied with the evening ahead. He found Emily in the lodge's dining area, where she was discussing the setting up of the large marquee tent for the dance.

Ryder waited patiently, not wanting to get involved with organizing that. He was filled to the brim with organizing things at the moment and was only too glad to let Emily take the lead on the dance setup.

Once she was finished with the man, she looked up and saw him leaning against the door frame.

"Did you need me for something?" Emily asked him, checking her wristwatch. "Because I could really use a cup of coffee before I have to go and make sure the food and beverage order for the dance is correct."

"Hey, Em," Ryder greeted her, pushing himself off the doorframe and walking toward her. "I came to ask you for a favor."

Emily raised an eyebrow and said, "Sure, as long as I can grab a cup of coffee." She walked over to the coffee machine that stood on the long table near the window for the guests throughout the day.

"No, go ahead," Ryder said, gesturing with his hands. "And the favor is for this evening."

Ryder followed Emily to the table. "Coffee?" She offered, and he shook his head.

"No thanks," Ryder said, taking off his hat and running a hand through his hair. "I was wondering if you could watch Rosie for a couple of hours tonight."

Emily's eyes narrowed, and she studied her brother's face. "Why? What are you up to?"

Ryder knew that with Emily's keen sense of perception it would be useless to try and evade her question. He let out a sigh, his gaze dropping momentarily.

"I've made plans, and I need someone to watch Rosie," Ryder told her.

Emily's eyes narrowed suspiciously. "And what kind of plans are we talking about here?"

"Just plans." Ryder shrugged while playing with the brim of his hat. "I'd usually ask Gran, but she and Heather are staying overnight in Denver to conclude whatever urgent business took her there."

"Heather's with Gran?" Emily asked in surprise. "In Denver?"

"Yes," Ryder answered, his brow creasing. "You didn't know that?"

"No, I was coming to call Gran to ask if she knew where Heather was, as I hadn't seen her the whole day," Emily explained, taking a sip of her coffee, pulling a face, and pouring in some more sugar. "When did you say they were coming home?"

"I didn't," Ryder pointed out. "But Gran said they'd be home sometime tomorrow afternoon."

"Yes!" Emily pulled her fist down in a victorious gesture and had a huge smile on her face.

"And that makes you happy because..." Ryder's brows creased tighter together as he gave his sister a curious sideways glance.

"Now Avery and I can go to Silverthorne on our own without Heather." Emily squealed, grabbing her brother for a hug and pecking him on the cheek. "Thank you for that good news, big brother."

"I'm glad I could make your day," Ryder told her. "Now about taking Rosie for a few hours tonight."

"Oh, yes, of course," Emily told him. "She can stay with us." She raised a brow once again and pinned him with curious eyes. "So, about your plans..."

Ryder's shoulders sagged in defeat and he sighed. He couldn't hide anything from his sister. "I've asked Avery to dinner."

Emily's expression turned serious, and concern flickered in her eyes. "Ryder, you know what you're doing, right?"

Ryder ran a hand through his hair again, offering a half-hearted smile. "Yeah, Em. We're just two old friends catching up. It's nothing serious."

Emily's gaze held a mix of worry and understanding. "You do remember what happened the last time you two tried to have a relationship, right? I just don't want to see you or Avery hurt again."

Ryder nodded, his eyes distant. "I know, Em. We're not kids anymore. We're just trying to make up for lost time." He swallowed, not sure if he was trying to convince his sister or himself, as he said. "As friends this time."

Emily let out a sigh, her concern not fully eased. "Okay, big brother."

Ryder's lips curled into a grateful smile. "Thanks, Em. I appreciate it."

Emily shook her head, her smile returning. "But don't say I didn't warn you when she goes home to Los Angeles, and this time it's you left alone in Frisco with a broken heart."

"I'm okay, Em. I promise you; I'm not falling in love with Avery," Ryder lied. *I never fell out of love with her.* He gave himself a mental shake to rid himself of the thoughts that echoed from his heart and soul.

"So, where are you having dinner?" Emily asked him.

"I thought I'd get Nora to make us Avery's favorite dinner and set up cabin number five for her," Ryder told her.

"You do know that Gran booked someone into Cabin Five for tomorrow afternoon, right?" Emily told him.

"But what about the problems the cabin has?" Ryder's eyes widened in alarm.

"Oh, don't worry about it," Emily assured him. "I meant to tell you a few days ago, but the time just got away from me because of how busy we've been with the festival."

"Tell me what?" Ryder's eyes narrowed.

"Gran paid to get a contractor in to fix the cabin and have it redecorated for her guest." Emily's words sent zaps of disbelief down his spine.

"You two never mentioned you were going to do this because?" Ryder's eyes narrowed.

"You were busy, and Gran knew you'd try to talk her out of it, and she said the guest was a VIP." Emily spoke quickly. Oh, and probably because she knew you'd react like you are right now, and I might have lied about the reason I didn't tell you." She bit her lip. "She actually made me promise not to until it was too late and the cabin was finished." She grinned and held her hands in a ta-dah gesture. "So—Surprise?"

Ryder stood staring at her in disbelief, and before he could feel angry with her for not telling him what was going on, he remembered he'd also kept the matter of the funding of the festival from her.

"It's okay, Em," Ryder told her, seeing the surprise in her eyes. "I understand, and the guest must be important to Gran for her to want to do that."

"Yes, apparently." Emily shrugged. "She didn't say who he was, and she booked him in as Priscilla's guest."

"Oh!" Ryder said he felt tiny waves of shock tingle through him. "You don't think it's a *man* friend, do you?"

"And what if it is?" Emily looked at him in amazement. "She's entitled to a romantic life too, you know." Her brows raised a little higher. "Love doesn't discriminate against age."

"I know!" Ryder breathed, holding his hands out in front of him. "It's just a shock to think of Gran dating anyone." He bit his lip. "There are so many sharks out there and I'd worry they were after her for—"

"Her money!" Emily finished for him. "Trust me. I'm sure the Venters have all their money tied up neatly and securely." She widened her eyes. "Remember when we tried to get our monthly allowances increased to help save the lodge?"

"Of course!" Ryder sighed. "So, what am I going to do about dinner if I can't use number five?"

"Oh, I never said you couldn't use number five," Emily pointed out. "I asked if you knew it had been booked out."

"No, I didn't," Ryder answered.

"Let's go take a look, and I'll help you set it up for dinner with Avery tonight," Emily offered, finishing her coffee. She put the mug down and linked her arm through his. "Let's go find a few items for the table and speak to Nora about your dinner menu."

"You don't have to do this," Ryder told her.

"Oh, yes, I do," Emily informed him. "Avery's from Los Angeles, and if you're going to be foolish enough to do this, you may as well go big."

"Thank you, little sister." Ryder grinned and kissed the top of her shiny head.

Ryder had been pleasantly surprised at the transformation of cabin number five when he and Emily had first gone in to set up his date with Avery. Thirty minutes later, he and Emily stood surveying what was mostly her handy work.

The table was adorned with a simple white tablecloth topped with rose-pink candles. A bunch of red, pink, and yellow roses was placed in a delicate crystal vase and set in the middle but off to the side.

Emily had insisted that he use candles on the table because the soft flickering light would cast a romantic ambiance over the room, and the flowers added a touch of elegance to the setting. Emily had given Ryder strict instructions to start the fire in the fireplace twenty minutes before Avery arrived to make sure the cabin was warm.

As he surveyed the room, he couldn't help but feel grateful for Emily's advice and assistance in setting the stage for a memorable evening. She'd given him so many instructions that Ryder's head was getting sore, but he loved her idea of offering Avery a pink rose from the vase and then retiring to the sitting room for hot chocolate in front of the fire.

Once the cabin was set up, Emily promised to make sure their dinner was delivered ten minutes after Avery arrived, enough time for them to start with a glass of wine. Emily was walking around the cabin, appraising their handiwork with a discerning eye. "I think that's all set and ready for tonight." She turned and grinned at her brother. "Don't you?"

Ryder nodded as he glanced around the room. "Thank you for helping me make it special."

Emily's gaze softened, and she gave her brother a gentle smile. She put her arms around his waist while he put his around her shoulders, and they stood looking at the room in front of them.

"Please, big brother, be careful with your heart and with Avery's," Emily said softly. "I don't want to see either of your hearts broken again." She tilted her head to look at him. "You've both come so far after going through so much these past fifteen years."

"I know, Em." Ryder nodded. "Don't worry. This time Avery and I know that one of us is leaving."

"I just hope that one of us won't take another fifteen years to come home again." Emily sighed.

Ryder pursed his lips and nodded in agreement with his sister.

They stood in silence for a few minutes before Emily broke away from their embrace.

"Alright. Now, let's go over that list of things you need to do before and when Avery arrives." Emily gave him a tight smile as he rolled his eyes.

Ryder may have teased his sister about her instructions, but he was following them as he lit the fire on time, and it blazed to life. He couldn't help the tingle of excitement that surged through him for the evening ahead. Emily might be cautious, but Ryder was determined to make the most of this chance with Avery, even if it meant savoring the present and letting go of expectations for the future.

The last time they were together, there was a weight of expectations for their future, and they hadn't paid much heed to the present as they were too much in love. Ryder swallowed as he checked his wristwatch and lit the candles as a thought struck him.

What if his mother and Avery's had been right to interfere? Ryder gave his head a shake as the revelation settled in his heart. His mother always said that if he and Avery were meant to find each other again, they would, but this time when the time was right.

Am I sure this isn't the right time? Ryder's brows knit together as his mind started to buzz with his train of thought. "No, surely not."

He busied himself opening Avery's favorite red wine to let it breathe as he contemplated.

"Avery's going back to Los Angeles after New Year's," Ryder told himself, pouring some of the wine and taking a big sip to steady his nerves.

Before he could ponder his thoughts more, there was a knock on the door, and his heart slammed against his rib cage, knowing it was Avery. He took another quick sip of wine and a deep breath, then went to answer the door. Ryder felt his breath catch in his throat when he saw Avery standing with her coat dangling over her arms and her cheeks pinkened by the icy cold evening air.

"Hi," Ryder greeted her and stepped aside, taking her coat from her as she walked past him. "Come in and make yourself at home."

"It's so nice and warm in here," Avery said, rubbing the tops of her arms as she walked into the living room and warmed her hands by the fire. "I'm sorry if I'm a little early." She turned to look at him as he walked into the living room. "But my parents came early, and I decided to slip away because the booth was getting busy."

"Yes, the evenings are quite busy," Ryder agreed, picking up two glasses and the wine as he walked over to join her. "Especially with only two days to go before Christmas."

"I did feel a bit guilty about leaving my parents on their own," Avery admitted, accepting the glass of wine he handed her.

"We can eat later if you'd like to go help them." Ryder put the bottle on the coffee table.

"No, my mother told me to go and do something fun." Avery's smile widened.

323

"You have been at the booth on your own the whole day," Ryder pointed out.

"Yes, but my parents had to be at the store," Avery told him, frowning. "Are you sure you and Hank are going to be alright helping out with the hardware booth tomorrow?"

"Of course," Ryder assured her. "Emily's already set out our schedule."

They laughed, knowing how Emily loved scheduling things.

"What smells so delightful?" Avery tilted her head and took in the aroma of the Pizza warming in the oven.

"Your favorite pizza," Ryder told her. "And Nora prepared your favorite green salad for you as well as cherry pie with caramel marshmallow cream."

"No way!" Avery's eyes widened, and she licked her lips. "While the pizza and salad sound amazing, can we maybe have dessert first?"

"Nope!" Ryder shook his head, wide-eyed. "Emily knew that when you found out what was for dessert, you might suggest that, and she demanded that I stand my ground and make you eat food first."

"But what Emily doesn't know..." Avery gave him her biggest smile as she tried to change his mind.

"Nope, sorry," Ryder laughed. "While I'd gladly try to lasso the moon for you, you know I can't go against Emily's wishes because she somehow always knows."

Avery sighed, and her shoulders sagged in defeat as she nodded with a sad face. "Fine, be a scaredy cat," she teased him, and he noted she didn't reference his comment about lassoing the moon for her.

"Are you hungry?" Ryder asked.

"I'm starving," Avery admitted. "I skipped lunch."

"Don't let Nora hear that," Ryder joked. "Would you like to eat?"

"If it's ready?" Avery said.

Ryder seated her at the table.

"Oh, this is lovely, Ryder." Avery's voice was hoarse with emotion, which touched her eyes as she sat.

"Thank you," Ryder said. "But I can't take all the credit. Emily helped."

Ryder left the room to get the pizza, and as they ate, they spoke about the festival and how he and Emily were going to try and bring it back as an annual affair. The time flew by, and they finally retired to the living room to have some hot chocolate. They sat side by side on the sofa, lost in their thoughts as they sipped the sweet beverage.

"Did you manage to conclude the business you needed to do while you were here?" Ryder broke the silence.

"Part of it," Avery told him.

"Oh, we never had that meeting you wanted to have," Ryder suddenly remembered. "Do you still need to meet?"

"Yes," Avery said, nodding and putting her mug on a coaster on the coffee table. "But I just need to finalize some things first."

"Okay," Ryder said, not wanting to push her and not really interested in discussing business either.

Avery turned, and their eyes locked as he put his mug down.

"I have to admit that I was worried about coming home." Avery's voice was soft and throaty, and her eyes never left his. "But now I'm glad I did."

"I'm glad you did too," Ryder admitted as they moved toward each other.

Before they could say another word, their lips melded together, and whatever it was he was about to say was forgotten.

CHAPTER 19

The crisp morning air held a sense of excitement as Avery and Emily set off for Silverthorne. The second last day of the festival was dawning, and Avery's anticipation for the upcoming Winter Festival Dance was building. She glanced at Emily, who was humming along to a tune on the radio, her eyes shining with eagerness as she drove her SUV.

"Em, I can't believe the dance is tomorrow night," Avery said, her voice tinged with excitement. "Where did the time go?"

Emily grinned, her hands tapping on the steering wheel to the beat of the song. "I know, right?" She shook her head and blew out a breath. "But I must admit that I can't wait to see everyone dressed up and dancing the night away."

Avery nodded, her thoughts drifting to her plans for the evening. She was looking forward to spending time with Ryder again, even though she knew their time together was limited. She hoped the dance would be a memorable end to her time in Frisco.

As they drove, Avery suddenly realized they were one person short, and she was sure that Heather was supposed to be joining them.

"Where's Heather?" Avery asked Emily.

Emily's triumphant expression piqued Avery's interest, and she raised an eyebrow.

"Oh no!" Avery breathed. "Please don't tell me you really did sneak off and leave her behind."

Emily burst out laughing at Avery's shocked expression.

"No, although I did think about it more than once," she admitted. "But Heather's in Denver with my grandmother until later this afternoon," Emily revealed with a twinkle in her eye. "She stayed over with my grandmother last night."

Avery chuckled and couldn't help feeling a little relieved that Emily hadn't ditched her cousin like they used to do when they were young and Heather was getting on their nerves.

"Well, I guess it's just us then. A best friend's day out." Avery turned, and they grinned at each other.

"Just like the good old days." Emily's enthusiasm and excitement filled the car.

They reached Silverthorne and parked at a bustling shopping mall. Their first stop was a cozy cafe, where they enjoyed a leisurely breakfast.

Avery knew that Emily knew about her date with Ryder the previous night and that she was bursting to ask Avery about it. She was about to say something about her dinner, but Emily beat her to it.

Emily couldn't contain her curiosity any longer and blurted, "So, how was your date with Ryder?"

Avery smiled, her heartwarming at the memory. "It was really nice, Em. We had dinner and just talked and caught up. We've finally managed to put our past behind us."

Emily's eyes softened with relief. "I'm glad to hear that. But you know, I worry about you two, and let's be honest here." She raised her eyebrows at Avery. "The two of you have been spending a *lot* of time together." She gave Avery a knowing smile. "Hank and I aren't blind, you know," Emily reminded her. "We see how the two of you look at each other." She sighed and shook her head. "Avery, I worry that the two of you are going to end up with broken hearts again."

Their coffees arrived and Emily sat back, waiting for the server to finish and leave before continuing her conversation. "I know I'm a worrier, but I've loved having you home again, and I'd hate for you to take another fifteen years for your heart to heal before you visit us again." She gave Avery a tight smile. "So yes, I'm worried."

Avery chuckled, shaking her head. "Em, you have the biggest heart and I know you worry." She smiled reassuringly at her friend. "But this time, things are different. We're older and wiser, and we're not putting any pressure on ourselves."

Emily sighed, still looking a bit concerned. "I just don't want to see either of you hurt again."

Avery reached over and squeezed Emily's hand. "I appreciate your concern, Em. But trust me, we're fine. No more broken hearts. Just a stronger-than-ever friendship."

"Alright, I'll trust you on this." Her eyes narrowed. "But now you need to trust me on this." Her eyes widened seriously. "If anything goes wrong between the two of you, this time I'll be the one who doesn't speak to either of you."

"Noted!" Avery laughed.

Avery shifted the conversation, turning the attention to Emily. "So, how's married life treating you?" She stirred her coffee. "You and Hank look so good together."

Emily's eyes lit up, and she grinned like a kid on Christmas morning. "Oh, it's amazing, Avery. And yes, Hank and I are so happy." She bit her bottom lip and smiled sheepishly. "We're actually trying to start a family."

Avery's heart swelled with happiness for her friend. "Em, that's wonderful! I'm so happy for you."

"Thanks, Avery." Emily's smile was radiant. "We're really excited about the prospect."

With their bellies full and spirits high, they embarked on their shopping adventure. The next few hours were a whirlwind of trying on dresses, laughing in front of mirrors, and discussing the merits of different shoes.

They browsed through various shops, exploring a range of styles and colors, until they finally found the perfect dresses that made them both feel glamorous and confident.

As they took a break for lunch, Emily spotted a nail salon nearby. Her eyes gleamed with excitement. "Hey,

Avery, let's check if they have any openings for us to get our nails done."

Avery smiled, taken in by her friend's enthusiasm. "Sure, why not? A little pampering sounds like a great idea." She looked at her nails. "And after the week we've had, I'm sure our nails are in desperate need of attention."

"I couldn't agree more." Emily's eyes widened in dismay and she looked at her hands.

They enjoyed a delicious lunch and then headed to the salon. Luckily, they were able to secure spots for nail appointments and allowed themselves to be pampered for the next hour before deciding it was getting late and they needed to head back to Frisco.

As Emily drove them toward home, Avery's phone chimed, signaling a new message. She glanced at the screen and couldn't suppress her grin. Avery's heart raced as her eyes scanned the message.

Avery, I'm sorry about the delay in getting back to you. I'm on my way to Frisco to discuss your proposal with you.

GH

Avery messaged him straight back and couldn't help but admire her fresh manicure as her nails clicked against the screen.

When will you get here?

To her surprise, he answered right away.
Today.

Avery breathed a sigh of relief because she knew that the man wouldn't be coming to meet with her if he wasn't interested in her proposal. She'd known him well and long enough to know how he did business.

Emily's eyes widened as she looked at Avery. "That looks like good news."

Avery nodded, excitement bubbling within her. "Yes, I think it just might be."

Emily grinned. "Does this mean you've finally concluded your business and can now relax for the rest of your vacation?"

Avery laughed, feeling a rush of happiness. "I hope so, Em."

Emily's smile was infectious. "That's fantastic, Avery!" She glanced at her. "After the festival finishes and everything's packed up, you can breathe and finally relax."

As they continued on the road, Avery's mind was abuzz with possibilities. The festival, the dance, and now the potential deal with Holland Corporation—it was all coming together in a whirlwind of excitement and joy. She looked out at the snow-covered landscape, feeling grateful for the adventures and friendships that had rekindled during her time in Frisco.

As they neared Frisco, Avery looked at her phone and tried to call Ryder but found she had no signal.

"What's wrong?" Emily asked.

"I'm trying to call Ryder to find out how things are going with my parent's booth, but I've got no signal." Avery frowned, holding her phone in different positions, hoping to get a few bars.

"It's this pass," Emily told her. "It has a few mobile dead zones, I'm afraid." She chuckled. "Avery, relax. They've got this. Hank and Ryder are capable." She glanced at Avery. "Trust me, everything's fine."

Avery gave a small smile, but she still felt a bit restless; a feeling of unease was creeping up her spine. It was like that feeling you get when something is going right but you're waiting for the other shoe to drop.

"Ugh!" Avery groaned, shaking her phone in frustration. "I just wanted to make sure."

"Don't worry about it," Emily reassured her. "We're almost back at the lodge. You can check then."

As they pulled into the lodge's parking area, Emily turned to Avery. "See, we're back safe and sound. Now let's go reassure you that your parents' booth is as well, and the guys haven't burned it down or something," she teased.

Avery nodded, her unease still lingering. They hurried to the booth, but as they approached, they were met with an unexpected frostiness from Hank. Emily exchanged a puzzled look with Avery, and they both greeted him with cautious smiles.

"Hey, Hank. How's everything been here?" Emily asked cheerfully.

Hank's response was a curt, "Fine." His eyes narrowed into a glare as they met Avery's

Avery frowned, a little taken aback at Hank's coldness toward her all of a sudden. "Hank, is everything okay?" Alarm bells started going off in her head.

He gave a stiff nod. "Someone's been waiting for you at the lodge."

Avery exchanged a puzzled glance with Emily before quickly heading towards the lodge, her heart pounding with uncertainty. Leaving Emily with Hank, Avery took off toward the lodge. As she neared it, her phone suddenly beeped, indicating a signal. She checked her messages and saw an alert from her boss, Harry. Her heart sank as she read the message.

Pembrook Group was proceeding with the acquisition of both the Slope Hotel and Mistletoe Lodge. They were buying the lodges' debt, and the deal would be finalized by early January. The last words of the message made her blood freeze in her veins.

Oh, and be warned. Larry is on his way there if he isn't already, as he's the one who reopened the deal for the lodge.

Avery's breath caught in her throat. She couldn't believe what she was reading. She was still processing the message when she reached the lodge and walked into Ryder's office. He was not alone. Her heart dropped when he saw Ryder, his expression tense, and his eyes angrily locked onto the man standing in front of him in an expensive suit—Larry Grimes!

As Avery approached, Ryder's eyes moved from the man and met hers, and Avery felt a rush of anxiety. She barely registered Larry Grimes beside Ryder as he turned toward her with a smug smile. Avery's heart sank further; she'd hoped that there may have been the slightest possibility that Larry hadn't spoken to Ryder yet. But by the look on Ryder's face, she knew that was a false hope.

Before she could speak, Larry's brow raised as he drawled. "Hello Avery."

"Larry!" Avery's greeting was icy, and her eyes narrowed angrily. "What are you doing here?" She already knew the answer but wanted to hear it from the rat's mouth.

"Oh, so Harry didn't get hold of you?" His grin widened. "I've come to finish what you couldn't." He showed her the file in his hand. "I'm surprised you didn't realize the value for Pembrook Group in acquiring *both* properties." She reached for the file, but he snapped it away. "Oh, no, this is my deal now." He smirked.

"Pembrook is no longer interested in this lodge," Avery hissed, her newly manicured nails biting into the palms of her hands as her fists curled into balls at her side.

"Yes, but I pointed out that they'd be fools not to take both properties," Larry told her, clearly enjoying his triumph. "With the financial state of this..." He gazed around the lodge and shuddered. "...place, if Pembrook didn't acquire the property, they were leaving it wide open for any of their competitors to swoop in."

"You snake, Larry." Avery gritted her teeth, barely restraining herself from slapping his smirk from his arrogant face. But she remembered the message she'd received a while ago, and her heart flinched with some hope. "But I fear Pembrook is too late."

"How so?" Larry folded his arms, the file dangling from his fingers.

"There is another deal in place, and trust me, Pembrook has no chance of going up against this corporation." Avery lifted her chin defiantly. "And how dare you come here and worm your way into *my* project?"

"A project, I might add, that you couldn't close." Larry couldn't wait to throw it in her face. "It doesn't matter what you're planning, Avery." He gave a laugh. "You lose and I get the deal; the customer, oh—" His smirk widened. "And the promotion."

With that, he pushed past her, waving the file as he left Avery standing, staring at a stone-faced Ryder, who'd heard the entire conversation.

"Ryder—" Avery took a step toward him, but he stepped back and held his hand up. "I can explain." She swallowed as his eyes narrowed with disbelief and shone with betrayal. "I was going to tell you everything."

"This is what you wanted to meet about?" Ryder's voice was clipped.

"Yes and—" Avery was going to step closer but thought better of it when his glare warned her to stay where she was. "Please, Ryder, I don't know what Larry has told you but—"

"That's the real reason you came home, isn't it?" Ryder's words slid from between his gritted teeth while a nerve ticked at the side of his clenched jaw. "To get revenge on me?" His eyes narrowed to slits as he shot sparks of anger at her. "Do you hate us so much that you pounced on an opportunity to bully us out of our home?" His anger hit her like a flaming arrow in the heart.

"No, Ryder, no!" Avery's voice was hoarse with emotion that vibrated through her system, making her hands shake. "I only took the deal because I thought it would be better coming from me than anyone else if I couldn't find another property."

She tried to persuade him to listen to her, but he was too angry, and she saw that any attempt to reach him was futile. It was not just the rage that drove him; it was the gut-wrenching feeling of betrayal that amplified the pain. Avery knew that feeling all too well, and ironically, she'd been standing in this office the last time she'd felt it.

"Of course you did!" Ryder sneered. "This way, you were the one that got to swing the ax into my heart."

"No, Ryder, please, if you'd just stop and listen," Avery pleaded, fighting the tears stinging the back of her eyes.

"What fun you must've been having this past week playing with me like a cat playing with a little mouse, just waiting to pounce and go in for the kill." His words were chosen with precision, like an assassin choosing his weapon to end his target. "How triumphant you must be feeling right now." His eyes gave her an insulting once-over. "Not only were you neatly setting up the lodge for your clients, but you got to twist the knife in my heart this time too." He gave an ugly laugh. "I hope I gave you all the satisfaction you needed by running after you like a needy puppy dog."

Avery's eyes widened in shock. "No, Ryder, that's not true." She felt physically ill as his words hit home and she realized what he was insinuating. "Yes, I took the contract and came here to assess the lodge for the Pembrook Group. And yes, I came here with a purpose, but it wasn't so Pembrook could acquire the lodge, and I never intended for my feelings for you to resurface." Her brows knit tightly together. "I never once thought about you as a needy puppy dog."

Ryder's expression remained hard. "Please save it, Avery. I don't want to hear your excuses." He pointed to the door. "Please, just go." He swallowed, and Avery saw he was fighting for control. "You can go back to Los Angeles knowing what you came there to accomplish has been accomplished." His fists curled at his sides. "So, congratulations on your new promotion and extracting your revenge." He shrugged. "You get to walk away a queen and me the fool this time."

"No, Ryder!" Avery made one more desperate attempt to make him listen to her. "Please, listen to me." Tears welled up in Avery's eyes, her heart aching at the misunderstanding. She reached out a hand toward him. "Ryder, please—"

He cut her off. "Go, Avery. I don't want to hear anything from you." He dropped into his office chair, and her heart broke at the look of defeat on his face.

Feeling a mixture of hurt, confusion, and frustration, Avery turned and walked out of his office. Her vision blurred by tears, she nearly ran over Emily, who was rushing into the lobby.

"Avery, Hank just told me what's going on—" Emily's words died in her throat as her eyes met Avery's. "Please tell me it's not true."

Emily's words rang in Avery's ears as her heart splintered into a million pieces like a block of ice being gradually crushed by a machine. Her mind raced as she tried to comprehend and make sense of what had just happened.

She couldn't trust her voice at the moment. Avery knew if she said too much, she'd risk bursting into tears, and she wouldn't let Ryder have the satisfaction of seeing her cry.

"I'm sorry, Emily," Avery said, drawing in a shaky breath. "I can't talk right now." She swallowed. "I have to go."

Avery rushed past Emily and didn't stop until she was in the car, heading toward the exit of Mistletoe Lodge. She was so distraught that she didn't see the large helicopter with the Holland Corporation logo landing nearby. Her heart was weighed down with pain, anger, and despair like a swollen rain cloud.

As she turned onto the road to take her home, the dam of tears burst. As the salty drops of pain dripped down her cheeks, she refused to look back as she drove away, leaving behind the painful aftermath of the mess she'd made.

As soon as Avery got home, she didn't stop to greet her parents. She rushed upstairs to her room and started stuffing her clothes into her suitcase.

"Avery?" Judy's voice resonated with worry as she knocked on the bedroom door and pushed her head around it. "Oh, honey!" Her eyes widened, and she rushed into the room. "Sweetheart, what's going on?"

"Nothing!" Avery snapped, swiping furiously at her tears as she shoved her toiletries into the round case.

"Where are you going?" Judy asked, watching her daughter in confusion. Before grabbing her by the top of her arms and making her stand still. "Avery, stop and talk to me."

"To you!" Avery growled and gave a harsh, watery laugh before rudely knocking her mother's hands aside.

"Avery!" Judy said in shock. "What on earth?"

"Please, can you just leave me alone and let me finish packing?" Avery told her, keeping her distance. She was on emotional overload at the moment and learning about her mother's betrayal recently was still smoldering within her. "I do *not* want to get into anything with you right now."

"Get into anything with me?" Judy's confusion grew before her eyes narrowed, and her mom-voice cracked through Avery's room like a whip. "You'll stop right now, young lady, and explain yourself." Her hands balled into fists as she pointed to the ground with her index finger. "You know we don't keep things from each other in this house or let anything fester."

That was all it took to fully ignite the spark of anger flickering inside her over her mother's betrayal. Any tiny thread of control Avery had been holding onto for dear life snapped like a rubber band that had been fraying around the edges for too long.

"Oh, that's rich!" Avery sneered.

She knew what was happening to her right now had nothing to do with her mother. Avery was well aware of how unfair it was of her to take it out on her mother. But it was too late, and logic had twanged and flown off with the fraying rubber band keeping her self-control in check.

"What do you mean by that?" Judy's own anger sparked as she glared at her daughter.

"How dare you!" Avery's voice was hoarse, like it was being dragged over hot coals. "How dare you stand there and tell me we don't keep things from each other?"

"Avery…" Judy warned her. "I've no idea what's gotten into you or what's happened. But I don't appreciate you taking it out on me." She raised her eyebrows. "I'm trying to help you here."

"Help me?" Avery burst into hysterical laughter. "Like you were *helping* me fifteen years ago when you and your accomplice broke myself and Ryder up?"

Avery watched her mother's face pale, and she flinched as if Avery had struck her as she gaped in disbelief at Avery.

"So, it's true." Avery swallowed the fresh set of tears, trying to push them past her eyelids. She nodded when her mother said nothing but stood staring at her. "Please, just leave and let me finish packing so I can get the last flight from Denver."

Without a word, Judy spun on her heel and left the room, pulling the door closed behind her with a soft click. Avery's hand shook as she finished packing and breathed a sigh of relief when her phone dinged, indicating her taxi had arrived. Without another word, she left her parents' house without a backward glance, sliding into the cab as the driver put her luggage in the trunk.

As they drove out of Frisco, Avery forced herself to ignore the scenery that usually took her breath away and made her proud of where she was born. At that particular moment, she wasn't too proud of herself and was feeling the weight of the boot, not the shoe, that fate had dropped right onto her head.

So much for not leaving Frisco behind in tears and with a broken heart. She gave a soft, self-mocking laugh. *At least this time, I'm not wearing a wedding dress as I flee Frisco.*

CHAPTER 20

The atmosphere in Ryder's office was tense. His anger was palpable as he swiped items off his desk in a fit of frustration. Emily entered the room, her expression a mix of concern and bewilderment at the chaos.

"Ryder, calm down!" Emily's voice carried a hint of exasperation as she hurried to his side, starting to pick up the scattered objects from the floor.

Ryder let out a frustrated sigh and plopped down into his office chair, his hands covering his face for a moment before he looked up at his sister. "It's a disaster, Em."

Emily's brows furrowed as she continued to collect the items. "What's a disaster? What's going on?"

Ryder's voice was laced with bitterness as he began to explain the situation. "Larry Grimes, Pembrook Group, Mistletoe Lodge. We're about to lose everything, Em. All our hard work, all our effort—it's all for nothing."

Emily's eyes widened in shock. "Wait, what do you mean?" Her brow furrowed in confusion. "You're not making any sense."

Ryder's hands clenched into fists as he recounted the story, his frustration and anger clear in his voice. "Pembrook is making a hostile takeover bid. They're planning to acquire the lodge, and there's nothing we can do to stop it."

"What?" Emily's voice held disbelief. "No, there has to be a way." She looked toward the door. "What happened with Avery?" She asked, her confusion growing. "She rushed out of here like there was a fire, and I couldn't get much out of her."

Ryder's rage resurfaced at the mention of Avery's name. "Avery? She's the reason we're in this mess in the first place. She's been working with Larry and Pembrook all along."

Emily's eyes widened, her expression a mixture of shock and skepticism. "Avery? Are you sure?"

Ryder's jaw tightened as he nodded. "Yeah, she confirmed it. She admitted she'd been helping them."

Emily's brows furrowed in thought. "I find it hard to believe Avery would do something like this without a reason." She shook her head. "What did she tell you?"

"Tell me?" Ryder's eyes widened as his frustration flared again. "I didn't give her a chance to spew out more lies." He slammed his hand on the desk, making Emily jump along with what was left of the contents on it. "She played us all for fools."

Before Emily could respond, the office door swung open again, and Priscilla entered, accompanied by a tall, distinguished-looking man about Ryder's age.

"Ryder, Emily, I'd like you to meet Giles Holland." Priscilla introduced the man with a warm smile. "He's our guest who'll be staying in cabin number five."

Ryder nodded in acknowledgment, shaking Giles's hand, though his thoughts were still muddled with his anger. He really wasn't in the mood to make small talk with one of his grandmother's guests, even if they were one of the richest men in America. Priscilla turned to Emily, introducing her as well, and Ryder's mind was a whirlwind as he was still processing everything that had happened.

"Have either of you seen Avery?" Priscilla asked, her brows shooting up as Emily turned to her grandmother.

"Gran, now's not a good time to bring up Avery," Emily told her.

"What's happened?" Priscilla asked, her accusing gaze turning on Ryder. "What did you do this time?"

"What did I do?" Ryder looked at his grandmother in disbelief and had his angry tirade cut off by Emily clearing her throat and moving her eyes towards their guest. "I beg your pardon, Mr. Holland." He picked up his phone and messaged Hank. "You must be tired after your trip from..."

"Los Angeles," Giles filled in for him. "And please, call me Giles."

As Giles mentioned Los Angeles, a memory flashed through Ryder's mind, and he realized where he'd seen Giles before, other than on the cover of Fortune Five Hundred Magazine. He'd been one of the group with Avery fifteen years ago when Ryder went to try and visit her at UCLA.

Avery knew Giles Holland! For a second, he was impressed until he remembered her lies and betrayal.

"My brother-in-law, Hank, will be here in a few minutes with your luggage and to escort you to your cabin," Ryder informed him. "I don't want to be rude, but my sister and I have some pressing business to discuss with my grandmother."

"Of course," Giles said with a bow of his head.

As if on cue, Hank walked into the office to escort Giles to his cabin.

"We'll meet for dinner and finalize everything," Priscilla told Giles as he followed Hank out of the office.

After Giles left the room, Pricilla turned her shrewd eyes on Ryder and Emily. "Okay, you two, what is going on?"

"There's been a development," Ryder informed her. "And I'm afraid we've been betrayed and lied to by someone we took in and trusted."

"Oh?" Pricilla frowned for a few seconds before it dawned on her who Ryder was talking about. "Do you mean Avery?"

"Yes Grandmother, Avery," Ryder confirmed.

"Ryder suspects that Avery's behind the hostile takeover bid by the Pembrook Group, which is the company Avery works for," Emily explained to Priscilla.

Ryder's shoulders slumped as he recounted the story to his grandmother, his anger still simmering beneath the surface. "She lied to, betrayed, and played all of us for fools, Gran."

Ryder frowned as his grandmother said nothing but stood staring at him with a blank expression on her face.

Emily still wouldn't believe that Avery had deliberately betrayed or harmed them in any way. "I personally think there's more to the story," she defended Avery to her grandmother. "But Ryder won't hear of it." Her eyes narrowed accusingly as she glared at him. "In fact, he didn't even let her tell her side of the story."

"Where is Avery now?" Priscilla's voice and expression were void of emotion as her eyes traveled from her granddaughter to her grandson.

"I don't know," Ryder informed her. "And quite frankly, none of us should care." He shook his head, the anger still burning in his stomach. "She lied to us."

Emily's voice was gentle. Her concern for her brother was clear, but she was also trying to figure out why her friend would do something like this. "I know you're hurt, Ryder, but let's not jump to conclusions. There might be something we're missing."

"And you, my dear, would be right to think that!" Priscilla's voice was firm, and she turned to Ryder. "While you are running on pure emotion and looking for any excuse to cut Avery off before she leaves you to be the one holding your heart in pieces in Frisco—"

"Gran!" Emily hissed. "That's unfair."

"Is it?" Priscilla raised her eyebrows pointedly at Ryder. "You're still carrying around so much guilt for the way you left Avery fifteen years ago that you're lashing out like an angry octopus with its tentacles flaying out willy-nilly, not caring what it hits."

Ryder heard a giggle and turned to see his sister trying hard not to find their grandmother comparing him to an octopus funny.

"Gran, you don't know what's been going on at the lodge," Ryder told her.

"I'm going to stop you right there, young man." Pricilla held her hand up. "I'm going to be the one talking right now." She raised her brows as she looked from Ryder to Emily. "The two of you are going to take a seat and not say a word until I've finished what I have to say."

"Gran, we really don't have time for a lecture on—" Ryder was cut off by his grandmother, who closed her fingers together in a gesture for him to be quiet and do as she said. So, Ryder sat, as did Emily.

"I knew weeks ago about Avery being put on the Pembrook Group project to acquire the lodge," Priscilla scolded Ryder and Emily by saying. "She also told me about a week ago." She fiddled with the briefcase that Ryder had only just seen in her hand and pulled out a proposal. "She also told me what her plan was and had been all along since the moment she agreed to handle the contract for Pembrook Group."

"You knew all this time?" Ryder hissed, feeling his anger flare.

"I did, and I suggest you reign that red-hot temper of yours in, young man," Priscilla warned him. "If you'd given Avery the chance to explain herself to you before you kicked her out—"

"How do you know I kicked her out?" Ryder asked his grandmother suspiciously.

"I assumed that to be the case," Priscilla told him. "And now I know my assumption was correct." Her eyes narrowed, and she shook her head. "How many times have I told you to stop, think, and then look both ways before stepping off the curb so you don't get hit by a bus?"

"Once or twice," Ryder mumbled.

"Well, guess what? You just got hit by a bus!" Priscilla slapped the proposal on the desk in front of him. "When I went to meet Giles Holland, who by the way is a lovely man, I asked him why he'd invested in the many companies he had over the years." She told them. "I'm not talking about the massive corporate companies he's acquired, but the smaller ones. Mom and Pop type establishments."

"I wasn't aware that the Holland Corporation invested in anything that wasn't worth over a couple of million dollars," Ryder said, sitting back in his chair and clasping his hands in front of him.

"Well, he does," Pricilla told him. "Not to make a profit off them, but rather to save them and help the smaller businesses survive."

"Good for him," Ryder scoffed. "I don't see what that's got to do with what's happening to us."

"Did I say I was finished speaking?" Priscilla asked him primly, and Ryder shook his head.

"Sorry," Ryder grumbled.

"Giles told me that he does it to honor his parents." Pricilla informed them. "He was adopted by a nice couple after being abandoned at a fire station when he was four years old."

"Four years old?" Emily choked. "Oh no, that's awful."

"One of the firefighters, Patrick Holland, took him home," Pricilla continued the story. "He and his wife were childless, but not for a lack of trying. His wife took one look at Giles and fell in love. They adopted him and gave him the best life they possibly could."

"That's a happy, sad story, Gran," Ryder said. "I still don't know what it's got to do with our situation."

Priscilla ignored him and continued, "Giles's mother had a bakery, which they lived over until the whole block on which it was situated was bought by a large corporation." She shook her head. "His mother lost everything, and they lost their home."

"Oh, Gran, what a heartbreaking story." Emily's eyes shone with unshed tears.

"They had to move into a one-bedroom apartment until his father was promoted to fire captain." Priscilla gave Emily's hand a squeeze. "His mother never opened another bakery, although baking was her life. He also watched his neighborhood being torn down to make way for big chain stores." She shook her head. "He swore that one day, if he came into money, he'd do what he could to protect the smaller businesses being pushed out by the larger chain stores."

"Great story," Ryder said again. "I'm still not seeing the connection."

"Avery has helped Giles do that over the years she worked as an acquisitions and mergers consultant," Pricilla's words struck a chord with Ryder.

A horrible feeling started to churn inside him and he figured out where his grandmother was going with her story but he wasn't ready to believe she had good intentions. "If you're trying to tell us Avery was trying to save the lodge. You can save your breath, Gran." He told her. "Avery as much as admitted to her sleazy colleague Larry that she'd come here to acquire the lodge for the Pembrook Group."

"But did she?" Emily's brows furrowed as she looked questioningly at her brother.

"What do you mean?" Ryder shook his head and raised his shoulder. "Obviously she did because that Larry person flashed the bid in front of me."

"Yes, but that was Larry," Emily pointed out. "Not Avery, and if she was going to do it and was out for revenge like you accused her of being, wouldn't she have been the one to do that?"

"She was waiting for the right moment," Ryder said, defending his reasoning and decision.

"She was waiting for the right moment," Pricilla told him. "But not to hit you with what Larry did, but for an investor who wanted to invest in the lodge to help us get it back into full operational capacity."

"Why are you defending Avery?" Ryder was starting to feel like an absolute malicious idiot, and regret flooded through him at the nasty thing he'd spewed at Avery.

"I'm not defending her, Ryder," Pricilla argued. "I'm merely stating the facts."

"Something you'd have known if you'd given Avery a chance to tell her side of the story," Emily pointed out a little smugly. "I told you there was more to the story."

"She still lied to us and left us in the dark about the situation," Ryder said stubbornly.

"Giles speaks very highly of Avery." Heather's voice had them all turning toward the door.

"How long have you been standing there?" Ryder hissed.

"Long enough to know that you can be an arrogant, stubborn fool." Heather shrugged unabashedly at having been eavesdropping and was not apologetic for it either. "Giles told me the reason he only works with Avery to help these businesses is because of her heart."

"Her heart!" Ryder harrumphed. "Yeah right."

Heather ignored his rude outburst and continued, "He said that Avery was one of the only mergers and acquisition consultants that didn't go raging into a deal, not caring who got hurt." She walked into the office and took a seat next to Priscilla. "Avery painstakingly goes over the deal before approaching the property about to be acquired." She stretched out on the chair. "If they aren't wanting to sell, she'll do what she can to try and save the business while finding another suitable one for her client."

"Just like she did with Mistletoe Lodge," Emily said with a smile. "I knew it." Her smile grew. "Avery would do everything she could to save the lodge."

"Yes, my dear, you're right," Pricilla agreed. "Avery did just that regardless of whether or not it cost her, her job, a lucrative promotion, or the client."

"May I see the proposal, please, Gran?" Emily asked.

"It's a really good one," Heather assured them. "Gran and I went over it on the way to Denver to meet Giles."

Something in Heather's eyes and her voice caught Ryder's attention, and he frowned at his cousin. "Why are you blushing?" he asked. "It's not something you often do."

"That's because our Heather and Giles hit it off together," Priscilla said, letting the cat out of the bag with a grin.

"Well, he is gorgeous," Heather stated.

"I'll give you that," Emily agreed with a warm smile for her cousin. "Not to mention being a self-made millionaire."

"Yes, but it's not the money," Heather assured them and she sighed, her eyes getting a glazed look as she thought of Giles.

"Great!" Ryder hissed, throwing up his hands. "The man has charmed my grandma and my cousin."

"While Giles is a very charming young man," Priscilla told Ryder, "I can assure you that no amount of charm sways me when it comes to business."

"Sorry, I didn't mean that, Gran," Ryder assured her.

"I've gone over the proposal, both the original and Giles's amended one," Priscilla said, pulling the conversation back to the business at hand. "It is a very good one, and it will save our home and keep the sharks like the Pembrook Group from circling, especially when we're under the Holland umbrella."

Ryder took the proposal from his sister and started to flick through it.

"As the lodge's legal and financial advisor, I'm telling you we're taking this deal," Pricilla's instructed. "We keep the lodge and have full control of it," she pointed out. "All Giles wants is a small share, which is to go to an animal shelter he supports." She pushed herself to her feet. "There is one more clause in the proposal." She raised her eyebrows and looked at Ryder. "I think when you read it, you'll want a good few mouthfuls of humble pie, Ryder."

Heather helped Pricilla up.

"Come on, Gran," Heather said. "Let's go get something to eat."

"Yes, I'm starving." Pricilla took her granddaughter's arm, and she stopped at the door to the office. "In case either of you is interested, my contacts told me that Avery booked a flight to Los Angeles, which leaves first thing tomorrow morning."

With that, she left the office, and two pairs of eyes stared after her.

"Why did grandmother say you're about to want a healthy dose of humble pie?" Emily looked at her brother questioningly.

"I'm not sure," Ryder told her with a frown as he flipped through the pages of a very generous proposal. His eyes widened as he came to the last page. "Oh!"

"Oh?" Emily said, getting impatient, that she leaned over the desk and snatched the document away. Her eyes widening as she saw the last clause and the signature agreeing to the terms beneath it. "OH!"

"Yes, OH!" Ryder pulled a face and took a breath as what he'd done hit him like a ton of bricks falling on his head. He dipped his head into his hands. "Oh, no, Emily, what have I done?"

"Made a right mess of things *again*!" Emily told him. "Only this time you have no one to blame but your quick-judgy attitude and your stubborn as a mule streak."

"Thanks for the support and understanding," Ryder drawled sarcastically. "Emily, I've made a right pig's

CHRISTMAS AT MISTLETOE LODGE

ear of this, and I doubt Avery will ever talk to me again, let alone forgive me."

"Well, you did say some nasty things to her," Emily told him. "Then you basically told her to get lost and take her lies with her," she reminded him. "Only they weren't lies or excuses." She bit her lip. "They were surprises and solutions to help us keep our home and protect our legacy."

"Fine!" Ryder hissed, feeling worse and worse with every word that popped out of his sister's mouth. "I'm an ogre. I get it." He ran a shaky hand through his hair as his feelings suddenly hit like a freight train. "Gran was right; I never look both ways, and now I've been hit by a freight train, not a truck."

"Yup!" Emily agreed with him and laughed when he threw his stress ball at her. "So instead of sitting here feeling sorry for yourself, what are you going to do about it?"

"I don't know, Em," Ryder said, leaning forward and rubbing his forehead. "I really don't know."

"I'll tell you what you're not going to do, Ryder Carlisle!" Emily pushed herself up, sliding the chair back with an exaggerated scraping noise. "You're not going to lick your wounds for another fifteen years before you decide to do something about it."

"I haven't been licking my wounds!" Ryder took offense to his sister's words.

"No, of course not," Emily said sarcastically. "Grab your cowboy hat and coat. It's time to hit the trail."

"Where are we headed?" Ryder asked, standing up and following his sister through the door and to the entrance of the lodge, where she ordered the town car.

"To the airport, of course," Emily told him.

"But Avery's flight doesn't leave until tomorrow," Ryder reminded her. "She won't be at the airport now."

"No, but I've got a good idea where she will be," Emily assured him, grabbing his coat for him. "Do you have your wallet and phone?"

Ryder patted his pocket. "Why?"

"Because you're going to need them." Emily gave him a silly look and pushed him out the door as the town car pulled up.

"I don't think we should do this," Ryder told her as their driver opened the back door for him. "This isn't a good idea. What do we say to her if she'll even talk to us?"

"*You'll* start by apologizing for being a douche," Emily told him. "And then *you'll* take her somewhere nice for a meal. Somewhere where it's nice and private." She leaned in the car after he'd slid in. "Then you'll do your best to talk her out of going, and hopefully she'll forgive you and still go to the dance with you tomorrow night."

"Wait, why aren't you getting in the car?" Ryder asked, feeling a little alarmed.

"Because I'm not going," Emily told him, giving him a smug smile as she closed the door, then waved him off, calling, "Good luck. You're going to need it."

CHAPTER 21

Avery stormed through the airport terminal, her frustration simmering just beneath the surface. She'd missed the last flight to Los Angeles, and the realization only fueled her anger.

Her hurried footsteps echoed through the empty terminal as she approached the airline counter to book the earliest flight for the next day. The attendant offered her a sympathetic smile as Avery handed over her credit card and confirmed her booking.

With a sigh, Avery turned away from the counter and headed towards the exit. She needed a place to stay for the night. A picture of a picturesque bed and breakfast flashed through her mind and brought a smile to Avery's lips.

As she stepped outside, the cold Denver air hit her, and she shivered slightly, wrapping her coat tighter around herself.

Spotting a line of taxis waiting, she hailed one and climbed into the backseat. She gave the driver the address of the bed and breakfast that held memories from her teenage years—Emily and she used to stay there during their weekend trips to Denver.

Avery just hoped that something was going to go right today and she'd manage to get a room at May's Cottage Bed and Breakfast.

The taxi pulled up in front of a charming house that looked like something out of a fairy tale. The building resembled a gingerbread house or a Swiss chalet, its architecture quaint and inviting.

Avery felt a rush of nostalgia as she stepped out of the taxi and paid the fare. She stood there for a moment, taking in the sight of the place that held so many memories for her, Emily, and even Ryder.

His name brought about a spurt of red-hot anger and frustration, and she felt another piece of her crack as she bit back the tears she'd been determined to keep at bay. Avery's footsteps crunched through the soft snow that had recently fallen on the path to the front door.

Her mood was as heavy as the weight of her suitcase. Trying to think positively about them having room for her, Avery's fingers wrapped around the cold doorknob. She pushed the door open, and a rush of warm air and the tantalizing aroma of something hearty bubbling on a stove tantalized her nostrils and made her stomach rumble.

Avery stepped inside, feeling the warmth of the cozy interior envelop her. The inside of the house was just as charming as the outside, with wooden floors, vintage furniture, and the crackling sound of a fire in the fireplace. It felt like a comforting embrace, a respite from the chaos of her day. As Avery walked toward the front desk, a figure emerged from around the corner.

A familiar voice exclaimed, "Avery Hawthorn, is that you?"

Avery's eyebrows shot up in surprise that the woman would remember her after all these years as she locked eyes with the smiling face of May Partridge, the owner of the bed and breakfast.

"Hello, May." Avery greeted the woman, the dark cloud floating above her head lifted momentarily by May's joyous voice and genuine welcoming persona. "Wow, I can't believe you remember me."

May Partridge's eyes twinkled with delight as she crossed the room to envelop Avery in a warm hug. "Oh, my dear, I never forget a guest. Especially not one of my favorites."

Avery returned the hug, her heart swelling. She always had a fondness for the woman whenever Avery and Emily came to stay here.

"I'm sorry to just drop in on you without a booking," Avery began. "But—"

"Say no more, dear." May cut her off and walked around the front desk, pushing the register toward Avery. "Just sign in for me, and we'll get you settled in a room."

"I'm surprised you have one available," Avery said, filling in the register. "Your bed and breakfast is always so popular at this time of year."

"Well, you're in luck," May told her. "We had a cancellation not more than forty minutes ago. So, there's a room all ready and waiting for you." May dipped below the desk and pulled out a key. "Come on, honey, let's get you to your room." She smiled and said, "Cherrie, my new chef, will bring you up a nice cup of hot cocoa to warm you up."

"That sounds heavenly." Avery breathed a sigh of relief that she wouldn't have to find a hotel.

Avery followed May up a flight of stairs and down a hallway adorned with framed photographs. May opened the door to a room that was like something out of a dream.

A wooden four-poster bed with a canopy dominated the space, and a fire was already roaring in the fireplace. The room was bathed in a warm, inviting light that made Avery's tense shoulders relax for the first time in hours.

"Oh, this is lovely," Avery breathed, stepping into the room and looking around in awe.

"I'm glad you like it, dear," May said with a smile. "You make yourself comfortable, and if you need anything, don't hesitate to ask. We serve breakfast in the dining room from 7 to 9. But I'm sure you remember that."

"Yes." Avery nodded, putting her luggage down and unraveling her scarf, then taking off her coat.

"I can get a tray sent up to your room for dinner if you like," May offered.

Avery's stomach rumbled, reminding her that she hadn't eaten since the disastrous turn of events back in Frisco. "A tray in my room sounds perfect; thank you."

May chuckled. "We have thick country vegetable soup and freshly baked bread tonight." She looked at her wristwatch. "It will be ready in two hours, and as soon as it is, I'll have some sent up to you."

As May left the room, Avery finally allowed herself to sink onto the bed, the events of the day catching up to her. She stared into the dancing flames of the fire, her thoughts a whirlwind of hurt, frustration, and confusion.

She couldn't believe how quickly things had spiraled out of control and how misunderstandings and miscommunications had led to this mess.

I could've prevented it, though! The thought ran through Avery's mind. "Yes, I should've told Ryder right away." She kicked off her shoes and laid down on the soft bed.

Despite the comforting surroundings, her mind refused to let go of what had happened earlier. She closed her eyes and finally let the scene at Mistletoe Lodge replay in her mind.

The anger, the hurt, the betrayal—it all swirled within her like a tempest that refused to be contained. But the thing that sliced through her the most was Ryder. The look on his face and the hurt in his eyes.

Another scene flashed before her, making her breath catch in her throat and her heart throb—it was the look on her mother's face when Avery had flung painful accusations at her.

"Oh no, Avery, what a mess you've created!" Avery whispered to the walls of the cozy room before the dam of emotions she'd been holding back for a few hours burst.

Her body was racked with sobs, and she curled into a ball, hugging one of the soft, fluffy pillows, and cried herself to sleep. The soft crackling of the fire lulled her as she drifted into a dreamland and sought respite from the heartache that plagued her.

The persistent knocking on Avery's room door interrupted her dreamy slumber. She groaned, wanting to retreat back into the pleasant world of her dreams, but the knocking continued, more insistent this time. With a grumble, she pushed herself up from the bed, her mind still foggy from sleep.

Dragging herself to the door, Avery cracked it open, her eyes squinting against the sudden light. And then, as if her dream had slipped into reality, her heart skipped a beat. There stood Ryder, looking both sheepish and determined, holding a tray laden with steaming bowls of soup and an assortment of other foods. For a moment, Avery questioned if she was still dreaming.

"Ryder?" Avery's voice was a mix of disbelief and confusion. She blinked, wondering if her sleepy mind was playing tricks on her.

Ryder greeted her with a sheepish smile, his expression a mix of apprehension and hope. "Hi. Mind if I come in?" His brow furrowed. "I'd really like to talk." He held up the tray as if it were a peace offering, a tangible olive branch between them. "I brought some food."

Avery's sleepy haze began to clear as her heart raced within her chest. Her mind swirled with a flurry of emotions, each one vying for her attention. She crossed her arms, regarding him with a mix of wariness and curiosity.

"That depends," she replied, her voice steady despite the tumultuous feelings inside her. "If by talk it means I get a chance to do so too?"

Ryder hesitated for a moment, his gaze searching hers, and she could see his were as clouded with emotions as the turmoil roiling inside her.

"Of course." Ryder's voice was hoarse. "I'm so sorry I was such a pig head before."

Avery studied him for a few seconds, her heart warring between caution and a flicker of hope. With a small nod, she stepped back, allowing him to enter. Ryder walked past her, his presence filling the room with a mix of tension and anticipation.

"You were also a grade-A douche!" Avery added, making him laugh, then nod in agreement.

"I know," Ryder admitted before scanning the room. "This is a nice room."

"Yes, it's cozy," Avery agreed and pointed to the small table by the window. "You can put the tray down there."

Avery closed the door while Ryder placed the tray on the table. The aroma of warm soup filled the air, and she could feel her belly rumble. He turned to her. His eyes filled with regret.

"Avery," Ryder began, his voice soft yet filled with a weight of emotions. "I really am sorry for how I reacted earlier." He swallowed, but his eyes never left hers. "It was wrong of me not to give you a chance to explain and hear your side of the story."

"Yes, it was," Avery agreed with him again. Her stomach drew her toward the food. "Can we eat?" She looked at him. "Sorry, but I'm starving."

"Of course," Ryder said, joining her at the table. "My stomach also complained when I got a waft of aroma from the soup."

"How did you get May to allow you to bring me my dinner?" Avery asked, buttering some soft, warm bread.

"Oh, she interrogated me for about thirty minutes before she'd even let me know if you were here or not!" Ryder blew out a breath. "I had to basically explain everything to her."

"Aw, she's such a honey." Avery grinned, taking a bite of the bread she dunked in her soup. "Oh wow!" Her taste buds did a little dance in her mouth at how good the soup was. "This is delicious." She pointed to the bread. "And the bread. You have to taste it."

Ryder did as she said, and his eyes widened. "Oh wow!" He took another bite. "I wonder if I can steal May's chef?"

"That's not nice!" Avery pointed out. "She's been so nice to you, and you want to steal from her," she teased.

"Okay, then maybe just the recipe for this soup and the bread!" Ryder relented, the air of tension sizzling between them easing a bit. "Avery, I feel I need to apologize a thousand times over for being such a—"

"Jerk?" Avery raised her eyebrows.

"Okay, I was going to say idiot, but I guess jerk works as well," Ryder said, and Avery nodded. "I should never have let that arrogant Larry Grimes wind me up like that."

"Larry has that effect on everyone," Avery told him. "He feels entitled to the Grimes empire, but his uncle told him he had to earn his place in the company like everyone else." She took another bite of the soup-dunked bread and paused while she ate. "So now to get ahead, Larry tries to steal everyone else's business and ideas because he thinks it will fast-track him through the ranks."

"Nice guy, then?" The sarcasm dripped from Ryder's tongue.

Avery put her spoon back, wiped her hands, and sat back, holding Ryder's gaze. "You're not the only one to blame for what happened." Her voice was soft as the words tumbled from her lips. "I should've told you that first day I called and then canceled a meeting with you and Emily."

"That's what you wanted to talk to us about?" Ryder leaned forward on his elbows as he watched her intently.

"Yes." Avery nodded.

"Then why didn't you?" Ryder asked her. "Why did you put the meeting off?"

"Because I wanted to bring you good news and the confirmation of an investor interested in helping you get Mistletoe Lodge operating like it used to," Avery admitted.

"Ah, by investor, you mean Giles Holland?" Ryder's eyes shone with a teasing glint.

"Yes." Avery nodded, and her eyes widened. "Wait!" She held up her hand. "Is Giles at the lodge?"

"Yes, he arrived with my grandmother only moments after you left," Ryder told her.

"Giles arrived with Priscilla." Avery's brows furrowed in confusion.

"Turns out Giles contacted our legal department for some information," Ryder explained. "All legal information for the lodge still goes through my grandmother."

"She said so," Avery said, distractedly. Her nerve ends were zinging. "If Giles is there and contacted the lodge's legal team, that means—"

Avery looked at Ryder in wide-eyed wonder.

"Yes, he wants to invest in the lodge, and my grandmother insists we take the deal." Ryder smiled. "Which, after reading through it with Emily, we agree with her that it is an amazing deal." He nodded. "And Giles is a silent partner who, other than us wanting to sell the place, will leave the running and decisions to us."

"Ryder, that's fantastic." Avery grinned, silently sighing in relief. Giles had come through for her once again. "Giles is a really good guy. He's not what people think, and he's from a humble background."

"Yes, my grandmother filled us in on his history." Ryder rolled his eyes. "I think she was vetting him for Heather."

"Heather?" Avery looked at Ryder, her brow once again creased in a confused frown.

"Yes, my cousin and Giles seem to have hit it off and are quite *smitten,* I think is the term my grandmother used, with each other," Ryder told her.

"Oh!" Avery was surprised. "That's interesting."

"Why?" Ryder looked at her questioningly.

"Giles is more introverted, and Heather is a larger-than-life explorer," Avery said.

"Well, opposites usually attract, and maybe Heather is as good for him as he is for her," Ryder pointed out.

"You could be right," Avery agreed, and the room fell into a charged silence.

Ryder was the first to break the silence. He reached across the table and took Avery's hand.

"Thank you, Avery." Ryder's voice was gruff with emotion. "Thank you for pointing Pembrook in the direction of the Slopes Hotel to buy time for Giles to swoop in and help us." His thumb caressed her knuckles. "And thank you for bringing the lodge to Giles's attention." He gave her a small smile, his voice dropping even more. "You saved our home and our family's legacy."

"You're very welcome." Avery's own voice was gruff, and her heart was beating wildly as Ryder's soft caress woke the butterflies in her stomach. "And I'm sorry for not being upfront and honest with all of you when I arrived at the lodge."

"I understand why you weren't," Ryder assured her. "I know you were fighting for us all along."

"So, where do we go from here?" Avery asked, her eyes falling on their linked hands.

"Well, according to the last clause in the proposal you drew up for us, you're going to go through quite a change in the near future," Ryder pointed out.

"Ah, you saw that?" Avery nodded. "It's the right thing to do and what Giles has been pushing me to do for years."

"You didn't have to do that for us," Ryder told her.

"No, it was only partly for the lodge," Avery confessed. "It was also because I made a promise to Giles the next time I found a worthy investment."

"That you'd quit Grimes Mergers and Acquisitions to start an investment property consultation for Giles?" Ryder asked curiously. "So, you could save small businesses like mine and as many others as you could?"

"Yes, and to save my soul too," Avery told him with a small smile.

"After meeting a Grimes," Ryder said, "I think it's a wise move to make." His eyes narrowed. "Although Giles is an incredibly handsome guy,"

"Yes, he is!" Avery teased. "But he and I are just really good friends and have been since our first day at UCLA."

"You have impressive friends!" Ryder's eyes widened.

"I do!" Avery nodded. "Including a whole lot who own a lodge on the outskirts of Frisco."

"That's kind of you to say." Ryder smiled. "Avery, can you forgive me?"

"Can you forgive me?" Avery countered.

"How about we forgive each other on the count of three?" Ryder suggested, his eyes sparkling with nostalgia.

"Like your mother used to make us do when we all had a fight." Avery laughed, remembering. "Only Emily was always so competitive."

"Yes, she even had to forgive everyone first." Ryder remembered.

"So, before your mother could get to three, Emily would blurt out, I forgive and love you!" Avery shook her head.

"Ready?" Ryder asked, and he took her other hand in his as she nodded. "You count."

"Okay," Avery agreed. "One, two—"

"I forgive you, and I love you, Avery!" Ryder blurted it out before she could finish.

Her heart jolted, and her breath caught in her throat as her eyes widened. She blinked in surprise as she sat staring at him, speechless.

"Avery?" Ryder asked, looking at her worriedly. "Oh, no. Did I break you?"

A hysterical giggle at what he just asked started to bubble up inside her, and her chest jiggled as the mirth tickled her insides. And before she could stop herself, the laughter bubbled over and spilled through her lips.

"Avery?" Ryder's eyes widened in surprise.

"I'm sorry!" Avery pulled her hands from his and covered her mouth. "It's been a very emotional day." She held up her hands and gained control of her giggles. She took his hands, cleared her throat, and fought down the bubbles of mirth. "I forgive you Ryder, and—" She paused, catching his eyes with hers. "I love you too."

Before she had a chance to breathe, Ryder shot out of his chair, pulled her up out of hers, and his lips found hers as he poured all the love he felt for her into the kiss. The sound of a knock on her door broke them apart.

It was May, with two cups of steaming cocoa. Once May had left, Ryder and Avery snuggled close together on the small sofa that was in front of the fire as they drank their sweet beverage.

"So where are you going to be opening this new Holland Investments?" Ryder asked her.

"I don't know," Avery said. "I was thinking about opening it in Frisco." She grinned mischievously, and then a thought struck her like lightning. "Oh no!" She breathed. "My mother."

"She's okay," Ryder assured her.

"How would you..." Avery's voice trailed off.

"She called the lodge after you left the house and spoke to my grandmother," Ryder explained. "My grandmother apparently told her what had happened." He put the mug on the coffee table. "I wasn't there, but my sister called to let me know when she was wanting updates on whether or not I'd found you."

"I'm going to have to call her and work things out."
Avery blew out a breath.

"You will," Ryder said encouragingly, wrapping his
arm around her shoulders. "Will you come home to Frisco
and go to the dance with me tomorrow night?"

"I will." Avery accepted his invitation. "But I'll have
to go home and patch things up with my mother first."

"Of course," Ryder agreed, and they fell into a
companionable silence before he turned to her. "I have a
crazy thought."

"Oh, yes?" Avery frowned.

"I know this is impulsive and, like I said, crazy...."
Ryder spun off the couch and went down on one knee in
front of Avery. "Marry me, Avery."

"What?" Avery blinked at him, and before her brain
had time to process, her heart pushed the words out. "Yes."

"Tomorrow!" Ryder said.

"Tomorrow?" Avery's brow knit together in confusion. "What do you mean tomorrow?"

"The licensing department is still open tomorrow," Ryder told her. "I'll go get us a license first thing in the morning and book us a court to get married in the afternoon."

"Are you joking?" Avery looked at him in amazement.

Her heart pounded as the idea of marrying Ryder the next day started to take root, and excitement coursed through her.

"No." Ryder gave a soft laugh. "I've never been more serious in my life."

Avery's eyes searched his for a few seconds before a breathtaking smile turned up her lips, and she answered, "Let's do it."

Ryder grabbed her and pulled her to him for another soul-shattering kiss. An hour later, he reluctantly left her after another lingering kiss.

"I'll pick you up tomorrow morning around ten." Ryder said.

"Yes." Avery nodded, still not quite believing what was happening and sure she was still dreaming.

After Ryder left, Avery showered and forced herself to go to bed, where she tossed and turned until finally falling into an excited sleep in the early hours of the morning.

EPILOGUE

Something tickled Avery's nose, pulling her from the amazing dream. She swatted at it, but it tickled her nose again. Her arm searched the bed beside her and hit something warm and solid, making her eyes fly open and her heart start to pound in fright. She turned to see a face real close to hers and screamed as she tried to shoot out of bed. She fell off the side and thumped to the floor.

"Avery?" The familiar female voice called as its owner peaked over the side of the bed. "Are you okay?"

"Emily!" Avery hissed through gritted teeth, rubbing her eyes and breathing to contain her wildly beating heart. "What on earth are you doing here?"

"I'm here to help the bride get ready!" Emily's words sent zaps of shock throughout her system.

So, it wasn't a dream! Avery's mind screamed at her, and she sat up, pulling herself off the floor.

"How did you know about that?" Avery asked and glanced at the clock. Her eyes widening. "Oh no, it's eight thirty."

"Yup," Emily nodded. "And I think you'd better hit the showers and put on your wedding gown."

Avery started grabbing her toiletries and heading for the bathroom, but stopped at the bathroom door and turned to Emily curiously.

"How are you here?" Avery asked her. "Ryder Called you didn't he?"

Emily nodded. "We have access to a helicopter," Emily explained with a grin, and she pointed to the closets. "You won't believe what my grandmother can achieve when she has access to one of those."

Avery followed the direction Emily was pointing, and her breath caught in her throat. Like a sleepwalker, she was drawn to the simple yet elegant white gown hanging on a closet handle.

"Is this the dress we looked at in that boutique in Silverthorne yesterday?" Avery turned and looked at Emily in awe.

"Yup," Emily said with a nod. "You said if you were ever to attempt getting married again, you thought that would be the gown for you."

"But when did you get this?" Avery ran her fingers through the silky-soft chiffon fabric.

"We've been up since the crack of dawn," Emily told her. "Trust me, the sparrows are out to get us, as we rose before they did."

"Em, we're just getting married at court," Avery told her.

"Yeah, about that...." Emily pulled a face.

"What's going on?" Avery's eyes narrowed suspiciously.

"I can't say." Emily made a zip and then locked her lips. "But you'd better go shower."

"I can't believe this is happening." Avery called over her shoulder as she went to the shower.

An hour later, Emily had styled Avery's hair and done her make-up, then helped Avery into the gown. She stood in front of the mirror, holding her breath, still unable to believe this was happening as she took in the gown.

It had an A-line V-neck dress with split beading appliques and a lace top that was pulled in at the waist, flowed down her legs, and stopped before it touched the floor.

"You look beautiful," Emily breathed, her eyes filled with tears. She sniffed and wiped one that escaped. "Sorry, I'm getting all emotional." She looked at Avery. "I don't want to distract you from your day," she told her. "Because we've all been waiting a long time for it." She sniffed again. "Please don't tell anyone, as we're not telling anyone until after Christmas."

"No!" Avery swung around and looked at Emily in amazement. "Are you?"

Emily nodded and gave Avery a watery smile. "Turns out we've already started our family."

Avery pulled Emily into a hug. "Oh, Em, I'm so happy for you both."

A soft knock on the door interrupted them.

"Oh, um!" Emily glanced guiltily at the clock. "Don't be mad." She fidgeted with her hands. "But there's someone else here to see you before you get married."

Before Avery could say more, Emily went to the door and opened it to reveal Avery's mother standing there.

"Mom!" Avery breathed, and as Emily excused herself, promising to come back in ten minutes, Avery flew into her mother's arms. "I'm so sorry, Mom."

"It's okay, honey," Judy said, her voice wobbly and her eyes filled with tears. "I should've told you years ago, like your father warned me."

They stepped back, and Judy quickly contained herself to look Avery over.

"You look lovely, sweetheart," Judy told her.

"How did you —" Avery looked at her, confused.

"Dad and I got a lift with Priscilla in Giles's helicopter," Judy explained. "Your father was thrilled, although I was scared to death."

"Is Giles here too?" Avery asked.

"Yes, I believe he's Heather's date," Judy laughed. "And the helicopter pilot."

"Oh, Mom," Avery said before Judy could say another word. "I should never have attacked you like that."

"It's okay, honey," Judy assured her. "If I were in your shoes, I would've done the same thing." She swallowed. "I'm so sorry, honey."

"Mom, please, it's okay." Avery assured her.

"No, it's not, and I need to explain why myself and Ryder's mother felt we needed to intervene," Judy told her. "It was two days before your wedding when you finally got your acceptance to UCLA." She bit her bottom lip. "I saw the look in your eyes and heard you tell Emily that it was too late. You'd made your choice and were settling on CU."

"I remember that day," Avery said. "You asked me if I was sure CU was really what I wanted because you didn't want me to just settle, you wanted me to follow my dreams."

"Yes, but I saw that dark spot in your eyes," Judy explained. "I'd seen that exact same spot every time I looked at my mother." She swallowed. "She too gave up on her dreams and settled to be with my father." She blew out a breath. "And that didn't end well for her."

"Mom, I'm not your mother, and Ryder isn't your father," Avery pointed out.

"No, but disappointment and regret live in all of us," Judy pointed out. "It's the monster that lives in everyone's subconscious closet and comes out to haunt your dreams or whenever it feels a rift in your happiness."

"Oh, Mom," Avery said and sighed. "I understand." And suddenly she did. "You never wanted me or Ryder to have disappointment or regret come between us."

"While love is a powerful force, it's also blinding, can mislead a person, and can knock you off a path you were meant to take." Judy ran her hand over Avery's face. "It also forces people to take shortcuts at times to rush into attaching their lives to each other." She squeezed Avery's hands. "When you're on that speeding train of love like you and Ryder were, it always derails, sweetheart." She gave a wobbly smile. "But if you allow it to run its natural course and slowly forge its path, it will always lead you to who you're supposed to be with."

"Like a slow, meandering river finding its way to the ocean and an infinite source of water," Avery recited what her grandmother used to say.

"You and Ryder have found your way back to each other," Judy told her. "You can't stop the river of true love from eventually joining up with the body of water it's meant to join."

"I love you, Mom," Avery said, hugging her. "And I'm glad you're here today." She pulled back and smiled. "Although we're getting married in court."

"Oh!" Judy's eyes widened, and she blinked. Her cheeks pinkened, and she started to look uncomfortable, making Avery's eyes narrow suspiciously.

"Mom?" Avery looked at her questioningly.

"Honey, I'd uh," Judy pointed to the door, "I'd better get Emily." She glanced at her wristwatch. "Goodness, is that the time?"

Before Avery could say anything more, Judy slipped out of the room, and a few minutes later Emily returned.

"Why is my mother acting so weird all of a sudden?" Avery stood blinking at the door.

"Maybe because you were mean to her?" Emily teased.

"No, that's not it." Avery suddenly started to get the feeling that something big was going on, and she turned to look accusingly at Emily. "Okay, what is going on?"

Emily glanced at the clock beside her. "You're about to find out." She grinned.

"You look lovely." Avery suddenly noticed the soft pink, A-line, form-fitting dress Emily had on. "When did you get dressed?"

"When your mother came to distract you," Emily told her. "I'm your matron of honor, and your flower girl is waiting in the hall for you."

Avery opened the door, and Rosie, dressed in the same color pink and in a beautiful outfit befitting a flower girl, launched herself into Avery's arms.

"I'm so glad you're going to be my new mom," Rosie whispered, stepping back as she held up her basket of rose petals. "I get to throw these for you."

Avery straightened and looked at Emily. "You do know I'm getting married in court, right?"

"Uh-huh!" Emily nodded and gave Avery a sheepish smile. "Speaking of which, we'd better get going."

Emily pulled a bouquet of flowers from the top of the dresser that Avery hadn't noticed until then and shoved them into Avery's hand before picking up another for herself and shoveling them all out the bedroom door.

As Avery walked down the stairs with an excited Rosie and a nervous Emily, alarm bells started to go off in her head. The bed and breakfast was eerily quiet, like it was holding its breath, while Emily and Rosie led her through the living room and into the back garden.

Avery froze, and her heart lurched as the garden opened into rows of chairs filled with only four of the five faces, she knew. The chairs were parted in the middle, and a long red carpet rolled out towards an arch where Ryder and Hank were standing staring at her in front of someone Avery recognized as a Judge friend of her parents.

"When did all this happen?" Avery asked stupidly.

"I told you," Emily whispered. "Give my grandmother a helicopter, and amazing things happen, and so fast too."

Avery's father hobbled toward her, beaming in pride.

"Dad!" Avery whispered, and he kissed her on the cheek.

"You look beautiful, sweetheart," Frank said, holding out his arm. "Sorry about the crutches, honey."

"I'm just glad you're here," Avery assured him.

Rosie skipped and followed Emily towards the wedding arch, dropping rose petals as the wedding music started. Avery's breath caught, and her heart started to pound as she began her walk down the carpet. Her eyes met Ryder's.

When their hands clasped and they turned to look at each other in front of the judge, Avery was convinced she was still dreaming.

"You look gorgeous," Ryder whispered.

"And you look so handsome." Avery returned the compliment, eyeing out his tux. "You did all this?"

"My grandmother, your mother, sister, and cousin," Ryder told her.

Before they could say more, the judge started the ceremony, and Avery knew that her's and Ryder's had finally come together as they had always meant to after they had each forged their own paths in the world.

CONTINUE READING...
NEW YEAR AT MISTLETOE LODGE

Sweet Colorado Romance – Book 2

CHAPTER 1

Heather Jessop moved stealthily in the heart of the Amazon rainforest, where the verdant canopy stretched endlessly overhead. Her senses heightened to the symphony of life surrounding her. The dense undergrowth beneath her boots whispered with every step she took, each rustle and chirp telling a story of creatures hidden from view. She was on a mission, guided by her unwavering dedication to preserving wildlife.

It was early July, the heart of the wet season, and the jungle was alive with a vibrant energy. Drenched by the unrelenting tropical rains, Heather's khaki-clad form was a splash of earthy color against the lush, green backdrop. Her golden ginger hair was tucked under a practical safari hat. At the same time, a knapsack filled with medical supplies rested on her back, and a small medical cage swayed in her hand.

The call had come in earlier in the day. A local tribe had reported a baby jaguar caught in a poacher's snare. Without hesitation, Heather had embarked on a solo rescue mission. Her heart pounded with anticipation and concern as she navigated through the tangled flora and vines, guided by the tribe's descriptions.

Sweat glistened on her brow as she pushed forward. Heather had always been at home in the wild, and her life's mission had led her to confront situations most would deem dangerous. But in the face of danger, she stood resolute.

"Come on, Heather," she whispered to herself. "You've got this."

The sounds of the jungle enveloped her—the distant cries of howler monkeys, the rhythmic hum of cicadas, and the occasional ripple of water from a hidden stream. She knew she was drawing closer to her destination.

As she pushed through a particularly dense thicket, Heather spotted the faint glimmer of sunlight reflecting off the jagged metal wire of the snare. Her heart ached at the sight. She had to act quickly. Every moment counted.

She approached with caution, her trained eyes assessing the situation. The baby jaguar—a small, spotted ball of fur—was trapped, its panicked eyes filled with terror. The jaguar's mother had likely abandoned it, unable to free her cub from the cruel trap.

"Hey there, little one," Heather murmured, her voice soothing. She reached for a tranquilizer dart in her bag, slowly loading it into her tranquilizer gun. Heather knew she had only one chance to make this count. She steadied her aim, breathed in deeply, and squeezed the trigger.

The dart found its mark, and the tiny jaguar slumped to the ground, its frantic struggles ceasing. Heather rushed to its side, her heart heavy with worry and relief. The snare was still caught around the cub's leg, and she carefully began to untangle the metal wire, her hands trembling with urgency.

Heather couldn't help but marvel at the jaguar's beauty as she worked. Its fur was a tapestry of intricate spots and rosettes, a testament to nature's artistry. This creature deserved a chance to roam the wild, to grow into the magnificent predator it was meant to be.

Finally, the jaguar's leg was free from the snare, and Heather wasted no time administering first aid. She checked the cub's vital signs, cleaned and dressed the wound, and carefully monitored its condition. She stood and radioed her team for a rendezvous, her voice filled with triumph and concern.

"Team, I've got the cub. We need an extraction ASAP. Meet me at the designated coordinates."

Heather felt a sudden, sharp pain in her leg as she spoke. Startled, she glanced down to find the baby jaguar had woken from the tranquilizer, and in its disoriented state, it had lashed out with its claws, deeply embedding themselves in her calf.

Heather gritted her teeth against the searing pain and continued her call, fully aware of the situation's urgency. The extraction team promptly acknowledged her request, assuring her they were en route. Heather managed to sedate the cub again and secured it inside the cage she'd brought.

Realizing the importance of stopping the flow of blood streaming from her leg and ensuring her safety from potential predators, she swiftly wrapped a makeshift bandage around her wounded calf. With the jaguar safely secured, Heather returned to her rendezvous point. The relentless rain drenched her clothes, but her determination propelled her forward. Her leg throbbed with fiery pain, and she was starting to realize that her injury was more severe than she had initially thought.

Time seemed to stretch endlessly as Heather navigated the rainforest, her senses attuned to every sound and movement. The cub, now calmer, slumbered in the cage she held against her, finding solace in her presence. In moments like this, Heather deeply connected with the wild creatures she dedicated her life to protecting. It made all the risks and pain worthwhile.

Finally, the welcome sound of the extraction team's approaching helicopter echoed through the trees. Heather's heart soared with relief, and she signaled their location with a flare. The helicopter descended, and the team swiftly took charge of the injured jaguar and their fearless leader.

Heather was lifted to safety, her leg still throbbing. As the helicopter rose into the sky, the rainforest fell away beneath her. She couldn't shake the feeling of a deep connection forged in that jungle. Her heart sank with the realization that it would be some time before she could continue her mission to save the jaguars due to her injury.

The helicopter's blades sliced through the humid air, carrying Heather and the rescued jaguar away from the dense Amazon rainforest. The roar of the engine was deafening, but Heather hardly noticed. Her focus was on the small, wounded cub nestled in its cage. Despite her pain, she couldn't help but feel a deep sense of satisfaction in saving this young jaguar's life.

The journey back to civilization felt like an eternity. Rain pounded against the chopper's windows, its relentless rhythm a backdrop to the anxious whirring of the helicopter's blades. Heather clutched her injured leg, willing herself to stay conscious. She knew her survival was crucial to the cub's chances of a full recovery.

After what felt like hours, the helicopter touched down in a clearing near a small village on the outskirts of the rainforest. The local rescue team was waiting, their faces etched with relief as they saw the injured jaguar. Heather carefully handed the cub over to their capable hands, her fingers trembling from pain and exhaustion.

"Take good care of him. I've called him Savior," she told them, her voice weak but resolute. "And make sure he's released back into the wild when he's ready."

The team nodded in understanding. With the cub safely in their care, the rescue team wasted no time preparing Heather for her evacuation. Her leg ached mercilessly, and the telltale signs of infection were already setting in. She was carefully loaded onto a stretcher and transported by ambulance to a nearby medical facility, the bumpy ride causing every jolt of pain to shoot through her body.

The clinic, a modest building in the heart of the village, was basic but well-equipped. Heather's face was drawn as she was wheeled inside, her vision blurring from a mix of pain and exhaustion. Though lacking in resources, the local medical staff were skilled and dedicated. They immediately began assessing her injury and treating the jagged wound on her calf.

Over several days, Heather's fever raged. Her days blurred into a haze of sweat-soaked nightmares and fits of delirium as the medical team battled to control the infection in her leg. She was lost in fevered dreams of the jungle, jaguars, and her determination to protect the wild.

In her moments of lucidity, she would glance out the small window of her hospital room. The village starkly contrasted with the lush jungle she had left behind. Simple huts were scattered along the muddy streets, and the villagers went about their daily routines with a sense of calm foreign to Heather's fast-paced world.

One evening, as the sun cast a warm glow over the village, a young girl from the village approached her bedside. The girl's eyes were curious, and she carried a bouquet of vibrant tropical flowers.

"For you," she said with a shy smile, offering the flowers to Heather. "You saved the baby jaguar."

Heather managed a weak smile in return and accepted the gift. The act of kindness from a stranger in this remote corner of the world warmed her heart. It reminded her of the inherent beauty amid adversity and renewed her determination to heal. That memory was the last of the memories of the village as Heather's fever once again spiked.

The medical capability of the small village clinic proved insufficient to provide Heather with the specialized care her deteriorating condition required. With the infection rapidly spreading and her leg deteriorating at an alarming pace, Heather's life hung in the balance. She was urgently airlifted by air ambulance to Los Angeles, a journey she barely remembered as she waned in and out of consciousness.

Upon her arrival in Los Angeles, she was rushed to St. Mark's Hospital, a renowned medical center known for its expertise in complex cases. The infection had taken a severe toll on her leg, necessitating multiple surgeries to remove the affected tissue and repair the damage to save her leg from amputation.

Weeks turned into slow, arduous months of recovery. The infection had been successfully treated, and Heather's leg began to heal, but the journey ahead was long. It would be some time before she could return to work in the jungle or walk properly. After several months of rehabilitation and two additional surgeries to address complications caused by the prolonged infection, Heather was finally released from the hospital.

However, she faced another challenge, as her mobility was still far from perfect. She would require ongoing physical therapy to regain her strength and ensure her leg's full functionality. In addition, her doctors strongly recommended that she take it easy and allow her body time to heal fully. The toll of the months-long ordeal had left her physically and emotionally drained.

By the beginning of December, her injuries had healed to a point where she could walk without too much pain, and the doctors were confident she'd need no more operations. She was at a point where if she never saw another hospital again in her life, it would be too soon.

Her first stop after her latest doctor's visit was to see her boss at the Los Angeles offices of Wildlife Vets International.

Heather was eager to get back to the jungle and her quest to save the jaguars. She knocked on Nancy Dulling's office door and entered when her boss's cheerful voice invited her to.

"Hi, Nancy," Heather greeted the well-groomed and dressed director of the Los Angeles branch of the organization. Nancy was a retired wildlife vet who had been forced into retirement after an incident with a bison nearly ended her life.

"Hello, Heather," Nancy greeted her with a warm smile, her brown eyes assessing Heather. "How are you?"

"I'm all healed and ready to return to the jungle." Heather sat in the chair Nancy waved to.

"I applaud your eagerness to get back to the jaguars," Nancy told her, pushing her designer glasses onto her head as she leaned back in her plush office chair. "But, sweetie, I've received the letter from your doctor, and they have not signed you fit for duty yet." She handed Heather the letter. "They recommend at least three more months of recuperation."

"The operative word being recommended," Heather pointed out, handing the document back to Nancy. "I feel fine and eager to get back to work."

"How's the pain?" Nancy asked her.

"Gone," Heather lied, a twinge of guilt surging through her. "My only pain now is in my heart for the animals I should be helping but can't."

"Nice try," Nancy said with a knowing smile. "But I noticed your slight wince as you sat down and knocked your leg on the desk."

"That was because I knocked my leg," Heather defended her actions and grinned. "I think everyone would wince if they hit a part of their body on a desk." She knocked the oak top. "Especially as this is old solid oak."

Nancy tilted her head and stared at Heather for a few seconds in contemplative silence before sighing and shaking her head. "I'm sorry, Heather." Her eyes filled with worry. "You're our best vet and team leader, and while it pains me to do this, I have to go by the doctor's recommendations." She gave Heather an encouraging smile. "I know you're eager to get out there. But chancing it now may lead you to give up going out in the field altogether." Her brow furrowed. "Don't forget I've been where you are now, and I went back into the field too soon and against doctor's orders." She opened her arms, gesturing to her office. "Now I'm desk-bound."

"But your injuries had you near death's door," Heather pointed out. "Mine was just my leg that is now healed."

"Oh, sweetie," Nancy sighed. "Your injury was just as severe and had you near death, too. You just don't remember it. I was at the hospital when you were brought back to Los Angeles."

"Okay!" Heather gave up the fight, knowing she was not going to win. "Fine. But can we revisit this in a month instead of three?" Her brow knitted together pleadingly. "I'm going to go insane if I don't get back out in the field soon."

"Fine, it's a deal," Nancy agreed to Heather's terms. "But we let the doctors decide."

"Agreed," Heather said with a nod and blew out a breath. "I just wish it wasn't over the festive season."

"When did you last spend Christmas or New Year with your family?" Nancy asked her.

"I'm not sure," Heather shrugged. "Three, maybe four years ago."

"Then it's high time you did," Nancy told her. "As your boss, I'm ordering you to relax and have a family festive season this year and see the new one in with them, too."

"That's a bit impossible as my grandmother is in Frisco, Colorado, for Christmas," Heather explained. "And I'm not supposed to squish onto an airplane for three to four months."

"Well, it's lucky for you that we have a few helicopters at our disposal," Nancy reminded her. "Let me know when you'd like to go to Colorado, and I'll organize it for you."

"Seriously?" Heather shook her head, trying to look pained about the thought of having to fly to Colorado for Christmas, but the idea was more appealing than she let on.

"Yup," Nancy nodded. "Pack your bags and get ready to head to Colorado."

It was eleven days to Christmas when Heather found herself in one of the organization's jets, making her way to Denver. Once there, she was met by one of the organization's helicopter pilots who was going to fly her to her family's cherished lodge nestled on the outskirts of Frisco. The anticipation swirled within her as she gazed out the window, her eyes drinking in the snow-covered landscape below. The mountainous terrain, cloaked in a blanket of pristine snow, unfolded in all its majestic splendor.

The helicopter's descent marked her first return to Mistletoe Lodge in four years. While Heather spoke to her grandmother at least twice a week when she could, she'd not told her grandmother about her injury. Heather had also not spoken to her cousins, Ryder or Emily, since she'd voted to sell the lodge a year ago. The whirring of the blades against the crisp mountain air filled her ears, a comforting and familiar sound. Her heart danced with the prospect of reuniting with her family and relishing in the holiday season she had missed in recent years.

With a soft thud, the helicopter gently landed, and the scenery before her seemed straight out of a winter postcard. The snow-laden trees sparkled in the winter sunlight, and the lodge, which held many cherished memories, stood resolute against the elements. Heather pushed the door open once the pilot, Wally, gave her the go-ahead. She thanked him, hopped out, and leaned in to retrieve her backpack and Stetson.

With a friendly wave to the pilot, Heather closed the door behind her, her gloved hand twisting the handle before she released it. The helicopter's engines roared to life again, and Heather stepped out of harm's way. With a powerful surge, it lifted off the ground, ascending back into the sky with a sense of graceful power.

The helicopter incited a swirling mist of snow that wrapped around Heather. She plopped her Stetson on her head and watched the aircraft rise into the sky, flying off in the direction it had come. She sighed and turned to scan the scene before her. Heather was delighted and surprised to see her cousins standing watching her from the other side of the driveway that separated them.

Her face lit up with a warm smile, and she waved at them before shouldering her backpack filled with the essentials she would need for her vacation and headed toward them. Heather forced herself not to limp as the cold gripped her injured leg, making it feel like an icy hand dug its long nails into her calf.

"Hello, hello!" Heather beamed, her cheeks pink from the chilly air. Dropping her pack carelessly in the snow, she bounced into her cousin Ryder's arms, kissing his cheek. "Hey, Ry, it's good to see you."

Not waiting for his greeting, Heather greeted his sister, Emily.

"Emmy!" Heather wrapped her arms around Emily. As small as she was, she lifted Emily off her feet as she squeezed, once again ignoring the slicing pain the exertion caused her leg. "I've missed you soooo much."

"Hey, Heather," Emily greeted her.

"Rosie?" Heather dumped Emily back onto her feet and turned to Rosie, Ryder's nine-year-old daughter, who took a step behind Ryder. "My word!" She observed Rosie. "How you've grown in two years."

"Hi," Rosie said shyly, cowering behind Ryder.

Heather turned her attention to Hank, whose eyes narrowed at her warningly, but that didn't deter Heather. She gave him a cheeky grin and went in for a hug.

"You're still making grand entrances, I see, Heather," Ryder said as Heather unfolded herself from hugging Hank.

"Gran always says a lady must make an entrance to be noticed." Heather laughed, saying, "I heard the festival was back on, so I thought I'd come to lend a hand."

"Aren't you supposed to be counting polar bears in the Arctic?" Emily asked.

"Tagging," Heather corrected her. "Tagging polar bears."

"You were tagging polar bears?" Rosie's curiosity outweighed her shyness as she looked at Heather and stepped away from her father.

"I did," Heather confirmed. "Do you want to see some pictures?" She pulled her phone from her bomber jacket pocket to show a fascinated Rosie.

"Oh, wow!" Rosie's eyes were huge. "Look, Daddy." She pointed to a picture of Heather sitting beside a polar bear that had been tranquilized.

"Yeah, Heather does a lot of dangerous stuff like that," Ryder said as if in warning, making Heather frown at him.

"I want to go work with polar bears, too," Rosie told him.

Heather's frown turned into a smile as she looked at the beautiful child, remembering how she, too, had been fascinated by wild animals at Rosie's age.

"Heather doesn't only work with polar bears, sweetheart," Ryder explained. "She's a wildlife vet, which means she works with all sorts of wild animals."

"That's so cool," Rosie said, staring at Heather in awe, and Heather's smile broadened.

"If you're trying to scare her away from being like Heather," Hank laughed, patting Ryder's shoulder. "You're not doing a good job of it."

"What's wrong with being like me?" Heather asked.

She pocketed her phone and picked up her well-worn backpack, glancing at Ryder questioningly and feeling hurt by his cutting remark.

"Nothing," Emily assured her, rolling her eyes at Ryder. "Just Ryder being a protective father."

"Ah!" Heather nodded and moved the conversation away from her work. Her family didn't know that her arctic trip had been over two years ago. "So, how's the preparation going?" She looked curiously at Ryder and Emily.

"Thanks to the weather, we've only just been able to get started," Emily told her.

"So that means you could use an extra hand around here?" Heather grinned at Ryder.

"You're always welcome at the lodge, Heather," Ryder said through gritted teeth, his shoulders tensing up, making Heather realize he was still angry with her. "This is your home too."

"Are you still mad at me for voting to sell this old place?" Heather tried to make light of their argument over a year ago.

"For the purpose of keeping the peace for the festive season, I'm going to ignore what you just said," Ryder informed her stiffly. "We're done here for the day."

"Come on, Heather, let's get you settled." Emily linked her arm through Heather's. "I'm sure Grandmother's going to be thrilled to see you. You're going to have to stay in her cottage with her as we're filled to capacity."

"Not a problem," Heather said, glancing at Ryder before they started walking toward the lodge and smiling at Emily. "It will be like the good old days."

"Daddy, can I go with them?" Rosie asked, stopping Emily and Heather as they waited for his reply, and he nodded.

Rosie's excited call summoned Rory, the golden retriever, and he bounded toward the trio before they continued their walk. As Heather walked, the crisp winter air kissed her cheeks, and her senses drank in the serene beauty of the landscape. The earthy scent of snow underfoot and the distant sounds of animals in the fields combined to create a feeling of peace.

When they rounded the bend, the lodge emerged from the surrounding woods, revealing its rustic charm and welcoming facade. Heather's heart swelled with a profound sense of belonging and nostalgia. The lodge was more than just a building; it was a repository of her family's history, love, and traditions. The towering pines and snow-draped eaves seemed to embrace her like old friends.

Once they crossed the threshold, the lodge's interior embraced them with its warm, cozy atmosphere. Heather was met with the delighted surprise of her grandmother, Priscilla Carlisle, and the lodge's chef, Nora Preston. Their warm smiles and welcoming presence tugged at Heather's heartstrings. The bonds she shared with her family were unbreakable, transcending the years and miles that had kept her away. With its rustic beauty and loving family, the lodge had a magical way of melting away the worries and hardships of the outside world.

At that moment, the fierce passion for preserving wildlife that had always driven her took a back seat. It was her calling, her purpose, but for now, it was on hold, allowing her spirit to embrace the tranquility of the holidays and focus on healing. The lodge was the perfect place for that, a sanctuary where time seemed to slow, and every creak of the wooden floor whispered tales of cherished moments.

AVAILABLE ON AMAZON

SWEET COLORADO ROMANCE SERIES

<u>Christmas at Mistletoe Lodge</u>

<u>New Year at Mistletoe Lodge</u>

<u>Reunion at Mistletoe Lodge</u>

AVAILABLE ON AMAZON

MORE BOOKS BY AMY RAFFERTY

SERIES

The Lighthouse on Plum Island - Book 1- *Cobble Beach Romance*

The Bakery in Bar Harbor ~ *Secrets in Maine Series*

Cupids Bow Ranch ~ *Montana Country Inn Romance Series*

Starting Over in Nantucket ~ *Cody Bay Inn Series*

Leave a Rose in the Sand ~ *Starting Over in Key West Series*

A Mystery at Summer Lodge ~ *A Coastal Vineyard Series*

Charming Bookshop Mysteries ~ *Small Town Beach Romance*

Moonlight Dream ~ *Honey Bay Cafe Series*

Nantucket Christmas Escape ~ *Second Chance Holiday Romance*

Retreat ~ *Manatee Bay Series*
Secrets of White Sands Cove ~ *A San Diego Sunset Series*
The Seabreeze Cottage ~ *La Jolla Cove Series*

STANDALONE NOVELS

The McCaid Sisters ~ *A Second Chance Romance Mystery Novel*

BOX SETS

Montana Country Inn: The Complete Collection ~ *Montana Country Inn Romance Series*
Cody Bay Inn: The Complete Collection ~ *Nantucket Romance Series*
Starting Over in Key West: The Complete Collection ~ *A Florida Keys Romance Series*
A Mystery at Summer Lodge: The Complete Collection ~ *A Coastal Vineyard Series*
Charming Bookshop Mysteries: The Complete Collection ~ *Small Town Beach Romance*

Honey Bay Cafe Series: The Complete Collection ~ *Second Chance Beach Mystery Romance*
Nantucket Christmas Escape: The Complete Collection ~ *Second Chance Holiday Romance*
Manatee Bay: The Complete Collection ~ *Treasure Seekers Beach Romance Series*
Secrets of White Sands Cove: The Complete Collection ~ *A San Diego Sunset Series*
The Seabreeze Cottage: The Complete Collection ~ *La Jolla Cove Series*

THREE IN ONE

Coastal Collection: Sea Breeze Cottage, Mystery at Summer Lodge, Secrets of White Sands Cove ~ *Three Series in One Book*

SPANISH VERSION

El Café de Bahía Honey ~ *Honey Bay Cafe (Spanish)*
Escapada Navideña a Nantucket ~ *Nantucket Christmas Escape (Spanish)*

Bahía de Manatee ~ *Manatee Bay (Spanish)*
La Posada de la Bahía Cody – *Cody Bay Inn (Spanish)*

AMY RAFFERTY VIP READERS

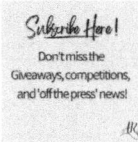

Don't want to miss out on my giveaways, competitions,

and 'hot off the press' news?

Subscribe to my email list.

It is FREE!

Click Here!

CONNECT WITH AMY RAFFERTY

Not only can you check out the latest news and deals, you can also get an email alert each time I release my next book.

Follow me on BookBub
I always love to hear from you and get your feedback.
Email me at ~ books@amyraffertyauthor.com
Follow on Amazon ~ Amy Rafferty
Sign up for my newsletter and free gift, Here
Join my 'Amy's Friends' group on Facebook

A NOTE FROM AMY RAFFERTY

Hi, wonderful people,

Known as 'The Queen of Gorgeous Clean Mystery Romance,' I write sweet and captivating women's romance fiction novels. My stories are filled with warmth, excitement, and memorable characters, as they navigate the joys and challenges of family and friendship.

I aim to bring my readers uplifting romantic reads and feel-good fiction that fill their hearts with love and emotion. You'll discover strong, inspiring female role models and the men who cherish them, along with the powerful bonds of family and friendship, second chances, and later-in-life romances.

I write books you cannot put down,
bringing
sunshine to your days and nights.

Thank you for being here and reading my books x

REVIEW

It would mean a lot to me if you would be so kind and leave me an honest review for ***Christmas at Mistletoe Lodge.***

The link I have placed below makes it so easy as it is a special link taking you straight to the review section.

Thank you in advance and I appreciate you.

[Review Christmas at Mistletoe Lodge Here!](#)

Printed in Great Britain
by Amazon

56421527R00260